Swatting at Butterflies

S.A. Fanning

Immortal Works LLC
1505 Glenrose Drive
Salt Lake City, Utah 84104
Tel: (385) 202-0116

Cover Art by Wilbert Stanton
wilbertstanton.com

ISBN 978-1-953491-35-0 (Paperback)
ASIN B09TZ9378S (Kindle)

To Diane Fanning, because who else?

Editor's Note

Swatting at Butterflies is a beautifully written book that covers some mature and serious subject matter. Though the author does a wonderful and sensitive job with these topics, it is necessary to let the readers know that Swatting at Butterflies contains scenes related to sexual assault and its aftermath that may be difficult for some survivors and their loved ones to read.

If you or someone you know has been sexually assaulted, help is available. The National Sexual Assault Hotline can be reached at 800-656-HOPE (4673) or via online chat at online.rainn.org .

Holli Anderson
Chief Editor
Immortal Works

Chapter 1

I sat in front of the coffin, trying not to laugh. But the whole thing was a mess. Half the town had shown up, *to celebrate the life of a very special lady.* And they were still showing up, fashionably late, slamming car doors and shushing each other as they huddled around the tent where it was share-your-story time. Friends dabbed their eyes, trying to speak over the wind, emotion, somebody's baby screaming like a demon.

Everyone had their own special story to tell about Mom—funny stories, tearjerkers, tales of strength and courage. Standard fare, I suppose, for this sort of thing. I had stories. I had so many stories I could have told had I wanted to be a part of the show, which I did not. And neither did Uncle Robbie, sitting next to me, silent and stoic as the wind gusts picked up, ruffling hats and plastic flowers, sending the world's tackiest wreath rolling down a hill of grave markers.

A group of little boys took off after the wreath, hurdling over headstones and giggling. All of this as a girl with a guitar took her place and plowed into a Joni Mitchell song. The latecomers continued to shimmy for seats, weeping along in chorus when the wind took on the wrath of a hurricane. The tent flapped and fluttered at the edges, cups and trash scraped down the curb. A faraway wind chime clanged like a dinner bell.

Mom would have laughed until she cried, had she been there. And through the confusion I thought I noticed a hint of mischief lurking beneath her pretty smile in the picture frame. The smile sitting on the casket, cutting through the distractions. The smile speaking to me like a secret.

Watch this, Chloe.

The frame landed at my feet with a crash. Guitar Girl jumped and nearly broke a string. She looked around like something was wrong as Grandpa sprang from his seat, igniting a gasp from the congregation. I bit my lip to keep from cracking up, but it was all so ridiculous, watching the old man scurrying about, his tie waving, the glass crunching, as he muttered to himself, "Someone shut that baby up," as he collected the mangled flowers and tried to fix Mom's cracked picture frame.

Guitar girl had it right, this *was* all wrong. We shouldn't have been there. Mom was too young and pretty to be dead. The casket was too new and shiny to have dirt slung onto it. None of it seemed real. And don't get me started on Grandpa. How people must have thought it was grief that made him snap, that the anguish of losing his only daughter had left him irrational, angry, ready to lash out at the world. Truth was, Papa Vanderbrooke was just the sort of righteous jerk who'd get embarrassed at his daughter's funeral.

Things got back on track, eventually, after Grandpa had chased off both baby and singer. The boys returned with the wreath, and the preacher stood and spoke to me directly. He made sure everyone considered the poor girl without a mother or a father. They launched into a prayer. They consoled me. They smothered me with fragrant hugs and sticky handshakes. It was like they wanted me to break down, to prove how much I loved my mother.

I could've told them I was glad it was over, that the cancer ravaged body in the casket didn't match the pretty face in the frame. How the last year of Mom's life had been a wasteland of waiting rooms and insurance battles. That we'd done our crying, in private, together over scan results and treatment plans. At least now there was no more hope.

Hope had done us no favors. Hanging around, lurking in the corner of my thoughts, whispering how *this* time the cancer was really gone, and after some reconstruction, Mom would be as good as new. We'd have a story to tell and celebrate her life as a survivor. A big party at the awareness garden, with real flowers and no plastic wreaths. We'd eat cake and make jolly. All eyes would be on Mom, not me, and there would be no hurricane winds, only a gentle breeze that would sweep back her hair—it would grow back—and carry the clinks of our glass flutes to the treetops as we said a toast, because damn it all, she was alive.

That kind of hope is exhausting.

We didn't stay long at the reception. Long enough for Uncle Robbie's annoying wife Glenda to have a glass of wine and make her rounds. Uncle Robbie drove. I cracked the window to escape the secret-smoker stench, ducking his worried glances in the rear-view mirror. Glenda went on about the beautiful ceremony. *Beautiful*, just *beautiful*. She must have said *beautiful* eleven times in three minutes. And when it wasn't *beautiful* it was *lovely* or *breathtaking*. Anything besides what it was—a train wreck.

We were on the way home. Their place. Where I'd spent the last few days. And up until that moment—when Glenda whipped around, gripping the seat with one tiny but ferocious hand—it had all felt more like a visit.

"Chloe, just remember, she's in a better place."

I avoided her eyes, nodding with my best grimace-smile/slow blink-of-the-eyes combo as I stored the little gem with the rest of my cliché collection. Although, honestly, the better place one didn't bother me. She was right, Mom *was* in a better place. If only that could have been the end of it. If only Glenda would've cranked up the Dave Matthews or whatever they were into, maybe things could've been bearable. But she didn't. Glenda was incapable of restraint. So she plunged right ahead the only way she knew how.

"You know, if you want to talk about it, I'm here for you, okay?" She stared at me through an entire traffic light. *Okay? Okay? Okay?*

She was only trying. But her giddiness irked me. And yeah, okay, I didn't expect the world to stop with Mom's death, but Glenda was almost overjoyed by it. Like she'd won a raffle drawing good for one teenage daughter at a charity event. Finally, I turned to the window to escape her skin-scraping stares. Wasn't happening.

She offered a stick of gum. "We're both here for you, right sweetie?" she said, tossing the support-baton to Uncle Robbie, looking suspect up there in his jacket and tie, recoiling at the thought of sitting down and swapping stories with his niece about his dead sister. But there we were, caught in a snag of traffic. A pickup truck rumbled to a stop beside us, and two hicks sneered at the well-dressed people in the car. Us. People must have thought we were a family.

Finally, Robbie cleared his throat and popped up in the rear-view. "That's right Chloe, we want, um, we want you to know that we are here for you, okay?"

I closed my eyes, nodding again, more out of respect for him getting through his lines than anything else. For months this thing had been planned out, mapped and navigated every step of the way as Mom faded. Before that even, when we first started *making arrangements*. When Mom and I would drop by Uncle Robbie and Glenda's house for dinner. And by dinner, I mean the four of us sitting at the table bawling our eyes out discussing Life After Mom. LAM, as I thought of it.

Robbie and Glenda's old gothic-type house overlooked the quaint downtown square. Madison Street was *the* place to be in the historic district, where it's all cobblestone streets and wrought iron fences, bronze plaques and such. They'd been restoring the place for as long as I could remember, and that house was like their child. There was always a saw or hammer or tools lying around where Glenda had Robbie on a project.

Of all the crap times in my life, those little sit-down dinners took center stage. Mom and Glenda holding hands and sniffling while Robbie stared off at the wall like he was just itching to get back to the crown molding. I sat at the table like an invalid, unsure what to do or say and wondering how I'd ever survive being Glenda's new restoration project. But it was important to Mom, so I went. And now here we were, fully prepared with nothing to do.

Robbie was a few years older than Mom. He used to be cool but now had the look of a guy in-between naps. I loved my uncle, he'd done more for us than anyone. He'd lent us money and even cosigned for Mom's car loan a few years ago. Even this move-in thing had been his idea. So yeah, Robbie was solid. But Glenda was too much. A realtor, even before we got Mom's body in the ground I'd heard her talking about selling the house on Dorchester. The one Mom and I rented from them.

When we got to Madison Street, I went to start unpacking. It had to be done, and after being watched and coddled all day I needed to be alone for a while. My room was right off the steps, beside the bathroom. Not that it was a bad spot, but any room in the world would have sucked because I wanted *my* room, across the hall from Mom, where I could hear her shuffling around in the middle of the night, even the sound of her peeing or coughing, something to let me know she was still there with me.

I stuffed my clothes into someone else's drawers, eyeing the unfamiliar faces in the unfamiliar frames. Everything was so neat and sterile, the house was old but posh, with all these high-tech gadgets, stainless steel and shiny hardwood floors that lit up in the sun. Right out back was a matching carriage house at the end of the driveway. It would have been the perfect spot for me, but it was being remodeled or something.

So began my new life. On a strange bed with a gloomy funeral hangover. Mom was gone. Dead. Buried. I wanted to forever erase that day from memory, but it was there, vivid and bright, even the sound of the wind dragging in my ears. All those people paying their respects. That preacher staring down on me. My emotionless grandparents. I told myself that my own funeral would be a party, not a soggy celebration-of-life deal but people dancing and laughing, getting faced and making bad decisions.

I lay back, clutching our phones, Mom's black and mine white. Our shared plan, shared data, our lifelines—now disconnected. The walls blurred. My nose stung. A big, fat teardrop hit the comforter.

She was really gone.

Chapter 2

The day of my return to Dunham Episcopal School was chilly, but the morning sun was bright and making promises. The buds in the cherry trees lining the path were beginning to loosen their grip, previewing the show to come. It felt like a lifetime since I'd walked beneath their cotton candy blossoms. And in a way, it had been.

Spring last year was a fight, and Mom fought hard. Summer came and she kept me laughing. We traveled some, to Charleston where we'd eaten outside, near the water, fighting the wind, the seagulls trying to steal our food. I saved some sand I kept in a jar. Just like I kept the ticket stub to the last movie we saw together. We went to the park and I had to help her back to the car, then she let me drive home even though it was two months before I could get my learner's permit.

Yesterday, Glenda had me fill out something like a hundred thank you cards to everyone who'd helped out with Mom's medical expenses. Not that I wasn't grateful, only, it was the day after the funeral. Even Uncle Robbie mentioned something about the timing, which Glenda dismissed like she did most everything he said.

I was starting to get a feel for the house, and things were dull. Uncle Robbie was a drag, not the same guy I remembered from when I was little. And Glenda was, well, Glenda. I was more than ready to be back at school and out of the house, where I could at least have my own thoughts.

In the courtyard, Vienna snatched me for a hug, then held me out at arm's length. She nodded. I nodded back. No crying today, even as her eyes went glossy. We turned and started down the path.

I never thought I'd be so happy to let my best friend go on about Spence as we strolled along, the sun slapping the monuments around campus, casting shadows on the stone pathways. It felt good to laugh, to forget for a few lovely minutes, to feel Vee's arm occasionally sweep against mine as she talked with her hands, gushing on about the love of her life, filling me in on everything I'd missed.

Vienna Summerset stood out on campus for two reasons. The first being she was gorgeous. Breathtaking, really, I kid you not, she was by far the most beautiful girl I've ever met. Her dad was white and her mom was black and they both looked like movie stars. As a result, Vee got her father's height and her mother's face and a pair of stunning green eyes that made you want to lean closer when you talked to her. Which brought up the second reason.

It's not that there weren't any black kids at D.E.S., there just happened to be a heck of a lot more white and Asian kids. Mostly the rich and mighty, kids shipped down from New England or Canada or abroad from Spain, Germany, England. A few scholarship kids from Africa, Vietnam. Only about a quarter of the kids were day students like Vee and me—and I was only there at all because of Mom's job. Anyway, Vee was sensitive about being biracial, so I was sensitive about it too.

School quickly became an extension of the funeral. Walking through the solemn nods and pity stares, all the early morning promise I'd felt clouded over. Since Mom had worked at Dunham Episcopal, everyone knew when she'd gotten sick. Everyone knew she was all I had.

I spent nearly an hour a day my first week back in crisis consultation, trying to get used to the new routine of secretly grieving and otherwise assuring everyone I was fine.

I wasn't prepared for how empty the school felt without her. Up until her final months, Mom stuck it out with her job as an administrative assistant, coming to school when she could manage. And though I would have never admitted it, I felt safe with her around. Just knowing she was somewhere on this earth, heart beating and fighting, helped me breathe when I lost control. During chemo, when I'd get my assignments and sit by her bed, I got used to the sound of her rasp, accustomed to her groans and signals, helping her turn or adjust, brewing tea and heating up her socks. Still, I never let myself believe she was dying,

After school, Glenda's car was waiting for me at the curb. She must have just finished her secret smoke, judging by the eye-stinging, industrial strength air freshener that hit me in the face when I opened the car door.

"How was it, girly?"

Girly. Already. "Okay, I guess."

I put the window down and wiggled my fingers at Dylan Kowalski. He nearly fell over getting his hand up to wave. I smiled. Glenda pounced.

"Ooh, who's that?"

"Oh, just a friend."

Dylan was tight with Vee's boyfriend, Spence. He was on the lacrosse team, tall and lanky, one-part athlete, one-part nerd. He was a senior, and we'd gotten close being how we were always thrown together when Vee and Spence snuck off to be alone. But it was kind of adorable how he squirmed when I caught him looking at me.

Glenda craned for the rear-view and I thought the car was going to hop the curb. "He's cute."

I checked my eye roll, hoping against hope she'd stop going on about it. She did, eventually, but only to tell me all about her little brother coming to town to work on the carriage house. She tapped the wheel as she drove, flicked her bangs back as we crossed town for the medical center. Poor Andrew had just broken up with his girlfriend, she told me between teeth clicks. It was for the best, if you asked her, Andrew could do so much better than Renee.

"Anyway, he's going to be staying with us for a bit," she said with a nudge. "So it's our job to cheer him up."

Yay.

We pulled in at the family practice center. Glenda parked the car, turned the key, and whipped out her phone to get set for her walkathon podcast. This quack visit was part of the deal. While Mom was able to fix things so I could finish my last two years at Dunham Episcopal, she also made me promise to continue seeing Doctor Ogelsby. Yay again.

Glenda yanked at the tangled earbuds. "Okay, see you in sixty."

"Oh, boy."

Dr. O was okay. She had a gentle face, nice to look at, with freckles and glasses. She hardly ever jotted down notes when I talked, like some of the school counselors did, which used to leave me wondering what it was I'd said that was so noteworthy. Instead she had this grip tight way of locking in on me, chewing her pen (despite hardly using it to write secret stuff about me), with an occasional nod and smile.

I have what I call outside thoughts and inside thoughts. Pretty self-explanatory—some things I keep to myself, others I choose to share. Not even Dr. O hears it all, because some things are mine and mine alone. Still, it wasn't so bad being the first time back after Mom. Doctor O didn't push too hard, we mostly just chit-chatted about school and guys and Miss Shelby—the thorn-in-my-side teacher—and Glenda—the thorn-in-my-side guardian. The one I found doing yoga stretches by the car when I came out of the building.

At dinner, Uncle Robbie sat at the table like a slab, ready to spoon up some brown rice cooked to a crunch and smothered with enough pepper to holster in a spray canister. Glenda launched into her workday recap—realtor meetings and showings, open houses and potential offers. The bebop jazz filled the background. Robbie nodded and grunted along, his eyes like two roaming search lights as Glenda blathered with incessant energy about fundraisers and galas, and maybe most of all, her brother Andrew.

Poor Robbie, the guy was like forty or something. I think he liked his own little routine, but now he had Glenda all revved up, taking in family members like stray cats. It was obvious he wasn't looking forward to more company or having to tip-toe around his sixteen-year-old niece.

I couldn't believe what my life had become. I yearned for Olive Garden night with Mom, when she'd make minestrone soup and salad and we'd heat up some bread sticks and sit down to a feast. So simple, yet the memory nearly folded me over.

❧

Apparently, Glenda had Doctor O on speed dial, because soon, dinners had become the main focus of our little chats. We were in her office. Me on the super comfy chair and Doctor O sitting with impeccably good posture in her no-nonsense chair. I was imagining the whack jobs before me who'd sprawled out and told all, spilling tears onto the armrest, prattling on about their jacked up childhood and unfulfilled dreams, when Doctor Oglesby said, "Something's different about you, did you cut your hair?"

I shot her a look, like, *just what sort of trap is this?* But she didn't flinch. I had to give it to her there, of all the professional types I'd come across, she was the only one who took my stares head on, her lips pursed nearly to a smile. I think she relished the challenge. Finally, I flipped my hair back and told her I'd lost four pounds.

"How'd you do it?" she asked, dead serious. I was kind of shocked because it was blatantly obvious I did not need to lose weight.

"I haven't been eating dinner."

"No?"

"No, Glenda can't cook to save her life." I sat up a little straighter, matching her posture, a little miffed how she wasn't alarmed but calmly scribbling notes. I mean seriously, all the eating disorders out there, and here I come along with a not-so-subtle cry for help and she's going to chew on her pen? Let it slide?

I flipped myself around, my arms draped over the couch. "I usually wait until they're asleep and come out and have a bowl of cereal, but that's about it." Again, I sat up straighter, let her take me in. "They're kind of worried about it—my weight." I emphasized *weight*, thinking, *what kind of doctor are you?*

"Hmm," she said, letting it hang there for a minute. A rash of ants skittered down my neck. Heat across my face. I couldn't hold it in any longer.

"Do *you* think I need to lose weight?"

"Chloe, of course not. Do you worry a lot about your weight?"

Ugh. I fell back into the chair. Dr. O eased our discussion back to Glenda and why I was being so "aggressive" towards my aunt. She spoke with practiced calm, assuring me the move was a big adjustment for everyone. Not just me. But I was too hung up on the whole weight thing to even look at her. Aggressive? I'd drop ten pounds just to show her if she kept this up.

By the time I found Glenda, all flushed and sweaty from her walk, I was too annoyed to talk. And she just sat in the parking lot, the car so quiet I could hear her panting. A plane flying over our heads.

"So, Chloe, I spoke with Mr. Suddith today."

"What? Why?" I turned to her, like, *what now?* She sucked down her water, big annoying gulps, then smacked her lips before granting me an answer.

"Well, about your activities."

Relentless. This woman was absolutely relentless. Since Mom had gotten sick, I'd had a pass on extracurriculars. I'd been able to skip out on such yawn-tastic pursuits as Communications Club, Writing Lab, Latin—so just what was Glenda doing, talking to Mr. Suddith, reaching across the seat to touch my arm?

"We just think, maybe it's time you get back to your obligations."

We, as in her. Because Mr. Suddith wouldn't force me to do anything right now. He'd even said, *take as much time as you need.* I took my arm back and stared out the window, watching an empty-eyed chubby boy being led into the office. Glenda kept on keeping on. Gulping water. Smacking her lips. Reaching for my arm. Talking.

"I mean, you don't want to just quit, and then—"

"Can we go to McDonald's?"

Silence. A grip of terror took hold on her face. She and Robbie were all rah-rah organic. Buy local, recycling bins, composting, and soy. Glenda loved a cause, be it nutrition or social justice or whatever else came with a free canvas bag or bumper sticker. I'd heard her rants against McDonald's, going on about chicken coops and wages, ethics. But I wanted a quarter pounder. And for her to stop. Stop with everything.

"Um, well," I watched the inner struggle in her eyes. Ethics clashing with maternal longing. Finally, she turned the key. "Well, I suppose just this once, but do you know what they put in that stuff?"

I found out in the drive thru.

Chapter 3

For the next few weeks, everyone continued to treat me like something damaged. Teachers, administrators, even the coaches spoke to me slow and soft, a hand on my shoulder as though my mother dying had made me not only emotional but dense. People I hardly knew hugged me. Grief counselors randomly pulled me from class to check in. I told them what they wanted to hear and kept my GPA intact as though to prove to everyone that I wasn't suddenly stupid. I'd already banged out my SAT's earlier in the year, and I had a good chance of being one of the few juniors selected for Cum Laude Society.

Vienna caught up with me during free period—study hall for those non-Cum Laude types. "Hey, have you talked to Dylan today?"

I shot her a look. "No. What are you up to?" Sometimes with Vee, you had to get to the point

"What do you mean?" she said with a big grin, eyes darting. It was clear she should never go out for theater. I stared at her until her shoulders drooped with a sigh. "Okay fine, I think he wants to ask you to the dance, but he's worried about—"

"The dance? Lame."

"—that. Look, I know you're still, you know, with what happened last year with Chris, but Spence's parents are in Quebec City for the week. We'll get fancied up and go to the lake house instead of the dance. Sound okay?"

The sudden plunge in my stomach caught me by surprise. The dance. Dylan. The quick pull of excitement in the wake of those thoughts. But I needed some answers first. "Why are you and Spence playing matchmaker?"

She nudged me along. "Come on, Dylan's cute."

Spence and Vienna had reached the highly annoying, public groping stage of their relationship. Spence would throw an arm around her waist whenever there wasn't a teacher around. I'd made the mistake of tagging along with them out to dinner one night, which meant watching them suck face while I chugged sweet tea. I mean, yeah, Spence was hot, but hanging out with them together was a spectator sport. Then again, maybe with Dylan it would be all right.

"I'm not playing matchmaker, I'm playing friend," Vee said, going into mood repair mode. "A friend who would like to see her best friend lighten up and have a good time."

Unlike Spence, Dylan was shy—the sensitive type. It might not be terrible. "Okay, all right," I said with a shrug. "If he asks me, I'll go. Oh gee, I'll go to the dance and have a jolly time."

"Has anyone ever told you you're impossible sometimes?"

I pretended to mull this over. "Hmm, nope, just you."

"Someone needs to keep you in check. We'll have fun, okay?"

"Yeah, swell."

Unfazed, Vee took my arm and led me down the hall.

I hadn't really seen anyone since Chris. And I couldn't think about Chris because it still knotted up my stomach. How our relationship had triggered everything with those dimwits, Stacey and Olivia. How he abandoned me during the worst time of my life.

But I did think about Dylan for most of the day, and I felt the first tiny crack of light come through the shadow of Mom's death. Even Glenda was okay on the way home, leaving me and my school day at peace because she was so amped about her brother being there to renovate the kitchenette in the carriage house.

What I couldn't do was bear to look at her anymore. She had this beyond annoying tick where she frantically shook her head to part her bangs. The other day I counted it off and it was like every ten to twelve seconds she'd shake her head to free the little-claw like hairs on her forehead only to have them slide right back to their home position. I cracked myself up thinking how every picture of her was a blur, catching her mid-shake and berserk, unable to stop twitching for one solid second to at least appear in a photo as a normal human being.

On Madison Street, we pulled into the driveway behind a dusty Toyota Forerunner with some boards on the rooftop canoe rack, the back bumper plastered with stickers.

"Oh, good. Andrew's here. Let's go see how it's coming along."

The carriage house door was wide open. A commercial blared from a radio. I hung back, keeping my customary two or three steps behind Glenda. As we entered I smiled, seeing Uncle Robbie sipping a beer, hovering over the counter-less cabinets in what used to be a kitchenette, enjoying some guy time.

Andrew—I presumed—stood, fixed his hat, and smiled. I knew from Glenda's gushing he was twenty-eight, but he was more boyish looking, tall like Robbie but rangy and thin. Glenda had said something about him just getting back from the beach, explaining his dark tan and sun-washed hair. His bluish/gray eyes were one-part spectacular and one-part creepy. But overall he seemed pretty chill.

"Hey guys," Glenda said, her eyes lingering on Robbie's beer, like she was debating whether to bust his balls.

Andrew smiled. "Hey, sis. So I was just telling Robbie we're going to need to special order this corner piece," he stopped, nodded to me, and Glenda tossed an arm around my shoulder.

"Oh, Andrew, you remember Chloe?"

"I don't think we've met," I said, ducking out from her grasp.

"Hey, Chloe," he said, followed by the obligatory *sorry to hear about your mom.* I nodded and things got quiet.

Glenda picked up the slack. "So Andrew, will you be joining us for dinner tonight?"

Robbie drained his beer. "It's nice out. I was thinking we should fire up the grill."

Glenda stood there, blinking rapidly, obviously wounded but trying to recover. I was all for it, anything to keep her out of the kitchen. Good job, Uncle Robbie.

"Um, okay sure," she said, making sure we all knew it wasn't *okay sure* at all. She took stock of the room, all the caulk tubes and tarps, dusty trash and beer bottles laying around. Not exactly a hub of productivity. Glenda nodded to me with a dent in her smile. "So Chloe, you want to go get changed and help me with the salad, okay?"

Andrew grinned at me, like he knew what I was dealing with. He turned for the fridge and grabbed two beer bottles by the neck, popped the top and handed one to Robbie. Glenda eyed him carefully.

I smiled, thinking this just might be okay.

Chapter 4

How Andrew and Glenda were related was a riddle to my young, impressionable mind. Glenda was a mess of nerves, always uptight, biting her nails and fighting her bangs to the point of cartilage damage. She was constantly stressed about something, unbelievably stupid things like whether or not the Azaleas in the front yard would bloom in time to accommodate the tulips or if the kitchen tile in the carriage house was the right shade of weathered gray to compliment the backsplash (I'd endured both of these mind-numbing conversations).

Then there was Andrew, Mr. Casual, with his cloudy gaze and lazy man-spreading. Sometimes, when Glenda wasn't looking, he'd shoot me a look, like, *can you believe this?*

He'd done all sorts of cool stuff, too, like backpacking through Europe, crashing in hostels and riding the trains like Vee and I always talked about doing after graduation. He'd worked in a food truck in D.C. before making his way out to San Francisco to install solar panels. Glenda harassed him some about finishing his degree, but her eyes took on a proud shine when her little brother spoke, like, *Yeah, I'm the successful one, but isn't he something?*

From what I could tell, Glenda and Andrew had never really been close, what with the ten-year gap in their ages. She'd been more like a surrogate parent after their dad died, which kind of explained her borderline weird affection towards him. Andrew was a baby when his dad passed, and he seemed to be without the dumpster-load of issues rattling around in Glenda's trap.

Robbie and I took refuge in the carriage house, "helping" Andrew while escaping Glenda's nonstop nagging. Uncle Robbie grinned more with Andrew around, covering his laugh with a cough when Andrew called Glenda out. It was nice to see my uncle cut loose like he used to, with real gut laughs instead of the empty chuckle I'd heard around the house. I think he liked having a guy to shoot the breeze with, anything to get some air in that house.

The next weekend, Robbie, Andrew, and I were hanging out in the carriage house when Robbie went on a beer run because the two of them had managed to clear out the garage fridge. You can probably guess how much flak Uncle Robbie caught for that. Glenda rode him about the pettiest things, like using too much butter on his toast. Anyway, as soon as Uncle Robbie was gone, Andrew looked back over his shoulder to the door. He turned to me and said, "That guy really needs to get laid some time."

He said it in an offhand way, like it was nothing more than two old friends shooting the breeze. I laughed, hopping off the bar to grab my water from the window ledge when his gaze slid down to my waist and kept sliding and he didn't even try to hide it. I tossed my hair back and took a sip. "Tell me about it."

He got back to his measurements in the far corner of the kitchen, inspected a piece of tile, then turned to me with a smile that made his dimples bloom. I could feel my cheeks flush. He leaned back against the cabinets, wiping off some excess glue or paste or whatever it was. "You know, my sister's always been wound pretty tight. Always been the worrier."

"Yeah, how so?"

"Well, you know." He watched me for a second before getting back to work, going on with the story. "When she was in school, well, she had those braces. And she was a little awkward." He gestured towards the house with the tile. "You've seen her. Anyway, she kind of had a hard time with it."

"Explains a lot," I laughed.

I was trying to decide if this was weird, what his eyes were doing, or maybe *I* was being weird, overreacting because Andrew was older and staring at me the way he was. He took a sip of his beer and smiled before going into the story of Glenda's high school trauma. Not so casual anymore.

"She used to come home crying every day."

"Seriously?"

He shrugged, keeping his eyes on the beer. "Then, you know, they can't have kids so, well, probably why she's so excited to have you around."

I wasn't sure what to say with all this new info. I'd just figured they were too busy for kids. Andrew turned up his beer, smacked his lips, and smiled. "Anyway, she's really trying though. I think she wants to win your approval."

I wasn't exactly prepped for the info dump. I didn't need it really. "Well, she could start by giving me some space."

"Yeah," he said, looking up slowly.

"What?"

I thought he was going to take up for his sister, launch into another heartfelt tale about their parents. Instead, he imitated her headshake thing, and I about lost it.

"Oh, wow. That is so dead on."

We were cracking up hard when the door brushed the floor. I swung around to see Big Sis standing there, and I covered my mouth to hide my giggling, which only made it worse.

Glenda's eyes shot like darts around the room. "What? What's so funny?"

Andrew set down his beer and pointed at me. "She is."

Glenda whipped her head my way with a suspicious smile, throwing shade across the room. "Well, I'm glad you two are having a good time. Chloe, I was wondering if you could help me out in the kitchen?"

"Oh, uh, okay." I slid past the bar to the living room, around the chair moved to the side and covered with plastic. But when I walked past Glenda and glanced back, Andrew did the head shake again and I folded over in laughter.

"My gosh, you two, what is so funny?"

"Just an inside joke," Andrew said.

It was harmless fun though, I mean, not counting Glenda's mini-freak-outs and her weird jealousy when Uncle Robbie and I hung out with Andrew. That was just plain creepy. Like the day we were putting groceries away and Andrew's Forerunner pulled up, and I made some stupid comment about the cute contractor being home and Glenda nearly had a stroke. She tossed the green bananas on the counter.

"What did you say?"

Her eyes sort of bulged out of her head. I looked around the room, thinking maybe there was something else going on. "I was making a joke."

She stared at me like I'd committed some awful crime. "Well, it's not funny. Andrew's got a lot on his mind right now."

I had no idea what she was talking about. "Uh, okay. Again, joking."

I should've kept my mouth shut. Because after that day, Glenda did all she could to keep us apart. I spent the rest of the week learning how to prepare and cook nauseating meals that would kill the grass if you tossed them out on the lawn. And whenever Andrew came around she would start in on him, asking rapid-fire questions about what was going on with his ex, Renee.

Finally, I mentioned the dance and Dylan just to shut her up about it. Only it made things worse, she went off like a rocket launch. "Chloe, how wonderful."

I regretted it immediately. Not so much because Glenda was foaming at the mouth, but because Dylan Kowalski had yet to actually ask me. And the dance was in three weeks, not that I cared or even planned on going, but still. Glenda tore into her closet like we were the same size.

"Okay, well, we'll have to go dress shopping this weekend, then I'll help you do your hair. This will be so much fun."

I guess it could be fun, if this were 1990 and you liked crimp irons or bangs, if you enjoyed such nerve-splicing conversations that made you contemplate the odds of death or coma from leaping out of the upstairs window. It was a bad move, telling Glenda about the dance, a moment of weakness I suppose. Just hearing her mention "boys" made my underarms sting.

A few days later Andrew took off—as he did a lot—leaving the three of us at the table with a pulsing hunk of vegetarian "meatloaf" between us, jiggling to the jumpy jazz horns and promising big, foamy leftovers to hold us over. Robbie took it hard, hiding in the bathroom for hours. Then again, it could have been the meatloaf.

Miss Shelby decided I was no longer exempt from the rules. The freaking bell hadn't even finished ringing before she pulled me to the side and gave me a warm, coffee-breath warning about being on my phone during class. I explained how the phone wasn't even hooked up—I'd kept both mine and Mom's phones just to peek at the pictures. Miss Shelby understood completely, but then reminded me I would be held responsible for my assignments, and from here on it was expected I would turn them in each morning like the rest of the class if I wanted credit. Sure, whatever.

She made us keep these journals, a page-long entry every day so she could grade our grammar and sentence structure like we were remedial or something. It was invasive and creepy and I'd quit keeping up with it for a while because when your mother dies you're granted some leniency. Now my leniency had expired.

So Monday was shot, even before the Dimwits of Dunham struck.

Stacey Calloway and Olivia Morgan, with their matching smirks —the same plastic smiles they used to welcome freshmen to Dunham as part of the student services committee—were carbon copies of the characters in the movies they watched. They spoke through a thinly veiled code of cutting glances and giggles. Attached by a nauseating cloud of jasmine. I suppose Stacey was the leader, being how she was somewhat attractive. But Olivia was the wild one of the two, always highlighting her hair until it took on a greenish hue.

They really thought they were something, like a camera crew was following them around, hanging on their every word. From the start I'd been done with them, and before we'd even finished the campus tour I could tell the feeling was mutual. I won't delve any further into their bitchography, but once it became clear that Vee and I would have no trouble making friends of our own—even some of theirs— well, they'd declared war.

As luck would have it, I just happened to pass by them on *that* particular day. I was off my game after the whole thing with Miss Shelby, and I only wanted to be alone. Normally, I'd roll my eyes and brush past their hysterical whispering. But Stacey had the nerve to call me over.

"I'm, uh, we're like, really sorry about your mom."

The little laugh tacked on the end rinsed the words of any sincerity. I nearly tripped, seeing fireworks, I was so blackout furious they would say my name or even mention Mom. Luckily, Vienna swooped in and took my shoulder, told me to breathe, and my throat loosened up and my chest uncoiled. Stacey whipped her hair as she spun back to her locker and giggled.

Vee pulled me along. "Relax, just relax."

Vienna had to pry open my clenched fist as we ducked into the stairwell. I fell into her.

"Don't Chloe. Just breathe. Breathe, Chloe."

I shook my head, words forming but washing away with the tears. I couldn't say why I was so upset about it, maybe I still had a right to be emotional, but still, it felt like they'd trespassed, broken in and trampled on sacred ground. It made me want to slap them until my hand was numb.

But Vienna had a way with words. Her voice was like a warm cushion, catching my freefall as she talked me down, and it wasn't long until she had me laughing through my cry, quoting some of the more desperate text messages Stacey had sent Spence over the summer, making silly emoji faces until I was cracking up.

She wiped away my tears as I regained my basic functions. Vee was good like that, putting me back together when I fell apart. And I did the same for her whenever she fell apart, which wasn't often. Vienna always seemed so normal and composed, at least when she wasn't freaking out about Spence Nottaway.

Chapter 5

Dress shopping with Glenda was an ordeal. We ate lunch outside, at this *most fabulous* café, where Glenda picked through a *most fabulous* salad, going on nonstop about her wonderful high school days and prom and who knows what else. Lies, as I'd learned about the braces and being flat (still is), all the nervous tics and head-banging. Things got awkward fast.

Since talking about her with Andrew I almost felt bad for the way I'd been treating her. The more she went on the clearer it became there was some major damage manifesting up there. Maybe it's why she couldn't stop moving or talking, like she was terrified of what her mind would cook up if she afforded it one free second of idle time. And so she babbled about, from childhood to college, and somewhere in the weeds of her life story I caught something about how she'd been the one who'd found their dad dead in his truck.

She took a few calls and answered a text message before getting back to her whimsical memories of campus. But I was still hung up on the dad thing, putting it all together. The look on my face must have made it obvious, because she stopped suddenly to rush off in search of the bathroom. Check please.

After lunch we trudged onward, to the shops, so she could buy organic hand-crafted junk, like misshapen hand soap that looked like a wad of chewed gum or jewelry suspiciously similar to a lamp chain.

Even worse was how Glenda made the dance and our dress shopping some major event, posting on Facebook where all her old friends liked it and said things like, *How exciting, She's stunning, Good for her!, Aww!,* and other comments you could have easily swapped under an adoption picture at your local Humane Society. I deactivated my account.

Social media wasn't the worst of my problems. Lately my conversations with Dylan went something like this:

Me: Oh, hey Dylan. What's up?

Dylan, a rash of pink spreading over his cheeks: Oh, um, hey Chloe.

I swear, the way he got nervous was all sorts of adorable. Endearing really, and it was almost like a ninja trick, how cute he'd become standing before me. Seriously, how had I never noticed how hot he was until now? If only he would speed things along.

Me, getting desperate, twirling my hair and sending ridiculously obvious signals that I was interested—not that he noticed: So what's new with you?

Dylan, staring at hall floor: Um, nothing much. I (unintelligible).

Bell rings, Dylan waves and shuffles off.

Me, big sigh, thinking: I shouldn't have to work this hard for a date.

It was all Vee's fault. This was her idea in the first place. Not to worry, she said, she'd talk to Spence who would "get his butt in gear." But as it stood, I was dress shopping for no other reason than to spend some quality time with Glenda. Not cool.

In the end, I did manage to find a nice little cream color dress that made me look tan. I found it at Tulip's, a dank little headshop that reeked of incense and patchouli. I could tell the dress wasn't Glenda's thing, it was light and semi-low cut, with straps and an open back. Her face went through a series of hilarious contortions. She asked me if I was sure a million times.

"I think this is the one I want," I said with my cutest smile. Melt. To the checkout counter we went, where the chick with the dreads and the nose ring eyed us with a smirk.

So I had the dress but no date. But again, if Dylan didn't tighten up, that would change. I could get a date, it was just that after Mom died people were under the impression I was all screwed up. And maybe I was, but I still looked good in a dress.

A FEW DAYS later I was wearing the dress in my room for no other reason than I liked the way it made me feel. I had the windows up and the whir of a saw from the carriage house got my attention. Andrew's Forerunner sat crookedly in the driveway, and it caught me by surprise, the small fluttering in my chest. Maybe it was the dress, or the thought of normal conversation, but I went to the mirror and set my hair up on my head.

Crunching across the pea-gravel driveway, some acoustic song drifted from the radio, a guy whining about the way a girl looks in her sleep. I found Andrew in the corner, still tiling away but not making much progress. I hung back until he noticed me. When he did, he stood up and smiled.

"Hey, Chloe. Wow, new dress?"

I nodded, shrugged, tried not to blush, but the dress did fit me perfectly, just right in every place. I leaned back on the little bar, cluttered with tools and trash. There was the slight hint of weed in the air. Andrew stepped forward and put his hand on the small of my back. I sort of jumped but caught myself. I didn't want to seem like a clueless little girl.

He smiled and nudged me closer. "Watch that, there's some caulk and all sorts of mess."

I stepped away from the bar and exhaled. "Oh, thanks."

He let me go and turned back to the corner, a pencil between his teeth as he hummed along. On the bar sat his phone. I picked it up, unlocked. His fault. With his back turned I snapped a few pictures of him hunched over. Stifling a giggle, I took some silly selfies, setting the phone down just before he stood up.

"Glenda said you're going to a dance?"

"Yeah, maybe."

I explained my dilemma, leaving out the finer details. He laughed and said he'd done the same thing. I pictured him in a suit, a little younger but not much because he didn't really seem all that old. He definitely didn't act like it.

He wiped his hands on his jeans. "Well, he's a lucky guy."

I shook my head, unsure what to say. But his eyes were stubborn, like he wasn't going to let me off the hook without a reaction. I looked back at the open door, the easy sun and sounds of the evening, crickets, a distant lawn mower, thinking Robbie and Glenda should be home soon.

Andrew snorted and turned to the fridge. "Glenda had to work late. I don't know where Robbie is. You want something to drink?"

Obviously he didn't mean a juice box. I shrugged. He dug through the fridge. "Let's see, there's some old wine coolers in here, somewhere. You don't seem like a beer type of chick."

He came out with a cherry red wine cooler. "Wild berry?"

Before I could answer he twisted off the cap and handed it to me. I took it. Why not? In my new dress, with my hair up, a cold drink felt right in my hand. Everything felt better without Glenda marching around, getting in the way, controlling every second of what was being said or done. Andrew watched as I took a small sip.

"Yum."

He turned up his beer then set it on the counter. "I didn't mean anything by what I said you know, just saying you're a bright girl and all."

Another sip. And one more. It wasn't like I'd never had a drink before. One time at Vienna's party we'd stolen a fifth of rum and made a big punch bowl, but there was hardly enough rum so we only got a little buzz before Spence and the boys drank it all. Someone puked in the fish tank. But the wine cooler snuck up on me. It was sweet, like Kool-Aid, only with a hint of sour, and it went straight to my head. Halfway down and it felt like I was sitting in a canoe, bobbing along with the rapids.

Andrew slid beside me. "You okay?"

"Huh? Oh, yeah." I set my chin down towards my chest because he was acting like a boy acts when he wants to kiss you. And yeah, the flirting was okay, had been okay, at least. But now he was basically panting, and I could hear my own heart thumping in my breaths.

I started to bring the bottle to my lips, but he reached for it and stopped me. He came in and pressed his lips to mine, hard. I wasn't expecting it, wasn't ready for him to be so close, for his nostril-y breath on my cheek. I pulled away, still smiling, but freaking out some. "What are you doing?"

He backed off. "Is it okay?"

Okay? I didn't know if he meant the drink or the kiss. It took a moment to register what happened, how he'd set his leg out against the bar and his arm on the other side, kind of blocking me in. But his face was soft and concerned, those gray eyes stirring. I blinked a few times, a dumb laugh in my throat because I didn't know what else to do. I still had the bottle, so I took a drink. This time he reached for my other hand, fiddling with my fingers.

It was kind of gross. His hands were jacked up, stained with the caulk and grout and I didn't want them on my dress. He smelled okay —musky but clean—scents at odds like my buzz and panic. My face, scraped by his stubble, felt hot and rashy. It was weird, how from a distance I'd thought he was cute, but up close he was more threatening, like a force coming down on me.

He leaned in again. This time he shoved his tongue in my mouth. Before I knew it he was sucking on my face in the wreck of a kitchen. I jerked away but he hung on, pressing harder with a moan. He grabbed my back and I knew he was getting caulk on my new dress. Not only that, for some reason Dylan flashed into my thoughts, and I really wanted to pull myself free when a car door thumped shut outside.

Andrew drew back. He swiped my wine cooler and jumped away. Robbie stood at the doorway.

"Hey, guys."

I can't imagine what it looked like. Me in my dress, hair up and flushed, out of place in the carriage house with Andrew. At the same time, I was glad he was away from me, out of my airspace so I could breathe.

Andrew, back in his corner, sprung out like a jack in the box. "Robbie, my man. We were just talking about you guys."

"Yeah?" Robbie had his eyes on me—eyes like my mother's. I looked away, wanting to wipe my face, wanting to tell him what just happened. Heat blasted my cheeks. I needed to tell Robbie what just happened. But then, why *was* I in there?

"Yeah, we were wondering about dinner. We weren't sure what to do on our own." He looked back and winked at me. I was still kind of fuzzy. I kicked my feet out, trying to catch my breath without heaving.

"Where is Glenda, anyway?" I said. Like I cared, but I had to say something, with Robbie staring at me like that.

"She's on the way, caught up in traffic." Robbie's voice was deep. Careful. He glanced at the fridge. "I was thinking maybe we could grill out again."

The scattered tile pieces. The light buzzing with new urgency. Suddenly, in the garage, my dress felt like a clown costume. Robbie looked over to the saw, to the cabinets where Andrew had stashed the wine cooler. Andrew cleared his throat. "Sounds like a plan."

"Okay," Robbie said, heading for the house. I think he'd rushed home knowing his buddy Andrew was here, all excited for some guy time, now he seemed disappointed. "I'll just grab a few steaks from the freezer."

He left the door open and crunched across the driveway, stopping at the Jeep for his satchel, then heading up the steps into the kitchen. Andrew turned back to me and set his hand right on my thigh. "You okay?"

I slid away, glancing down at my new dress. Any semi-buzz I'd managed had been jolted back to reality, first by Andrew and his force, then by Robbie's face, the defeat in his voice. Everything was wrong. I felt gross, looking at Andrew's filthy hands, his fingernails on my leg. I slid past him, towards the door.

"I need to go take a shower."

Chapter 6

I almost told Vienna about Andrew at school the next day. Almost. But she was consumed with her own drama—a major fight about some picture Spence posted with another girl. Her brain was in output-only mode at the moment so I let her go on about it until she stopped to catch her breath. I did manage to tell her about the dress, and I immediately wished I hadn't.

"Oh, so now look who wants to go to the dance."

I swear, she was my best friend and all, but sometimes she needed a good smacking. "Not the dance, no. I'm only doing it because you said…"

"Relax, Chlo, yeah we're still going. Oh, and no lacrosse practice today. Dylan should be at the baseball game this afternoon."

Baseball. Whatever. Anything to keep me out of the kitchen and away from the carriage house. The smudges had come out of my dress, but it took some work. So baseball, lacrosse, cliff diving. Anything was better than sitting at home, reliving that awful kiss in the carriage house.

I wrote up my account just before Mrs. Shelby's class. I had to laugh, reading it over.

Yesterday was quite splendid. We sat down to a feast of cooked goose, red-skinned potatoes, and garlic bread. Aunt Glenda proposed an evening stroll afterwards, wherein we ambled along the courtyards, taking a particular delight at the notes of a sparrow's song, washed in the glow of the fading sun, nestling gently into the mountains…

It would do. My mind was too cluttered with thoughts to come up with anything better. I thought about telling Robbie and Glenda about Andrew, but what was there to tell? I was the one who'd gone in the carriage house, alone, dressed to the hilt. Ugh, it was too embarrassing to think about, so I decided to keep it hush and hope it went away. Especially after how Glenda reacted to my "cute" comment.

As the day went on I looked forward to the baseball game. Not that I was hung up on Dylan or anything. I mean sure, he was cute—tall, with a strong set jaw and tight, curly hair, and the shy thing was sweet, but this whole dance-but-not-dance thing was getting painful.

When we met up afterschool, Vee hooked my arm as we started for the field, weaving our way through the campus, across the impeccably groomed grounds, between the gothic style cathedral and the ivy-clad buildings, and down paths to the athletic fields.

When I'd first arrived at Dunham from public school, it was like some Camelot courtyard. Everything reeked of boxwoods and money. I didn't know how I'd ever fit in with these privileged blazer boys with shaggy hair and khakis. But with Vee's fairytale giggle and gum commercial smile, we did just fine, tromping down the hill in our skirts, watching their heads swivel as we took our seats on the grassy bank.

Vienna squealed, waving out to first base. Spence waved back. He tugged on his hat and slapped his little mitt. He was really muscular, with broad shoulders and a V-shaped torso, and I started going on about his body to mess with Vee until she slapped my arm. We were still laughing when I turned back and found Dylan hovering over us.

"Hey, there."

"Uh, hey, Chloe."

Some kids up on the hill screamed at the batter. Vee scooted and Dylan eased in between us, getting quiet, his hands fumbling in his lap. Behind his back Vee found my eyes, but I brushed her off. Dylan, wearing his Dunham baseball cap, his sandy blond curls peeking out at the ears, kept his face straight ahead. I tried to come up with a way to nudge him along.

Silence. The thwack of the baseball slapping the mitt. Parents yelling at the kids on the field. Vienna kept things from getting too quiet. "So Dylan, what are your plans for the weekend?"

I threw a sharp look at Vee. Dylan fixed his hat. "Oh, well, uh. I've got..." it took him a minute to catch on, and when he did he started blushing hard, smiling and being all kinds of irresistible. "I um, Chloe, I was wondering if you wanted to go to the Spring Formal?"

Well Halle-freaking-lujah. I gave him my best smile and kind of bumped him with my shoulder. "Yeah, okay."

"Oh, I'm so glad *that's* out of the way," Vienna gushed. She slung an arm around him, wasting no time. "Okay, the plan is to meet up at Cantini's Steakhouse. Is that okay with you guys? We should probably make reservations because it will be packed and all...after, we'll go to the lake."

She went on for a while, at least until she caught her breath because Spence was up to bat. I, for one, had no idea Vienna was such a baseball connoisseur. She even knew how to keep score. Not me, I spent the next hour occasionally brushing Dylan's hand and smiling, telling myself I was going to forget what happened with Andrew in the carriage house. I had a dress and a date. That was enough.

It was a little after eight when I got back to Madison Street. Glenda had a dinner plate ready for me in the fridge. Oh joy, tortellini, only with faux meat sauce that promised to put my stomach through a cheese grater. I slid it into the trash and covered it with a paper towel, grabbed a bowl of cereal, and headed to my room.

⌖

LATER, I set my playlist and opened up the window, hoping to let the fresh air and reggae bring a little breeze of Mom to me.

Mom and I loved reggae music. I grew up singing along with Bob Marley and Peter Tosh, Greggory Isaacs, Jimmy Cliff, and more, since I was crawling. Mom had worked on a cruise ship after high school. She'd been all over the Caribbean, then to her exile in Jamaica, where I'd been conceived. From birth, every Sunday when it was warm enough, we'd open the windows and sit in the shade out on the patio with Toots and the Maytals going strong.

People think reggae music is stoner music, and sure, some of it is, but I like the fight in it. The revolution and rights, the protest, the rising tide of freeing one's mind and soul and body from bondage. It was about living *on* the earth and *of* the earth, and it filled me with such righteousness I was tempted to drop everything and move to Jamaica like Mom. Get lost on an island.

The breeze came, sweeping in thoughts of Grandpa and the funeral instead of Mom. I remembered how his hair was dislodged in the wind. Honestly, I was still shocked they'd even shown up and sat beside me. Of course they hadn't stayed long—not after good old Grandpa caused such a scene with the wreaths—but it was all I could do to keep myself together.

They didn't deserve to be there or anywhere near Mom. With their big house out in East Dunham—a shrinking estate being sold off in chunks because Grandpa had little business sense and a hankering for Maker's Mark. All he had now was that Vanderbrooke name. Mom always said: to hear Grandpa say it, you could almost hear the fanning of money between the syllables.

Once, Mom had broken down and told me how he'd always considered her an embarrassment, how he'd even laughed in her face when she got accepted to art school. He disowned her completely when she took off to Jamaica with the guy formerly known as my dad.

He called her a whore. His own daughter. And in some twist of logic, he and Grandma Millie used religion to defend their decisions but never for the strength to find compassion. They never considered me anything but a reminder of their daughter's supposed bad decisions.

Imagine being ten and running into your own grandparents at the grocery store, your grandmother staring at you in the frozen section with trembling lips and pleading eyes like she never really thought you were real. Your grandfather turning around and heading the other way. So yeah, I took issue with being used as a prop at the funeral.

They'd spent years pretending we didn't exist, and it wasn't until Mom got her job at D.E.S. that they started reaching out to us—if you could call it that. But by then it was too late as far as I was concerned. I'm not good like my mother. Forgiveness doesn't come so easily for me. Like Papa Vanderbrooke, I'm better at grudges. And so I carry on, proud to serve as a burden to them—a blonde-haired, blue-eyed, dead-ringer of a reminder as to what they squandered with all their self-righteous judgment.

I scrolled through the pics on my phone. The whole incident with Andrew was bizarre, almost unreal in my memory. And maybe there was something more to it, something to help me realize just how much I liked Dylan, with his shy eyes, his hat and his curls.

I picked up the picture of Mom from my dresser, the one of her at the beach on the pier, her arms on the railing and her hair swept back by the breeze. Sometimes I spoke to her or kissed her pretty face before I went to sleep.

The music, the sun, Mom at the beach. I got my new dress out and put it on again. I danced around in my room, Dennis Brown's *Here I Come* filling me with hope and light.

I was dizzy with happiness, at least for a moment. For a moment everything was fake and I was a character on stage. Mom sat in the audience, and after the show she'd come running up to take me in her arms and we'd go home and laugh about my strange dream. I snapped a selfie in the mirror of me in the dress. Then I kept twirling around like a little girl, reversing the kiss with Andrew and the bitter taste of his tongue until the music and the breeze and the dress was perfect.

Although nothing was perfect. Not even close.

Chapter 7

I lay in bed, half awake, drifting in and out after a dream about Mom on the floating dock at the lake. It's a dream I've had before, several times, where she grabs my wrists but we're too wet and her grip slides from my wrists to my hands then to my fingers before she slides off completely and dissolves into the black, murky water. I can only scream, too paralyzed with fear to go in after her, and so I just watch her slip into the abyss.

Doctor O had said it was understandable, that it symbolized my mother's death and my loss. I guess it made sense, but still, whenever it happened I woke up out of breath and sweating, my mother's hands still wet in my grasp, wondering why I didn't help her.

I sat up, catching my breath. It was late, or early, in the blank part of the night where everything is still and quiet, the house groaning and ticking, settling like it's stretching in for sleep. But then I heard it.

Footsteps. Not bare feet, but boots, stopping at my door. I knew Robbie wouldn't even look in my room when the door was open, and Glenda usually fell into a deep hibernation every night around ten. Which left Andrew, wiggling the door handle.

When the door creaked open I wasn't sure if it was real or another nightmare, but as my eyes adjusted my whole body clenched.

"What are you doing?" I asked in a hiss, forcing a calmness in my voice when everything inside of me wanted to scream for Robbie.

"Shh." Andrew's silhouette appeared in the doorway, the soft light from downstairs on his back. He was sort of swaying, one foot to the other, a soft squeak in the planks. "It's okay, it's okay."

No. It wasn't okay. I'd already decided I'd never to go back into the carriage house, but now Andrew was here, in the house. In my room.

I pulled the covers to my chin. I was only wearing a t-shirt so I didn't want to get up. But I also didn't want him any closer. Luckily he stayed where he was, clicking and sniffing and making all sorts of little noises. "I wanted to see you."

Gross. There was a disgusting hint of baby-talk to his words. Everything and a million other thoughts raced through my head. *Wanted to see me?* Hairs I didn't know I had stood up. It was bad enough the other day had happened, but what now? Did he think this was okay? Again, I thought about screaming out for Robbie, but what then? What would I say to Glenda?

Maybe he was drunk. His speech was slurred. Panic set in and I could hardly get the words out. "Why are you—no. Get out."

Another step. I slid back farther with the comforter, my leg cocked and ready to kick like mad if he came any closer. The bed creaked like it was going to snap; it was one of those antique finds Glenda had discovered and it was noisy as all anyway. Another squeak in the floorboards and Andrew reached out for me in the dark. A hand found my leg and I jerked away.

So much for kicking. I scrambled back into the headboard. "What do you think you're doing?"

"Chloe."

"Out."

"It's okay, Chloe, it's okay." He kept saying it's okay, over and over, all slow and weird. His tone teetered, up and down, soft and strong. I couldn't see his eyes but I could feel them on me. It was crazy to think this was the same guy who'd eaten dinner with us.

I pointed to the door, trying to be as clear and calm as I could manage. "You need to leave. Glenda and Robbie," I said, as the floor let out another long, painful whine. Andrew leaned in again.

"It's just that, the other day... Come down to the carriage house."

Fear thrashed inside my chest. His minty breath stung my face. But with the door open and the light leaking in, I felt less trapped.

The words came out in a slow, cracking whisper. "You need to get out of my room."

His shadowy presence was like a cold threat in the dark. Maybe two seconds before I let go with a scream, he turned for the hall, looking back, "I just thought we could have some fun."

My throat closed, stifling the bile churning up from my stomach. Again, I pulled on the comforter, tight over my shoulders until his boots finally slid away, out to the hall and down the steps. When I was sure he was gone, I leaped up and shut the door. I hurried back to bed as the dry heaves came. The room felt contaminated. By the mint. By his whisper. Soured by the absolute horror. I would never be able to fall asleep in there again.

I spent the rest of the night watching the door, ears perked for the sound of steps. All I wanted to do was run and bang on Uncle Robbie's door, explain everything, but the kiss in the carriage house held me back. I was too ashamed to move.

The last I looked at the clock it was after four. I curled up tight against the wall and squeezed my pillow until the sun came up.

Chapter 8

The next morning, I enjoyed maybe ten seconds of fuzzy consciousness before the nightmare of Andrew's visit eclipsed the day. I whipped the covers off, got dressed, and hit the steps, pausing at the third stair to make sure he wasn't hanging around the kitchen.

A flush of relief passed through me. Uncle Robbie sat at the counter, alone, munching on cereal as he scrolled through the news on his iPad. My uncle was still getting used to having me around, it was on his face when he saw me—confusion, apprehension, unease—flashing in his eyes before he recovered with a smile and motioned to the cereal.

"Saved you a bowl."

"Thanks" Normally, I'd call him a tool or something in my head. Bad habit, I know, but this morning, after Andrew in the night, Uncle Robbie's dorkiness was as refreshing as the morning sun.

I thought about telling him. I did. But again, the dark cloud of guilt hung heavy over my head, like I'd brought this on myself. And what could I say? To Robbie with his man crush, or Glenda who'd nearly bludgeoned me with organic bananas for calling her brother cute. Cute, huh? Not so much.

Glenda bounced across the kitchen with a healthy shake of the bangs, shouting loud enough for the neighbors to hear. "Good morning, people. One more day to go."

Glenda was a morning person. A people person. A pain-in-the-butt person. Most of the time Uncle Robbie and I grunted our hellos before we got back to what we were doing. But grunts wouldn't do here, because not only was tomorrow Friday, it was the big dance.

"Are you excited, sweetie?" she gushed. The woman stayed full tilt. She fiddled with her phone and NPR hummed to life. Concerned yet pleasant voices discussed U.S. relations with China as she mixed together her usual pea-colored gruel. Robbie and I shivered in disgust.

Glenda hummed about, still blabbing on about the dance. I nodded but mostly kept my head down, focused on my cereal while Robbie scrolled away—keeping busy, doing anything to keep out of the line of fire—avoiding my eyes as I stared him down, like, *Seriously man, what were you thinking with this chick?*

Uncle Robbie was a tough read. At first I'd thought he just didn't like me at the house messing up his day-to-day, cluttering up the only upstairs bathroom with all my stuff. But over the weeks I was beginning to think it wasn't *me* so much he didn't like but *Glenda.* Sure, maybe he'd say he loved her, if asked, but to watch them in passing? I wasn't buying it.

I could tell he so badly wanted to tell her just to shut her yap for one glorious second. It was all over his face, glowing on his knuckles as he gripped his spoon. And the cereal itself was proof the guy liked normal food, unlike Glenda with her kale smoothie. I mean, who honestly likes kale? Nobody. If they say they do they're lying.

Sometimes I wondered if Robbie ever woke up and stared up at the recessed ceiling with the exquisite crown molding and thought, *Man, I used to be all right. Like that time I took little Chloe to the beach with my sister. We listened to the Ramones, I got a tattoo, I was the cool uncle. Now I don't have the gall to eat red meat in my own house.*

He did have a tattoo, this corny little crescent moon on his bicep. Glenda talked about it like it was a horrible birthmark or disfigurement, like it made him a hick or a loser. I still remember that beach trip though, I was five or six and it was the first time I'd ever seen the ocean or a tattoo. Mom was having a hard time, and Uncle Robbie wanted to step in and be a father figure. Then he met Glenda a year later and got neutered. Now he doesn't do or say much of anything.

I'd bet you a pile of money Uncle Robbie was a totally different guy at work. I'd bet people were always inviting him to go have drinks or whatnot, but instead he comes home and stares at the walls or reads, nodding along with things, any things, whatever it took to expedite the conversation so he could go to sleep and do it all again the next day. No more Ramones for that guy. Robbie doesn't have music, friends, or hobbies. They've all been consumed by the bottomless pit that is Glenda.

How observant of me putting all that together. But I sure didn't observe who was behind the steering wheel of Glenda's car after school. It was parked by the curb, and I was completely engulfed in something Miss Shelby had said in class earlier when I opened the door and tossed my bag in the back. I fell into the passenger seat, ready to begin my afternoon ritual of screwing with Glenda, when a thick blast of fast food hit my face just before I saw Andrew at the wheel.

The doors locked. We pulled away. He gave me a shrug. "So, I was hoping we could talk."

No words. Andrew stared ahead without blinking. I looked around, at the kids running for the buses, to activity vans, and SUVS. Mr. Maynard, the chubby gym teacher, chucking it up with some football players. For about a second I thought about opening the door, making a run for it. But it was too late. He was going too fast.

Andrew weaved around the buses before I could do much thinking. "Look, the other night, I need to explain." He talked as he drove. I tried to get it together. He wouldn't do anything in broad daylight, right? And the last thing I wanted was for skeevy Andy here to think I was scared of him—which I was, terrified, actually, especially now. I'd spent most of the day just trying to get the shakes out of my hands, now my whole body trembled.

I steadied my voice. "Where's Glenda?"

He leaned towards me. "Huh? Oh, she's tied up at work. I

dropped her off and told her I'd pick you up. I hope that's all right?" he said, like it mattered now. His crazy eyes fell to my chest before popping up. When did he get so sketchy? Or had he just been really good at hiding it?

"Look, the other night," he began.

"When you came in my room?"

A laugh, back to the surfer-boy act. All sun and smiles, Mr. *Right-on* and *No worries* again. "Look, Chloe, I thought, I don't know, the other day in the carriage house. That dress and all."

Was he saying this was my fault? Was it? No. I rolled my eyes, hoping for a bus to come careening across the lot and smack right into us. It would be better than this. I turned to face him, because I had to get this straight. "Look, I'm not sure what you think is happening here, but..."

"Yeah, what *is* happening?"

The way he snapped shut me up. Violence in his voice. We pulled out on East Ridge, fast, the wheels screaming as we ripped into the flow of traffic. I took a breath, widened my eyes to get the point across. "Nothing is happening. Will you just take me home?"

I leaned my head back and puffed out my cheeks. How obvious could I make this? I wanted nothing to do with him. I only wanted to get home and forget this. And yet, he continued on like everything was normal.

"Glenda said you're going to the dance tomorrow."

My fear turned to anger as my head rocketed off the seat rest. I could deal with him kissing me, even whatever had happened last night, if it ended there. But I wasn't going to let him interrogate me. "What does that have to do with anything?"

He turned his head to the road, calm, but not, his hands were all over the wheel, his jaw twitching. He looked my way with a laugh. "We used to ditch the dance, go get drunk and mess around." He took his wrist off the wheel and pointed. "Right up here."

"Whatever."

Andrew veered left and my heart took off galloping. I grabbed the seat. "Where are you going?"

He set the windows down as the car hurled onto a side street. All sorts of alarms fired off in my head as we bolted down a narrow little neighborhood street, passing cars so close I could've reached out and touched them.

"Seriously, take me home. Where are you going?"

When I grabbed the handle above my head, he looked over at me and grinned, having a real good time now. "Just wanted to show you the spot. Lighten up."

"No."

Another glance at my hand as it fell to the door handle. He gunned the engine and we skidded over to the next street, the houses getting farther apart, the trees taller, dense.

"It's right down here, used to be a nice little spot. No cops or neighbors," he said, checking the rearview. His eyes danced, darting from the windshield to me with his lunatic smile. "What do you think?"

That you're a freak. I tried to face him, mouth open in shock. I tried to convey how I was, you know, sixteen and all. "Andrew, I want to go home."

He wiped at his wet grin, the casual Andrew vanishing and a more Neanderthal Andrew arrived for the nightshift. His gaze on my legs. He clicked his teeth. "I'm not buying this innocent girl act, Chloe."

His hand fell on my knee and I jerked away. We were doing like eighty down this tiny street, Glenda's car like a roller coaster over the hills. Who knew what he'd do next? I swallowed down the lump of terror in my throat.

Again, how could I have ever thought this guy was cute? I eyed the door handle, envisioned flinging myself from the car, my body rolling to a stop in a much-deserved bloody tangle of scrapes and breaks. Because Andrew here was not cute at all. He was dangerous and easily capable of killing both of us. I'd rather do the job myself than give him the pleasure.

"Just thought we could be alone for a while," he was saying.

Well, what a romantic. But how did this happen? All because, I don't know...at the house with my new dress. It was too gross to think about. He turned the car again, wildly, taking a hard right entirely too fast, so the car slid as the tires bit and clawed for traction. We plunged into the cover of the trees, down a shaded, two-track gravel drive lined with splintered fence posts and barbed wire.

I jumped as he let out a yell, an almost inhuman shriek as we thundered down the narrow road, deeper into nowhere, filling Glenda's nice little car with a fog of dust like chalk in my mouth.

We skidded to a stop under a tree where the path opened to tall grass surrounding a filmy pond with an old, tilted dock. A faded green boat sat turned over, its bottom scraped with rust.

Andrew rubbed on my leg again. I recoiled. He dug into his pocket and produced a pill bottle. The label was peeled and fuzzy. Vicodin, maybe? Who knew at this point. We were completely alone down there, in the trees, with that scummy water. But words... I could hardly breathe.

"Andrew...please."

He tossed back the pills. His face was a stone. Eyes mean. His movements were sudden and violent. I counted his breaths, waiting for him to do something when he let it go, sat back, and squeezed the bridge of his nose. He took a deep breath, eyed the bottle, then fixed his hair under his hat, almost smiling. "You're such a tease, Chloe."

"No, I just, I'm really not feeling well."

He reached behind me and I jumped against the door with a scream, almost expecting a knife or gun. A bloody machete by the look on his face. Instead, he tossed a bag to me and a cheeseburger fell out. "There, I got you dinner."

It sat on my lap, lukewarm and gross like his hand. In one swift motion he turned the key in the ignition so hard I thought it would break. The car roared to life. Andrew shoved it into gear, and the tires spun on the gravel, flinging dirt as the car slid to a halt before ripping back into drive. My head hit the seat, burger and French fries spilling to the floorboard.

Everything blurred, from the drive down, the anger, the wheels digging into the gravel as the car slid to get back on the path. Now he was laughing, a bitter, lunatic laugh. He was still clutching the pill bottle in his hand as he turned to me. "Glenda was right. You're nothing but trash."

I snapped my head around to face him, tossing the bag to the floorboard. "What?"

The way he ogled me, the pulsing vein on his head, I couldn't imagine any girl at any time wanting him. To be near him. He knocked back a pill, shook his head. "I said you were trash."

For some reason, out of everything else, I got hung up on him calling me trash. That *Glenda* said I was trash. "I am not, you reject."

The car slammed to a stop, flinging me forward, my head crashing into the dashboard. "Ouch!"

A hand clasped my neck before I could move or think or even register the horror of what was happening. Quick flashes of pain. My vision bent, curled like the rust-eaten NO HUNTING sign nailed to a tree above the twist of the fencing, the snarl of the barbed wire. A sharp taint of B.O. hit me full on, as Andrew, the nomad, the laid-back bohemian back-packer, mashed his face into mine. His tongue wormed its way into my mouth while his other hand landed over my chest, down to my thighs, and back up, under my skirt.

It was no longer a game. I squirmed, kicked, grasped, and clawed. I ripped into his arms, dug into his wrists, groping for the hand crushing my windpipe. He overpowered me, and at some point I realized how hopeless it was to fight, how my muted screams never escaped the car or the woods surrounding us. I let go of his arms and went limp, giving up hope as he crushed my breath in his hand.

And then he stopped. His hand left my neck, my legs. He fell back to his seat, heaving and sweaty. It had taken only seconds for him to hurt me. And now the pain, fueled by the terror, revved its way down my neck to other places. I was his captive, held hostage by my own fear, blinking and waiting for him to come at me again. But he drove.

"We'd better get back. I've got to pick up Glen soon," he said, doing the head shake thing like he hadn't just kidnapped me and driven me down to a pond and nearly squeezed the life out of me. I forced back the hot tears, the throbbing in my forehead where it had banged the dashboard. My body rumbled with aftershocks. Andrew kept saying how I shouldn't mention this to Glenda. Coming to the pond and all. If I did, well... I just shouldn't say anything.

French fries were scattered all over the floorboard. The bag was ripped and grease-stained and I knew I would hate the smell of McDonald's for the rest of my life.

When we did get back, Andrew turned to me and smiled. I found my book bag from the back and got out of the car. My movements were rigid, mechanical. I slammed the door, ignoring the sting on my hips from where my underwear had been ripped down my leg as I hiked up the steps. All I could feel was his hand clamped around my neck.

Upstairs I let it out. I bit down on my pillow and grabbed my sides until I broke the skin. I found my phone, punched 9, ready to have him hauled off to jail. Then I punched 1—but the kiss in the carriage house stopped me in my tracks. The look on Robbie's face, the shame of what I'd brought on myself. It was nothing more than pride. I dropped my phone to the floor.

I got up, wiped my face, then took a shower. When I was done, I heard them downstairs. Glenda's voice was hushed and urgent. Andrew's was casual and joking around. It hit me then how I could never tell her what had happened. How I was completely alone in this. A deep breath and I fixed my hair. I squeezed my eyes tight, until it hurt, before I hit the steps. I'd take care of this reject myself.

"Hey, Chloe," Glenda called out when I came in the kitchen. Andrew looked up, surprised. He'd brought in the crumpled McDonald's bag. It sat on the table, wrinkled and smeared, like evidence. Glenda followed my eyes. "Oh, I hope you're not going to eat that stuff. I'm making tacos."

I hopped onto the counter and swept my hair back. I pulled out the soggy cheeseburger and looked at brother and sister, wondering what the whispering was all about. My gaze settled on Glenda, hers on Andrew. Andrew watched me.

I caught a quick snap in her confidence. She tossed her hands up. "Oh fine." She pulled a pan from the drawer. "But you guys know how I feel about McDonalds."

"Yeah, yeah" Andrew said, playing along. His stare gripping me while Glenda launched into her talking points. But as crazy as he was, I'd thrown him, coming downstairs, smirking and unfazed. I made a show of unwrapping the smushed burger and tore into it with a bite, staring right back at him. Because my mother was dead, and I was forced to live in this new kind of hell.

So screw him.

Chapter 9

Dylan picked me up in his dad's shiny BMW. He was especially handsome in a crisp gray suit, and between the car and the little bit of gel he'd put in his hair to go along with his hopeful smile, it was all just too adorable.

As for me, Vienna had stopped by earlier and swept my hair up into a braided crown. Nothing major, but I loved it. And when Glenda didn't start in with her compli-sults—the passive/aggressive compliments she usually gave me about what I wore—I worried maybe I was trying too hard. But she did tag along out to the driveway, phone in hand, snapping pics like we were five. It was embarrassing.

As far as the Andrew situation, I dealt with it by not dealing with it. My heart went ballistic whenever I closed my eyes and a flash of the pond came to mind, the way he attacked me in the car. It was only yesterday yet seemed like a lifetime ago after staying up all night, staring at the bedroom door, my ears pricked, waiting for him to bust in like a nightmare.

Whenever those flashes came, I felt dirty, defenseless, my hands trembled and my breath backed up in my throat. Because of what happened, yeah, but also because if Dylan ever found out he really would think I was trash. And I feared that as much as anything else.

According to plan, we met up with Spence and Vienna at Cantini's Steakhouse. Dylan held doors, scooted my chair in, allowed me to order first, and insisted on paying for my dinner. For one night —for a dinner at least—I was a princess, with waiters at my beck and call, exchanging smiles with a boy fraught with the fear of missing even the tiniest chance to pamper me, giggling in the bathroom with

Vee, admiring our dates and our dresses, each other. A glimpse in the mirror, my hair up like a Goddess, eyeliner still perfect. Yeah, okay, I was glad I went.

It was hard to believe I was even there, with these people, as though I belonged. I was only at Dunham Episcopal because of Mom's heroic efforts, starting as a secretary and working her way to the Associate Headmaster's office.

Mr. Suddith had become like a father to Mom, and by the time she'd gotten sick I'd already piled up so many AP credits and exceeded so many expectations that he'd promised her I'd finish there no matter what. A cancer scholarship or something.

Anyway, I'd spent a few years now with these Dunham types, gotten to know them, more or less. And sure, I was more like a stray cat hanging around the campus, but the rich were all I knew. Besides, I had nothing else to call my own.

After dinner we took off, speeding past the glittering dance-floor of the Radisson ballroom, straight to the lake house. Spence Nottaway's dad was a big-time lobbyist turned political advisor. A legit one-percenter for sure—we're talking golfing-with-the-governor, beach house at Martha's Vineyard type elite. I'd been to their estate with Vee a few times. The place was mega, sitting on a couple hundred acres on the outskirts of town.

But Spence basically lived at the "cabin" on the lake. And by cabin I mean enormous A-frame house with vaulted ceiling, huge windows, two giant fireplaces, three bedrooms, a cigar lounge/pool hall in the basement.

Glenda had been too shell-shocked by the Nottaway name to flog me with questions such as where I was staying for the night. And with my phone being disconnected I simply wouldn't be checking in. She could do what she wanted about it later.

At the cabin, Vee tore into the wine before she found a glass and the four of us ended up on the wrap-around deck right off the living room, taking in the lake. Spence sipped a beer while Vienna caught a buzz in record time. He set an arm around Vee, his tie loose off his neck, looking like a junior politician as he gave Dylan a hard time for not drinking.

I smiled and abstained as well. The peaceful croaks and crickets, along with Vienna's hiccups, served as the backdrop to Spence and Dylan's sports stories. Then Vee's hands went missing and things got quiet.

No shame, those two. It wasn't long before they went from kissing and being cute to nearly forgetting we were there altogether. Finally, Dylan told them to get a room, so they did, upstairs, leaving me with my cute little shy friend out there with the wildlife. I tried to make things less awkward by plopping down beside him.

"Are drunk people always so annoying?"

He pointed to the door. "Those two are."

He smelled nice. Axe or some sort of body wash. And it helped to have Spence and Vee to make fun of, to break the ice at their expense. Dylan joked how Spence got his hair cut every three days, and I told him how Vienna got a bikini wax.

Dylan smirked. "Is that like, you know, everything?"

"No, I think that's a Brazilian."

"How many?"

"No, it's a type of... Oh haha."

I fell headfirst into Dylan's innocence and dorky charm. It was like a warm light to my skin. Speaking of which, when he saw me shiver (my dress wasn't much against the chill), he shed his blazer and set it around my shoulders, leaving his hand on my arm. A simple gesture that sealed the deal.

"Thanks," I said, turning to him, lingering until he sat up closer, leaning towards me. Finally, I had him alone. I closed the space between us, to find his lips, to gently ease into things, but even that proved too much.

Andrew. Right in my face. His filthy hands on my thigh. His vicious breath against my face. His horrible begging. His crushing strength on my neck. My chest tightened. My head spun. I needed air.

Dylan pulled back. "Are, are you okay?"

"Yeah, it's just, it's nothing."

Oh boy. I stood and turned to the railing, aware of Dylan behind me, probably wondering what he'd done wrong, thinking I must be mental or menstrual, maybe even considering hopping in his dad's nice car and leaving the basket-case behind. I had to save this, save this night and how it felt to be around someone I liked. So I turned around and found his face.

It took him a minute to get going. But when he did it was nice. His smooth jawline, his fresh aftershave instead of cologne. I held his face in my hands and leaned into him. He put a hand on my back, and we found our way back into the chair.

We did that for a while, finding a comfortable pace, falling into each other and giggling, then kissing, then laughing again until we heard the banging around upstairs. Heavy footsteps coming down the stairs.

Spence appeared at the door. "Dude, she's puking everywhere." Then, breaking into a smile. "What are *you* kids doing out here?"

"Nothing, just, um, nothing," Dylan said.

I peeled off his jacket and stood, shivering from the cold, like leaving the warm glow of a campfire. "I'll go check on her."

I brushed past Spence, who eyed me with an amused look on his face. Upstairs, Vee was wrecked. She looked up from the toilet, eyeliner running down her cheeks like a derailed coal train. "Ugghhhh, Chlooooweeee..."

"Too much wine, my love?" I knelt beside her, lifting her hair off the commode like I always did when this happened. It was a shame though, because her had-been-perfect hair was now in clumps—like wet string. A couple of hours ago we were in the restaurant, living so glamorously. Now my best friend looked like a heroin addict. I rubbed her back and performed my duties.

"It's okay, get it out."

She tried to talk but managed only yakking into the toilet before she'd cry and yack and cry some more because she couldn't stop doing either. By the time I got her into a t-shirt and some soccer shorts I'd found in the bedroom, she looked like a twelve-year-old.

It was nearly one when I returned down the stairs and found Dylan and Spence had come inside. Spence hopped up. "How she's doing?"

I told him she was asleep, then shrugged into a yawn. "I'm tired."

"Okay." He started for the stairs, turned to Dylan. "Just take either room, I mean, if you two are sleeping, you know." He rubbed his head, smiling again.

Dylan buried his head in his hands. "Good*night*."

Spence rushed upstairs where I heard him enter the bedroom, talking softly. Dylan fixed his hair and just kind of stood there.

"So," I said, "Vienna's kind of a lightweight."

"Yeah."

I knew he was thinking about what we were going to do about the sleeping situation. I looked out the doors overlooking the deck. "Wow, look at the moon."

He turned to the windows like it was the most important thing in the world. Then he came to life. "Hey, do you want to take the boat out?"

"Now?"

He shrugged, a sheepish smile. "Yeah. I guess it is late."

I looked out to the deck. The moon shone like a force, backlighting the clouds and shining off the water. Why ruin the boy's spontaneity? "No, I mean, yeah. Why not?"

I found one of Spence's huge D.E.S. hoodies. It looked ridiculous over my dress. And my hair had loosened some, but it was dark and after seeing Vee's hair I guess it didn't matter. Dylan, back in his sports jacket and tie, reminded me of a special agent leading me down the path to the dock. He held onto my hand and surprised me with a gentle kiss before he helped me down into the boat. He stepped in carefully and we started out on the water, the paddles knocking loudly in the quiet night.

The houses on the hill were washed in the gray light. Every once in a while I'd start when a fish jumped out of the water. Dylan smiled, the moon on his pale face, shining off his perfectly crooked smile. "Nice out here, huh?"

"You were a Boy Scout, weren't you?"

He stopped rowing and smiled, blushing behind the cover of night. "How'd you know?"

"I can just tell."

He set the paddles down and I climbed into him, snuggling into his arms. He traced my back with his fingers, and I thought how funny it was the way he'd been almost like a stranger when he'd picked me up earlier but now it was perfect. Like we'd been doing this forever.

"When Vee said I should ask you to the dance, I laughed."

I turned to him, nuzzling my cheek on his shoulder. It was just so nice. "Why?"

"Because, you just, I don't know. You don't seem like the type of girl who, hmm, how should I say this?"

I broke free from his arms. "What?"

"No, I don't mean—" He shook his head, speaking to the moon now. "I should just stop talking."

I fingered a button on his blazer. "I don't seem like the type of girl who *what*?"

He put his hands back on the paddles. "No, I mean. I guess I thought you were out of my league, that's all."

I rolled my eyes. "Okay, try again. Now tell me what you really meant."

"I guess," he started, tilting his head like he was trying to look into me. "Just that you don't seem like the type of girl who would go to the dance."

I took a breath, pulling my hands into the long sleeves of the sweatshirt. "You think I'm a snob?"

"No, no, not at all, just," he sighed. "I really shouldn't have said anything."

"But I did go, now didn't I?"

He looked at me for a long time, until I realized no, we didn't go to the actual dance. I let go of him, rolled my head back. "Oh, I see what you mean. Come on, you didn't really want to go, did you?"

"I would've. Spence would have. Vee would have. I mean, yeah, it's cheesy, but, whatever, sometimes cheesy is fun."

I dipped my hand in the lake and flung some water at him. "So are you not having fun with me?"

He held up his hands, wiped his face. "Hey, come on now."

More splashing. "Did I ruin your night? Did you really want to dance?"

He splashed me back and that was it, we were at war. I knew my eyeliner was ruined, running down my cheeks as I giggled and flung handfuls of water at him. Pretty soon we were both sopping wet, and I was shivering when he leaned forward, rocking the boat some as he kissed me on the lips. A perfect, excellent, full kiss.

DYLAN DROPPED me off the next morning after brunch at the Waffle House where we'd sat at a window seat, our dresses wrecked, the boys' suits wrinkled and loose in the sun. Vienna took an oath never to drink a freaking thing again for as long as she lived. We all placed our bets as to how long it would last.

The carriage house door was wide open. Andrew and Uncle Robbie were at it again, this time standing around in the driveway near the saw. It sent a rash of heat up my neck, seeing Robbie out there with him, chumming it up, fooled by Andrew's little act. I tried to go through the front door, to avoid the whole thing, but it was locked, so I had to scrape up the driveway and past the cabinets and boxes of tile. Robbie was asking about some measurements. He waved and I waved back, ignoring the glare off Andrew's sunglasses.

In the kitchen, Glenda was jittery, eyes bulging, silently pleading for details. She must have been up to her eyeballs in fair-trade coffee by then, head-shaking and looking like she was trying to shed her skin.

"So tell me all about it." she said, pretending she hadn't been at the window and seen Dylan drop me off, or that she wasn't put off by me wearing a boy's hoody over my dress. I poured my own cup of coffee, stirred some milk in, and took a sip. Amazing. One thing I couldn't knock was Glenda's coffee. Always freshly ground, always top notch.

"It was fun." I shrugged and took my mug to go.

I knew it killed her not getting the details about the dance, or that Robbie wasn't giving me crap about being dropped off the next morning by my date. But I wasn't doing it to spite her this time, I just wasn't ready to let go of the night. The moon on the lake. Dancing with Dylan on the dock. The crickets and frogs and the soft sound of his breath in my ear. His warm lips and gentle hands. The promise of what might happen next. That's why I took to my bed without changing clothes and just stared at the ceiling, smiling like a girl who'd just returned from a fairytale.

Chapter 10

The four of us hung out most nights, going to movies, lounging at the lake, another baseball game. We even drove out to this lame-core party out in Dearington Springs and it was actually a really good time, although it was mostly just Dylan and me making fun of people and all the stupid things they said when they got wasted. For a while things were, well, normal.

It was probably the best time I'd had since, everything. Before finding out about Mom's cancer, which was approaching a year ago. Dylan, with his corny jokes, kept me cracking up, and whenever we hung out my cheeks hurt afterwards from smiling so much. Spence and Vee were bearable for the most part, with minimal groping and arguing, or maybe nothing changed but now I was too distracted to notice. Even Vee's little pouting spells were tolerable, because everything was so new and fresh.

"You two are such a cute couple," Vee said on the way to lunch. I was in a mood, annoyed because Miss Shelby thought I wasn't making an effort with my "accounts." What was this anyway, fifth grade? It was like she had a free pass to pry into our lives. Granted, I'd written a whole page about the scrumptious fruit smoothie I'd made last night—part of a new plan to bore her into submission—but still, I wasn't about to bear my soul for her entertainment.

I tossed Vienna a hard look. "I don't think we're a couple."

"Yeah, okay," she laughed.

"We haven't talked about it or anything."

"You looked like a couple in the backseat last night." She made sucking noises. I rolled my eyes. Okay, so maybe this was fifth grade.

Yeah, I liked Dylan. Like, *really* liked him. At the same time, I was still sorting out what happened with Andrew. I couldn't sleep at night, couldn't stop my hands from clattering across my desk in class sometimes. Yet, if it never happened again I'd be fine. Figure I'd learned the hard way just how careless I'd been. But if he thought I was some little girl he could, I don't know, *molest*, well then, Andrew had underestimated me.

For a few days Glenda gave me the cold shoulder. After the dance—when I stayed out all night—her conversations were shorter, more pointed. She'd even curbed all the constant blathering about charities or the fund raiser she was sponsoring. It was kind of a blessing, really. I only wished I'd ticked her off sooner.

But the silent treatment was temporary. Glenda couldn't help herself when it came to Dylan or my social life. And when Vee showed up one Saturday, Glenda whisked us into the kitchen for some girl time.

Vee jumped right in, and Glenda went all the more over-the-moon. It was all I could do just to stir the slop in a bowl while she flitted around, cranking the jazz and going DEFCON 1. "So Vienna, how are things with you and Spence Nottaway?"

Oh, make it stop, this woman. I finished peeling the purple skin off the eggplant in time to catch Glenda hurl herself to the oven where she was burning the bread to coal. Vee winked at me. "Oh, things are peachy. I want to have his babies."

Glenda stopped, the heat of the oven on her face. "What?"

"I'm only kidding, things are fine, Mrs. V."

"Oh," she said, chuckling. She set the pan on the counter with the grand slam of all head shakes, rubbing her forehead on her wrist, debating whether to go into her Planned Parenthood spiel. "I hope so, you have a lot ahead of you, Vienna."

Just as things were about to get serious, Vee smiled again. "Wow, Mrs. V," she said, pinching Glenda's arm. "You're a beast. What's that Pilates place you go to again?"

For the love of everything, Vee. I clamped down on my lip as Glenda went orgasmic. For the next ten minutes it was all breathing and muscle control. Vee about died when Glenda went down on the kitchen floor, her shirt hiking up to reveal her hip-riding, yellow granny-panties. It was too much, and we were both about to die laughing when Andrew appeared at the door.

Vee had joined Glenda on the floor as she lauded the importance of precision. Glenda straightened up, while Andrew's stare never left Vee. I gripped the chef's knife until my knuckles whitened. Andrew laughed, shook his head, and waltzed over to the fridge.

"Didn't know there was a party, I was just coming to check on the fire."

Vee hopped up and Glenda fixed her shirt and wiped her bangs back, red-faced and panting. "We're making eggplant parm. You joining us?"

He looked from me to Vee. "Yeah, okay."

Vee raised her eyebrows at me. I wanted to tell her no. Not to smile. Not to speak to him or tilt her head and blink those bright eyes that knocked guys back a step. I wanted to warn her not to be fooled by his boyish act, because he might corner her and press his filthy face against hers. I let go of the knife while I still had control. Andrew snatched a beer and Glenda scooted to the counter to start breading the eggplant, nodding to Vee. "Andrew this is Vienna Summerset, Chloe's bestie."

Andrew stepped over and shook her hand.

"Pleased to meet you," Vee giggled. Andrew's eyes scanned her all the way down, then back to those eyes.

"It's a pleasure."

"Oh, you two are a riot." Glenda let go with her high-pitched donkey chuckle. So many thoughts roared through my mind. What he had done. Only the stubborn lock of secrecy kept me from screaming it out in the kitchen. It held tight like a rusted latch I couldn't kick apart. And he knew I wouldn't do a damn thing as he stood there and ogled my best friend before turning his gaze to me. I escaped from the kitchen before anyone noticed I needed to breathe through a paper bag.

I slid out of the room and raced up the stairs. I left Vee in there with him, making small talk and giggling over the music, pretending to be interested in what Glenda said, probably tossing harmless but furtive looks Andrew's way while Glenda not-so-secretly wished her troubled "niece" was more like her gorgeous friend. I swallowed down the panic washing through my chest. I plunged into my room, tears rolling before I could fling myself onto the bed, into the pillow where I could scream.

Shaking. Worse than before, my breaths too fast, fleeing from my lungs before I could catch up with my heart. Or the other way around. I'm not sure how long I was up there, but after a while there were a few light taps on the door. I braced myself for the worst.

Uncle Robbie poked his head in. "Hey, Chlo."

I wiped my eyes. A bit of surprise showed on Robbie's face. Mine too. I had no idea he was home, upstairs sleeping or hiding. Now he looked like he wanted to slam the door and run away.

He took a step, halfway in and halfway out. "You okay?"

All I could do was nod, wheeze, tremble. Robbie turned his head the other way and plodded ahead. He eased closer in the room like he was intruding even though it was his own home. His beloved old house.

"I was just taking a nap, I wasn't feeling..." He looked back to the door. I wiped my face.

"I'm sorry, I didn't mean to wake you, it's—" My voice wasn't my own. It was strange, quivery, almost a whisper.

"No, I was up. It's just, is it, um. Is it your mom?"

New tears scraped down my cheeks. "It's just so hard to believe. She's gone."

He sat beside me, slowly, like an old man. I realized he might be the only person who I didn't mind asking me about Mom. How much his face was like hers. The same shaped eyes. The same gold flecks swimming in calm blue waters.

"I miss her too," he said.

He glanced around the room, to the dresser, the window. "I heard some Marley the other evening, sounded nice coming out of the window."

I forced a smile. We stared at the picture of Mom. I wondered what he thought about me, up there breaking down while my best friend was in the kitchen. Or the other day coming home the next morning after the dance. With Mom I would have jumped on the couch and told her every wonderful thing that had happened, and she would have trusted me. But here it was all I could do to put one foot out and test the water.

Robbie set his arm around me. And I found comfort in his embrace. The two of us hiding upstairs, where the room was safe in the sunlight. I trusted him. Not enough, but some. Enough to lean into him and sob quietly but not enough to tell him what his wife's brother was doing. Not enough to say if he did it again he might find the wrong end of the knife I'd hidden under my mattress. No, not that much, but some. Uncle Robbie was all right. Eventually the shaking stopped.

"Knock, knock."

Vee stood at the door, her smile falling, her face soft with concern. She rushed over and bent down in front of me. "Chlo, you okay?"

Robbie rose, somewhat relieved to let her take over. I gave him a weak smile and he brushed out the door. "Let me know if you need anything, okay?"

I nodded. Vee took his place on the bed and hugged me tight, perfectly, just right, and I tried to apologize but she shook her head and so we sat there on the bed, crying, Vee stroked my hair, talking to me until I finally got myself together. By the time Glenda called up to say dinner was ready, she had me laughing again about Pilates.

Chapter 11

"Chloe, I expect more out of you."

Miss Shelby's voice was nasally, warbled, spit-sticking and strained through a disgusting mixture of mouth noises, like macaroni and cheese being stirred between each word. Sometimes I had to look down, away, or start backtracking altogether, which was rude, yes. Just not as rude as puking all over the floor.

And now she wanted us to write about how we'd changed through the semester, stressing voice and tone and rhetorical strategies with relative evidence. I was ready to go after her with the staple gun, especially when she tapped my shoulder on the way out, asking to have a little chat with me.

Oh, how she knew this assignment might be hard for me, but she didn't think I'd want special treatment—her way of saying, "suck it up, buttercup."

"It doesn't have to be about your mother. It can be about class if you'd like."

She leaned in to get my attention, so I had no choice but to look at her beady little eyes, submerged in her doughy face. I wondered if she was gunning for a headmaster position. Lord knows she didn't stand a chance out in regular society.

I was lost in this thought when, in an act of horrifying compassion, she swooped in with a creased smile and set a chubby hand on my shoulder. "I know what you've been through, and I just want you to know that I'm here for you."

I regarded the raw chicken breast on my shoulder. If anything was worse than Miss Shelby's hit list, it was her good graces. I delicately weaved out of her arm's reach. "Thanks, Miss Shelby, I really appreciate it. I think I may have some ideas."

"Wonderful," she said, stiffening. "If you need anything, I'll be here."

Had I changed? Oh, please. What did she think? Mom was dead and Andrew was living in the carriage house. I could write about how if he touched me one more time he might end up in a sack of fertilizer for his sister's garden. I could certainly fill a page or two about the joys of living with Glenda, how the other day at dinner she wouldn't shut up about a study on gut microbes and fecal transplants.

I hurried to the auxiliary doors with trembling hands and rapid breaths. I managed a couple of fake smiles then I hipped the bar of the door and made a beeline through the campus dormitories. I crossed through the path, just like I had so many times, months ago, along the rubber coated chain link fencing that enclosed the tennis courts, down to the athletic fields, and towards Dorchester Street.

They could keep it—all of it—the creeping moss and the ivy climbing the brick, the century old roots coiling around the students and staff, endowing them with false security. From permission slips to honor codes, those shiny SUV's and sleek sedans, the army of landscapers working the grounds, the headmasters and chaplains, the selective societies, student councils and Latin clubs, fine arts, everything was in such precise order. My only entitlements were black-of-night bedroom terrors and throat-choking picnics by the pond.

Because I didn't belong here.

I stopped only once, stumbling over my own feet, my vision drowning in the muck of my memories. Pulling myself together, I hit the path in stride, passing the worn benches, the hump of smooth rocks, and the roots like stairs around the thick oaks until it opened up and I stepped out, a block away from our old house.

I thought about the spare key, wondering if the locks had been changed. Mom only worked half a day on Thursdays. She'd have Spearhead cranking on the speakers, a pot roast cooking in the fall or a garden salad in the spring. I'd come in, slink off my book bag, bemoaning the woes of the day—almost always Stacey and Olivia. I'd ask her if there was anything in their file concerning a brain lobotomy or scientific experiments. She'd tell me to be nice, and besides—she'd say with a smirk—she couldn't divulge such information.

It wasn't always perfect. Mom and I had our share of fights, especially before she got sick. Like when I wanted to stay out later with Chris but she wouldn't budge on my curfew. Then the whole thing with my phone. I said some awful things to her. Things I wished so badly I could take back. Things you say when tomorrow lies before you—assumed and waiting—wrapped tight with a bow. Now I clung to the hope Mom understood. Something told me she did.

The house seemed smaller and dirtier than I remembered. The lawn was patchy and the siding was speckled with red dust. Uncle Robbie had already hired cleaners and painters, they'd been there when I'd gone back for Mom's photo album and other keepsakes. Robbie held onto a few pieces of furniture he said I would want when I was older. Now, peeking in the windows, I saw only bare walls. A skeleton of our memories.

Around back, the patio had been left untouched. Our struggling plants, shards of terracotta, clumps of grass and weeds creeping up between the cracks. I sat down in Mom's chair, rubbing the arm rests until my hands were black. One of Mom's planters had some life in it.

"Mom, it looks like your Marigold's are blooming."

I said it out loud. What did I care? The burst of orange petals in the pot filled me with tears and happiness. It gave me strength. I looked to the kitchen window then peeked back to Mr. Franklin's house to make sure he wasn't milling around in his backyard.

The spare key was still under the planter where we'd left it. The key slid into place and I was home again. Easy as that.

Cleaning supplies lined the kitchen. Brooms, a mop, spray bottles, and trash bags. Some rubber gloves. A blast of lemon in my nose, but underneath it all was the familiar smells of my old life.

I opened the refrigerator and found three bottles of water and an open box of baking soda. The cable cord snaked across the living room floor. My mind filled in the blanks. I felt the warmth of our couch, Mom cuddled up beside me to watch reruns of *How I Met Your Mother* or *Gossip Girl*.

The floor creaked with my steps. I hadn't been back to Mom's gravesite because there was nothing there but death. But here, in the house with the refrigerator clicking and shuddering, was where she sang softly when she did dishes. Where the afternoon sun streamed through the bay window. Scuff marks where we slid the coffee table against the wall so we could hold our own fashion shows, searching our closets for the most ridiculous outfits. Here I found a breath of life. I inhaled it.

Paint cans lay scattered around my room, my lilac walls now beige and neutralized. All the holes patched, the nicks covered and mended. I saw Chris, stretching lazily on my bed while Mom was at work, the sound of her car pulling in. I traced my fingers along the sill where he'd made a clumsy getaway out the window.

I crossed the hallway and lost my breath. I found death clinging to the shadows. Mom's body buried in the layers of quilts. Her dry lips when she told me she was dying. I slid down to the floor in the corner of her room, covering my ears until I fell asleep.

I awoke at dusk, a noisy breeze at the window. Glenda was probably frantic, calling Vee's parents. I stood and looked over to the emptiness where Mom's bed had been, thinking how soon, someone would move in here and suck out the pain. Take our skeleton and make it their own. Soon these walls would absorb laughter and fights and love again. Soon, the house would forget all about us.

Chapter 12

U ncle Robbie was cracking me up, watching Dylan from the door, lauding the kid's impeccable posture as he came marching up the driveway. I rolled my eyes. I'd told Dylan I'd run out to the truck to avoid Glenda and her questions, but he'd refused, choosing to meet my aunt and uncle face to face. It was almost like he wanted to do it.

It was Thursday night and my uncle was looking spiffy in his going-out sport coat and jeans. And just as Dylan was set to knock, he swung the door open. "Hey Dylan, come on in."

Dylan flinched, smiled, then shuffled inside, all *thank you, sir* and nodding. His hair still wet and his t-shirt tight. I wanted so badly to rush up and kiss him, but Uncle Robbie was steadily pumping his hand. Dylan was tall and they were about the same height, but Dylan's posture gave him a slight advantage.

Uncle Robbie released him. "So Dylan, I've heard a lot about you."

"Okay, we're leaving," I said, trying to make it out of there without being humiliated.

"Hey," Dylan smiled at me. I loved the way his voice changed. How he looked at me like the world had just landed at his feet. Kissing him might have been the best thing I'd ever done, honestly.

Uncle Robbie plodded on. "So Chloe tells me you're on the lacrosse team."

"Yeah, and I play golf," he said, taking in the room. "Man, you guys sure have done some nice work here."

I closed my eyes, wishing I'd warned Dylan not to bring up the house within an earshot of Glenda, who appeared at the bannister, fixing an earring. "Oh!"

Sure enough, there she was, clomping to the foyer, all dressed up for one of their fundraiser thingies. With three quick shakes of the bangs she was down the staircase.

"It's going to be featured in the next *Dunham Weekly*. A photographer is coming this weekend. I'm trying to get Robbie to clean up the yard."

Again, I edged Dylan towards the door. Uncle Robbie got back on track. "So what do the two of you have planned?"

"I don't know, just going to hang out."

"Be home at ten, Chloe?"

This was a first. A quick, subtle curfew from my uncle. Nicely done. It must have been all my running around that had them tightening the reins. Glenda had my phone activated yesterday following the news that I'd skipped out on school. Now she was making a fuss over Dylan. I looked to Robbie.

"Well, we have to score the drugs first, then sell them, so..."

Glenda went crimson. "Chloe!"

Dylan blushed too. "We'll probably just grab a bite to eat, maybe hang out with Spence and Vienna?" he said, looking to me.

"I suppose, after we sell the drugs, of course."

I opened the door and made it to the porch. Robbie patted Dylan on the back. "Okay. Food, drugs, then home."

For a split second it was all good fun. Until Andrew's Forerunner swung into the driveway, radio blaring as he skidded to a stop and flung himself out. He stalked to the carriage house like a freak, ignoring Glenda's jingling wave.

I tugged at Dylan, ready to go that second. "Okay, well, bye."

In the truck, Dylan stuck the key in the ignition. "Who was that?" he said, as Glenda, yanking up her dress, hustled over to the carriage house.

I shook my head, not wanting to get into it, sort of fighting to keep my voice steady. "My aunt's brother. Kinda sketchy."

It was all I could manage. I felt terrible. If Dylan knew the story he'd toss me out and go find himself a normal D.E.S girl. We drove up the street, but I was thinking about what might happen when I got home, if Andrew would decide it was time for another visit. My arms prickled and I fought to get a breath. I studied a pair of work gloves on the floor mat.

"You okay, Chloe?"

I jerked myself out of a hole. "Yeah, sorry, I was spacing out. Hey, so you haven't kissed me yet."

He leaned over and gave me a soft kiss on the lips. Some guy behind us honked and I resisted the urge to flip him off.

Arriving at the lake house, it was Dylan's turn to start acting weird. He got quiet as we approached, ducking his head, looking around. I followed his darting glances. "Okay, what are you doing?"

"It's nothing," he said, pulling in front of the house, ducking his head, checking the wrap around porch, the trees, everywhere. "It's just that, well, I lost a bet with Spence."

"A bet?"

"Yeah, just a baseball thing, but with Spence you never know."

I shook my head. "So, a guy thing?"

Dylan nodded, still not looking to me. "Yeah."

We stepped out of the truck, hearing Vee's squeals down at the dock. As we came down the steps I noted she was already in her swimsuit. The day had been warm but was cooling quickly, maybe seventy, tops. Although when you looked like Vee you wore a swimsuit in a snowstorm.

"Chloe!" she squealed, and came hauling it up to me, her towel trailing behind her and her boobs bounding with her steps. She'd actually gone swimming, the loon.

"You're crazy."

"I know. It's sooo cold," she said, yanking a towel around her body. I glanced over at Dylan, who set his gaze to his feet, which, wow, I couldn't have blamed him for peeking.

Down at the dock, Spence was shirtless under a blue sports

blazer. He was also in his swimming trunks, so that when he turned to us and saluted, he looked the part of millionaire playboy. All he was missing was his yacht and maybe a cigar. This was weird.

"Well hello there, Chloe," then to Dylan. "Ah, the loser has come to pay his debts."

Dylan hung his head. From what I could tell it was a bet about whether Spence could hit a homerun in a game or something. It was all so ridiculous, but I was relieved Dylan wasn't asking me questions about home for a change. I found a Corona and we dared Spence to go swimming, which he did, only to hop out and toss Vienna in again. I held Dylan's hand while Spence and Vee screamed, giggled, slapped, kicked, then kissed. It pretty much summed up their relationship.

Dylan shook his head. He was safe and predictable. Chris would have tossed me in the water without a second thought, but Dylan was more talk and cuddle than wrestle and make out. It wasn't hard to picture him in ten years with the exact same look of slight concernment.

Spence, dripping all over the place, drained his beer. "Okay ladies, the time is upon us."

Vee bit her lip, smiling with anticipation. Spence toweled off and slipped his blazer back on. He grabbed his baseball bat by the fat part, using the handle to point towards the house. "I will need young Dylan here to join me. For he has to pay for his woeful lapse in judgment."

Dylan hung his head. Spence led his hostage to the house. I had no idea what was going on but trusted it was some kind of sports ritual. Vee, all curled up in her towel, shook her head and set her face into the sun. Silly boys.

It was just the two of us on the lake. Across the water I could see another house through the trees. The blush of dusk on its back. A boat dock, too far to swim to but close enough to see the flowers lining the walk. Something about the orange blooms reminded me of the house, the marigolds. I told Vee about going back home, to Dorchester, hoping she wouldn't think I was mental.

She turned to me, her eyes absorbing my thoughts. "Really? How was that? Weird?"

"A little, but not."

She set her hand on mine. "Did you tell Uncle Robbie?"

I shook my head. Vee was my girl, but I had to be careful. I couldn't tell her all of my secrets. Especially after the crying in my room thing. But it was nice, she leaned over and gave me a big wet hug. I hugged her back.

"I know you miss her."

She let me go and we both wiped our eyes, laughing at ourselves for getting so mushy so fast on such a nice day. The breeze off the water gave me a chill. We looked back at the house, waiting for whatever Spence had planned, when Vee surprised me. "So what's up with Andrew?"

My heart stumbled, fear blasting through my skin in the form of cold sweat on my back. "What?"

"The other day at your place. Sort of cute, I guess, but kind of a creep," she said, toweling her legs, wiping a speck of dirt from her foot. "Right?"

Needles of shock prickled my skin. I rolled my eyes and sighed, took a swig of beer and tried to play casual. "He's just, I don't know, supposedly he's fixing up the carriage house."

"Living at big sis's, huh? I'd watch him though."

I forced myself to swallow, my voice came out hollow and weak. "What do you mean?"

She laughed. "He kept staring at me, like, you know, *staring*," she said, her eyes growing. "In the kitchen the other night. I ran up to tell you and that's when, you know. Anyway, it was probably nothing, just a little weird. And by a little I mean a lot."

I looked at my friend, her hair clinging to her face. Eyes to the sun and smiling. She glanced at me and I looked away, frozen beside her. I wanted to find a way, so badly, to tell her about what had happened.

Just get the words out. Then she looked up and laughed, clapped her hands together. "Oh my, guess it's time for the show."

I followed her gaze to the lake house where Dylan, stripped to the skin, wore nothing but a teeny tiny Speedo as he reluctantly followed Spence down the path.

Spence cupped his hands to his mouth. "Ladies, may I have your attention."

I got to my feet. Dylan's head hung in shame. Spence had shed the blazer but now wore an even more ridiculous captain's hat. He prodded and pushed Dylan down the path with the handle of the bat.

Vee let out a cat call. "Wow, Dylan, I had no idea you were so ripped."

I gave Vee a playful nudge. But she was right. Dylan, pale as the moon, was actually nothing but muscle. He peeked up at me as they came aboard the dock.

"Let this serve as a lesson to anyone dumb enough as to doubt my batting skills, for they shall suffer the—"

Vee shook her head. "Spence, really?"

"Baby, I won a bet, let me gloat here."

Vee waved him off. With a grin, I strolled over to Dylan and pulled his head down so I could kiss him full on the lips.

"Young lady, do not excite a boy in a speedo. Or we *all* must suffer."

"Sorry."

"Okay, as a result of doubting my prowess, Young Kowalski must swim to the third buoy marker and back."

Vee shielded her eyes as she spied the marker. "That's kind of far. And the water is *freezing.*"

"No worries. I have faith in this fine specimen. A polar bear, right Kowalski?"

Dylan nodded.

"Ha, a Pol*ish* bear. Well then. Off you go."

Spence set his foot on Dylan's backside, sending him off. Dylan shot ahead with sleek strides. Vee and I cheered him on as he passed the first marker, his white back glowing against the water. We were all giggling, and it was the kind of silly fun I wished I could have enjoyed without the haunting echo of Vee's words about Andrew. Dylan reached the buoy and waved back. I blew him a kiss, half of me enjoying the moment and half shivering because of the wind, because of how close I'd been to telling Vee everything only moments ago.

Dylan made it back to the dock, dripping and chattering as we helped him up. Vee handed him a towel and he collapsed to the deck, arms out, beads of water running off his elbows and sinking into the boards, shining off of his ribs as he heaved. With that, Spence and Vee scurried off to the house, leaving Dylan and me alone. I hovered over him, falling onto his chest and getting wet as we kissed.

Eventually we climbed to the house, searching for his clothes, but instead we ended up on the pool table where Dylan surprised me by leaning in and going for it.

I wasn't expecting it. Maybe the water invigorated him. The way he kissed me so full, urgent, and it wasn't a bad thing. I kind of had to show him what to do with his hands. He started slow but warmed up, and he was catching on nicely when the door opened upstairs. Vienna squealed as she and Spence banged down the steps, singing and clapping, giving us time to get decent before they busted into the game room.

We watched a movie, Spence going on the whole time about a road trip. He thought the four of us should pack up for the beach the day after school ended. I was game, but Vienna, dry and clothed, had cranked up with the pouting. She'd started getting moody ever since Spence announced he was headed to Stanford in the fall. Being a junior, it was all but killing her to think about her dear pretty boy taking his charms out west, and when she got like that there was no changing the subject or reeling her in.

Glenda was already driving me crazy about schools, to the point I'd started messing with her by announcing my own plans not to go at all. Like gold, the horrified look on her face, followed by nervous laughter and head shakes. It was no secret poor Glenda was not exactly blessed with what one would call intellectual aptitude. She'd compensated for such shortcomings with her trademark energy. Through boundless tenacity and relentless studying, Glenda had gone on to receive her master's degree—something she never let anyone forget. To Glenda, college was it, the *be all end all*. But I couldn't see myself at school, or not at school. Without Mom, I was just floating.

Dylan got me home before curfew. Robbie and Glenda still weren't back from their fundraiser fun, and I almost invited him in, but he had a curfew too. For the best, being how I was too distracted by the lights in the carriage house to be much good at kissing him anyway.

Later, up in my room, I was listening to music and drawing up a fake account for Miss Shelby. I'd really taken to messing with her hardcore these days. My last entry had been a fictional romp about my menstrual cycle, how I was concerned about the color and flow, using my best descriptive powers and words like discharge and regularity to make it sound legit. Now I was on this one about the virtues of non-binary gender identity because Miss Shelby had already gone on a tangent about it so I figured I might as well stir the pot.

Anyway, I was in the midst of it when the door eased open and there was Andrew, leaning on the doorjamb, leering at me. My breath caught in my throat, but I recovered quickly, determined not to show any fear no matter the cost.

He shook his head. "We need to talk."

"No. Get out." I managed to keep my voice from cracking. But a scream was trapped in my throat. Andrew's lazy grin widened, his blue eyes slatted and mean.

"So you got a boyfriend now?"

"None of your business. Get *out*."

He stepped closer and I leaped to my feet without thinking, gripping the pen so hard I thought the cap would go through my thumb. "I swear if you touch me..." My heart pounded too hard to finish the thought. Andrew held up his hands, halfway smiling.

"Whoa, whoa. What? Nobody's here. Look, I just, the other day, at the pond..."

I stood guarding my bed. *Pressure Drop* churned through the Bluetooth speakers Robbie had gotten me for my phone. Andrew looked to the dresser and started bobbing like an idiot. I stared him down, my eyes glazed, holding back the misty hatred forming in my chest. He dropped the dance and kind of stepped back.

"Look, I miss hanging out."

I exhaled, finally, staring down the biggest sack of loser I'd ever seen. "Are you serious?"

To my relief the kitchen door downstairs opened, and I'd never been so utterly relieved to hear Glenda's incessant chattering. Her approaching heals clicked on the kitchen tile. Andrew's eyes widened. He leaned out the door and put a finger to his lips. When he spoke again it was light and happy and for an audience. "Hey guys, how was it?"

I smelled Glenda before she appeared in the doorway. She was slathered in enough Betsey Johnson to peel the wallpaper. She was buzzed, too, flitting past Andrew and into my room to join the party.

"Oh yeah," she said, clapping so hideously offbeat I thought she was trying to kill a mosquito. "This so reminds me of Key West, mon. Do you have any Jimmy Buffett?"

By then I'd forgotten about the music. Andrew took his sister and twirled her around while keeping an eye on me. I stared at the old door without a lock, only the antique wiggly doorknob left on because it was original hardware. I was too stunned—by him coming up here, by her, by everything happening in my room—to speak. I wanted to scream at them both to leave, but it wasn't my room or my house. Or even my life anymore, for that matter.

The song faded. I snatched my phone from the dresser, signaling the end of our little dance party. Glenda spun around like a goofball —with her horrible hair and overbite. Her old lady necklace jiggled with her constant movement. She was apparently ignorant of Andrew's heavy breathing, the film of sweat on his forehead, his wobbly eyes, the twitching. He looked like some kind of Oxy junkie.

Thankfully, Uncle Robbie stepped in the doorway, yanking at his tie and looking like he only wanted to go to bed. "How was your night?" he asked me, keeping a level gaze on Andrew. I mumbled that it was fun because I wasn't about to waste any extra words around Andrew. Or Glenda for that matter, who whirled around to me all bug-eyed and stupid.

"Oh, sweetie, Dylan is a cutie," she said, hitting a high note with "cutie." My adrenaline, already humming, accelerated my irritation. Andrew's sneering and Glenda's cutesy routine had me back to mashing the clicker of the pen with my thumb.

"Okay," Robbie said, swooping in for Glenda. But she just couldn't leave it alone.

"Let's have him over for dinner," she glanced over to Robbie, mistaking his arm for affection. "Wouldn't that be fun? And you could join us too, Andrew."

Andrew, bugging out, gnashing his teeth and working his jaw like a crackhead, either didn't hear or didn't care to respond. Robbie said goodnight and guided Glenda and Andrew out of my room. Andrew hung at the frame, looking back at me before he finally started down the hallway. I gave him the finger and shut my door.

Chapter 13

I stayed away from the house, studying late in the library or hanging at Vee's place. After three baseball games in one week, even I knew what was going on. I leaned close into Dylan, his lips brushing my ear as he explained the difference between a ball and a strike. Later we'd all go back to the lake house, watching movies and plotting our summer trip.

Andrew took off for a while, not long enough. When he returned, we fell into this routine of him saying something rude and me telling him to go screw a goat. All of this went on behind Robbie and Glenda's backs. But thankfully Andrew spent most of his time in the carriage house, popping pills and otherwise basking in loser-dom.

Robbie's little bromance with Andrew came to an abrupt end. I'd heard him complaining to Glenda that as slow as things were coming along it would have been cheaper to hire a contractor.

Glenda was aghast. "He *is* a contractor."

"No, a *real* contractor."

And so on.

In short, things were bearable for a while. And I was beginning to get past whatever happened. I didn't want to risk things getting weird with Dylan—who'd begun picking me up for school on days he didn't go early. Sometimes we'd go driving around, and he'd even let me drive on the back roads, showing me how to pump the brakes or handle the way it slid on gravel. One day he asked if I wanted go to his house. And that's when I realized just how different our worlds were.

His house was huge, the typical sprawl for Dunham kids—two-car garage, massive chimney, sandstone brick, a lush green lawn adorned with soccer goals. But what got me was Dylan's mom. She was very obviously not my biggest fan.

I felt the chill from the moment I entered. So I did what I always did in those situations—became a total snot. Dylan attempted to build me up with my academics. Little good it did. Mrs. Kowalski glossed me over with a scowl. She hardly smiled, and when she did speak to me it was curt and to the point. At one point I leaned in close to Dylan, and I thought she might whip out a pistol and crack a shot at me.

Dylan had two younger brothers, and Mrs. Kowalski was a stay at home mom. Not sure about Dylan's dad, but who could blame the guy for working late?

She was big with the religious talk, and I couldn't help thinking of Papa Vanderbrooke, the way her eyes avoided me when she spoke, as though I wasn't quite worthy of scripture—like maybe she saw something in me that wasn't worth saving. Either way, Mrs. Kowalski spoke nonstop about youth groups and pastors and church retreats and camps while we sat at the counter and ate cookies. It would have been cute, but I'd had something else in mind.

We started going to my place where we could be alone so I could properly corrupt the boy. Things were heating up but I was still holding out. I'd only been with Chris, a lifetime ago, so it was a big deal to me. But Dylan was getting closer each time, and I thought it might happen on a dark afternoon when we had the house to ourselves.

I was too excited to pay much attention to things like storm advisories or tornado warnings. Things like the Forerunner in the driveway. With Andrew backing off lately, maybe I let myself think he was patching things up with that Renee chick, or, more hopefully, gearing up for a soul-searching adventure.

We were in my room. I had Dylan's shirt over his head when I heard a familiar creak outside my door. By this time, Dylan and I were used to keeping an ear out for adults, our alone time so fragile and intense, that we were on our feet in a second. I swallowed a scream and shoved him behind the door as it cracked open.

Andrew, his face so hideously malfunctioning, his eyes downcast and wobbly, his posture rubbery, like that of a little boy. "Hey, I really need to talk to you."

There was so much in his tone. Intimacy, comfort, a closeness it didn't deserve. I searched for something to say. I couldn't exactly tell him to go get lost with Dylan behind the door. Andrew's leering fell to my chest where my shirt was loose and I quickly yanked it up but kept one hand on the door, ready to slam. I tried to nudge him back into the hallway, keeping my voice bubbly, almost comical considering our proximity—the squeaky door the only thing between Dylan and Andrew.

"Yeah, um okay. I'll meet you downstairs."

"Chloe, I'm serious," he reached for my waist and I could practically feel Dylan emanating from the other side of the door, smell his deodorant mingling with Andrew's pouty breaths on my face. I backed away and snorted like it was no big deal. Just a big, silly game.

Whatever I did set Andrew off. It didn't take much, the way he was tweaking, his shoulders rolling with his bent smile. His face twisted up and down like an audition, showcasing as many emotions as possible. Then he started talking. "Chloe, I need you. I miss you, I want to—"

I threw my shoulder into the door and jammed it shut on his face. And then there was Dylan, standing stock-still, lips parted, his eyes burning into me. Andrew slapped the door from the other side. His voice against my back, upbeat and fun again, spilling into the room. "Come on, Chloe. Let's have some fun."

Dylan clutched his shirt. I forced my eyes away and tried to shrug it off. But Andrew wouldn't give it a rest, shouting up the stairs now. I swallowed hard and held a finger to my lips, pleading with my eyes for Dylan to stay quiet. Then, unable to control myself, I threw the door open. "Go away, you disgusting pervert."

"What? Chloe, what's your problem? You're such a tease."

I slammed the door again, hating that he'd ever learned my name. Because he started calling me trash and all those other lazy names, horrible names I'd grown accustomed to from him, but, judging by the look of horror on Dylan's face, were all brand new to him. I shook my head, smiling for Dylan but wishing it away, wishing Andrew gone, wishing me gone, but most of all wishing Dylan gone so he would stop looking at me like I was a horrific car accident on the side of the road.

Finally, it did stop, and Andrew slunk off. Footsteps down the stairs. Dylan stepped out, fixing his belt, his voice shaky.

"Chloe. What's going on?"

A limb scraped my window. My room turned gray and the sky looked like a bruise. The wind pushed and shoved the trees, flipping the leaves silver. I tried to pull my hair back but my hands were useless. "Oh, him? He's dumb. It's nothing."

"No. It isn't 'nothing'." Dylan just stood there, waiting for answers. Answers that would only bring more questions. I wanted him to go away. I wanted Andrew to die. Or, *I* wanted to die.

Dylan yanked his shirt over his head, pulled it down over his stomach and fixed his hair. "Why was he talking to you like that?"

I turned my back and walked to the window. Dylan followed me, hovering. What did he want me to say? I leaned into his neck. "Let's not let him ruin this, okay?" I started to kiss him because I didn't have words. I was too scared about what was happening. At the house. Between us.

Dylan pulled away. "*I need you?*" His brow wrinkled with anger. I'd never seen him upset or irritated, but it was there, seeping into his voice. Judgment. Anger. Confusion. My face blushed with heat, anger, but I couldn't tell him. He'd think I was disgusting.

"Dylan, it's nothing, really. He just has a weird sense of humor."

I'd lost him. Lost his desire, his warmth, the wonderful place that had just been between us. He kept shaking his head. "I thought he was weird, but..." he turned to me, "Chloe, is he like, touching you and stuff?"

And stuff was more like it. I forced back the tears, not because I was upset with him, but myself. I felt bad for *him.* Not only was he dating a chick whose mother just died, but now this. I turned away from him and fixed my shirt again, feeling his stare on my back. I tried one last time to coax it over.

"Dylan, really, it's nothing."

"Did he... Or?"

"*What?*" I shook my head, the tears really wanting to come out to play, thick and heavy, harder to push back. The wind slung a few fat drops of rain at the window. Dylan stood before me, staring at me, trying to grasp something so far out of his reach.

"Chloe, tell me the truth. Has he like, touched you?"

I was about to tell him to drop it, but the tears pushed their way out. I spun away from him, wanting to run and hide or even die. I waited for him to make his escape. Instead he took my hand. "Let's get out of here."

I clutched his hand as we rushed down the stairs, his grip hard and tight, absorbing my tremors. I squeezed back so he couldn't leave me. Our roles had flipped and shy little Dylan was in control. I followed along, confused, terrified, unable to trust myself because I'd actually thought things were starting to feel *okay.*

We scrambled out through the front door and to Dylan's truck. The gusts pressed at my back, I couldn't get my head around to see if Andrew had come out of the carriage house. Rain pelted my arms, the sharp tinge of wet asphalt filled my nostrils as Dylan helped me in. He ran to his side and we took off.

Neither of us said a word until we were through the traffic light, barreling down to the exit as the sky boomed. The wipers smeared the windshield, lightning flashing in the distance. Up on East Ridge, at the street that led to the little pond Andrew had taken me to, I pointed for Dylan to turn. A wash of tears filled my eyes as we drove into the neighborhood, down the same two-track road as the rain gushed into crevices and trenches alongside the trees and the NO HUNTING signs until we rattled over the cattle guard.

The sky unfolded, turning inside out. We came over the bank and Dylan turned the key back and the truck went silent under a row of low trees at the edge of the pond. The rain obliterated the windshield, washing out the silence in the truck. Washing out my feelings. My hope.

The storm hammered the roof and pummeled the trees. I thought about Dylan's family. His younger brothers were like six or seven and took tennis lessons. His family vacationed and planned their summer and invested in property and had a stock portfolio and retirement funds. There probably hadn't been much for Dylan to worry about until he met me. I turned to him, his chest heaving, his eyes straight ahead with his thoughts. I told him about Andrew.

His mouth opened when I got to the part about Andrew kissing me, *touching* me, as he'd called it. A few times his throat bobbed and he'd look at me, confused. I didn't exactly admit how I'd let that first kiss happen, and I wasn't so sure I had. I had to stop a few times to fight back the tears when I got to the part about Andrew sneaking inside my room, bringing me here, his hands groping between my legs. My voice was hardly more than a cracked whisper. I rubbed my arms, cold and wet, my legs flopping around.

I was shaking because of the rain. Because I knew Dylan couldn't do this. He lived in a good world, a given world—at least as he knew it —with expectations and rules. A place far away from the sickening horror show of my life. I'd thought I could handle both but it was clear I couldn't. I'd actually thought I could have his shyness, keep it somewhere locked away, safe from the carnage of Andrew and the night. I thought we could keep peeking at each other and smiling, holding hands innocently, looking forward to where it was all going while trying to shed the skin the monster in my room had touched.

The storm passed. Dylan seemed to wake up some as the rain dappled the scummy pond. I didn't know how or when to stop talking so I forced my mouth shut and only stared at the grass on my feet. We'd rushed out so fast I hadn't put on shoes.

For a while he stared out at nothing, clicking on the wipers for something to do. A layer of fog blanketed the windshield. He set his head on the steering wheel. He turned to me. "We have to do something."

Doing something was the last thing I wanted. And the way he said it gave me a chill. This wasn't something he was going to brush off. I tried to downplay what I'd just told him. What he'd just heard back there at the house. In my room.

"Look, Dylan, hopefully he's leaving soon and then—"

"Why haven't you told me? Or anyone? He should be in jail." I didn't like his voice. Or the way he glared at me like he was angry. Angry at me.

"Dylan," I started, my voice low. I reached across the seat. His hand felt dead to the touch. "I can't tell Glenda, she'll never believe me. Where would I go?"

Dylan slammed his hand down on the steering wheel. I jumped, then realized I had to pull it together, pull him together. "Look," I started softly, "I understand if this is too much for you. But, I'd rather you not tell anyone."

"What are you talking about? *Tell anyone?*" He shook his head, sighing. "What, you're just going to let him keep...let him...?"

"I'm not *letting* him do anything. I can take care of myself, Dylan. All that stuff, it's just talk. He's just a stupid druggie, okay?"

I scooted closer to him. I kissed his hand over and over before moving to his neck, his lips. He started to kiss me back. I whispered into his ear. I told him to let it go. But it wasn't warm, not like before. When I touched his leg I thought he was going to scream. He brushed my arm away.

"Chloe, I can't do this right now."

"Okay," I said, "okay."

So we sat at the pond, watching the fresh rain drip from the limbs, pretending to be okay for a while. There wasn't much else to say.

⁂

I SAT IN MY ROOM, clawing at the memories of Mom, forcing them to appear on demand. I shined them clean so they wouldn't fade or get lost in the sludge of reality. What would she think about all of this? How would she get me through it? I tried not to think how none of this would've have happened if she hadn't gotten sick.

Mom used to say there was nothing I could do to make her love me any less. So I kept telling myself that. But Dylan sure thought less of me now. I rolled over in my bed. It had been stupid of me to say anything, but I was thrown off with Andrew coming to the door, invading my safe place with Dylan. Now it was lost, that much had been clear on our silent ride home, how he sort of turned to the window when I tried to kiss him goodbye.

I'd be lucky to ever see him again, if I could face him. But not just that, what if he said something? If he told Spence and Spence told Vienna, she'd go straight to the crisis counselors at school. I'd no longer be the poor girl who lost her mom. I'd be the repulsive girl. I'd be looking at one big mess. All because I couldn't keep my mouth shut.

Downstairs, the zippy-bippy jazz music cranked in the kitchen. I rolled out of bed, knowing if I skipped dinner it would become a thing again. I found Glenda bopping along to a Charlie Parker song. Jeez, I was becoming a jazz expert. If I didn't get out of this house soon I'd be shaking my own bangs.

She whipped around to me, violently, her smile fit for a straitjacket. "Hey kiddo, would you do me a favor and go tell Andrew dinner's ready?"

I stopped in my tracks. "Actually, I'm not..."

"I'll get him," Robbie said from the living room.

Glenda looked me over. "How are you feeling, sweetie. You don't look so well."

No? Could it be that junkie stalker brother of yours in the carriage house?

I told her I needed to lie down. I think she bought it, considering my face was pinker than her chicken. Upstairs I couldn't help hearing Andrew's guffaws and wacky stories through dinner conversation. All the excuses about how the kitchen was coming along but this or that wasn't matching up and he needed to special order something.

He'd ruined my life. Ruined things with Dylan, and school—even my sleep was no longer mine because he crept around in there too. I jammed in my earbuds, falling into the good words of my friend Peter Tosh, biting into my pillow with my teeth, trying to breathe Mom back into my life.

I'm like a walking razor don't you watch my size...

I'm dangerous, said I'm dangerous

Chapter 14

On Saturday morning I found a note in the kitchen. Uncle Robbie and Glenda were off strawberry picking, which meant I had the house all to myself. The first thing I did was check the driveway to make sure Andrew's truck was still gone. Seeing only Uncle Robbie's Jeep, I vegged out on the couch in the den, sinking into a mindless reality TV show about pregnant teenagers.

It was nice for a while, stretching out, the sunshine on the windows, the kind of day you could enjoy inside or out. At least until a commercial came on and an urge struck me like a punch.

Even as I wandered to the kitchen window, I tried to talk myself out of doing something so stupid. But I was still seething over how Andrew had completely destroyed things between me and Dylan, and now, looking out the window, I was ready to retaliate.

I reminded myself Andrew would be gone for good soon, he never "stayed put," as Glenda said it. Whenever the remodeling was done he would be off to the next thing. And if he didn't leave, I would.

All that in my head and still, my hand found that key, I stepped out the kitchen door into the crisp sunny day, crunching off towards the carriage house, ready to put his toothbrush in the toilet—if he had one—maybe spit in his milk. Anything to exact my revenge.

With the weather so nice, I figured Glenda would want to take the parkway home, stopping at the overlooks to take selfies so she could post on Facebook. So I had the time and opportunity, and no shortage of spite. I stuck the key in the door and swung it open.

Some pizza boxes and beer bottles rested in the corner. Cans of paint were strewn about to go along with all the empty tile boxes and discarded caulk tubes. On the coffee table, it was more of the same. Mountain Dew bottles, Monster drink cans. Aspirin, pill bottles, various wrappers from energy supplements, and all sorts of the kind of stuff found sitting next to the register at a convenience store. I pushed my way in, watching my step, and there in plain sight was a bag of weed on the bookshelf.

I snatched it and brought it to my nose to smell it, about to pocket the bag when the Toyota barreled up the driveway and slid to a stop. My heart sprang from my chest. There wasn't time to do anything. Run. Run like mad and get out of there. But where? I was trapped. No back door, only the front that sat wide freaking open.

Ding. Ding. Ding.

The car alerted me like a warning.

Steps.

Running.

Andrew crashing into me.

He seized my wrist, crushing it in his grasp as he kicked the door shut, stealing the sunlight and sealing us off. His other hand, filthy and sour tasting, wrapped around my scream. He ripped the baggie from my fist and set his mouth to my ear. "You could have just asked me if you wanted to smoke."

Busted and vulnerable, I tried one last-ditch attempt to coax him out of it, wiggling my mouth from his death grip. "I didn't think you'd mind."

He started to smile but cut it off. His eyes went blank. None of his usual dumb-luck innocence, but sharp and cold. Acute. He tossed the baggie into the chair, half of it spilling out. He yanked my arms down, putting his face in mine. "I don't mind, Chloe."

Fresh beer hung on his breath. Locked in his grasp, I was shocked by the terror but hoping he couldn't tell. I was furious with myself for being in there in the first place. Again, I tried to play it casual.

"I was just looking around," I said, nodding to the kitchen. He scoffed at my desperate excuse. I struggled to pull away again but little good it did. He had nearly a hundred pounds on me.

He groped my chest. "Yeah, suddenly interested in the kitchen? Going to jump on my case like your Uncle Robbie?"

I gasped as he yanked me into him. His hand slid up my back, then down, lower until I tried to squirm away, trying to hide my fear, like I was playing a game when instead I was looking for something I could use to break his face.

"Oh, don't act like that. You came here for a reason, didn't you?"

He took my arm, his fingers pressing into my flesh before he slung me onto the couch. A silent gasp shot out from my stomach. I launched myself up to get away but he came in with his shoulder, tackling me. My head slammed into the wall, igniting an explosion of sparks. My throat closed. The room dimmed. I couldn't believe this was happening.

I flailed and swung, even as I realized it was hopeless. I'd promised not to underestimate him again, yet here I was, trapped. He smothered me, grabbed me until I had no choice but to go along. A blur of tears between us. I held out hope for a chance, just for a chance to do something, when he started moaning, mumbling into my ear, talking to himself. I turned away, eyed the glass vase in the corner of the room. Pans in the kitchen, a bag of tools that might crush his skull. All out of my reach.

His face pressed into mine. His rough stubble tore at my cheeks, his morning beer breath shooting up my nose as he came alive with anticipation. "That little boyfriend has you acting all righteous now? You doing things for him? Do you love him?"

His breaths came short and rapid. Harsh. I tried one last time to reason with him. "Please stop. Please."

Then I screamed. Again he smashed his hand onto my face. He was lost in some fantasy. Not in that room. Off my face, his arms coiled, like a constrictor wrapping itself around me. I pulled a little, managed one more, "Please." But there was nothing to do, nowhere to move. I was about to break.

When he licked my face my arms went dead. Life collapsed. I felt nothing, not as he tugged at my pajama pants. There was no escape, no chance left for me. No talking or outsmarting him. Only screams. Tears. But nothing would stop him. He licked me like an animal in the wild.

I slipped into a safe crevice in my mind. It wasn't consent but survival. I blanked, shut it down so he couldn't have me. He took what he wanted. I lay there, a body, immune to the burn of pain. My head turned to the side as I stared at the clock. Endured the minutes. His trash on the floor. Dirty socks and beer cans. Somewhere outside a chainsaw hummed, reminding me how ordinary things were happening out there. Then it was over.

He rolled away, regarding me like one of his discarded tools. I didn't move. Didn't jump up and run. Didn't scream. I just lay there, like nothing.

I blinked, imagining what it would feel like to put a fork through his eyes. And in those waking moments a blaze inside of me gave birth not to anger but a molten hatred, one that replaced even my own basic need to live. On the couch, I would have detonated an explosive vest if that's what it took to end him.

I heard his grin, like a snake shedding its skin. He lumbered off the couch, victoriously, lazily, easing back into his jeans. "I gotta head out. But I was thinking we could get together again tomorrow, Glenda and dummy ought to be gone."

His voice rang in my head. I refused to believe it was real. I was in this hellish apartment, my body as limp and lifeless as the tools and grout. Buckets I could've filled with tears if I let them go. The molting process began with quivering at the top of my head, rippling from my scalp as it worked down my neck and my shoulders. A scalding wave, scorching my insides as it slid down my chest to my legs, out through my feet. It left me barren.

Andrew with a clueless smile, like somehow, in the misfiring neurons of his malfunctioning ego, he allowed himself to believe I'd enjoyed what had just happened.

He sauntered with a certain bounce in his step, having conquered me. The bathroom door was wide open, a stream of urine hit the toilet as he belched. I thought about Vienna getting all glitzed up with Spence. To be served by the white-gloved staff, bowing and fake-smiling amid all the clinking crystal. They'd mingle amongst the merry swell of privilege and influence blowing over the ballroom, getting chummy in the name of charities and uplifting the impoverished while small-talking about hair styles and dresses. I thought how Vee would flinch if someone mentioned her "kinky" hair or remarked on her "exotic features." How she'd be so self-conscious about her black-half and guilty about her white-half that she'd simply excuse herself with a flash of those big green eyes.

Slowly, my brain stabilized. I pictured police officers and detectives in the room, discussing the matter amongst themselves, nodding along, jotting things down. Me trying to explain to Glenda what her brother had done. How it wasn't my fault. Rape kits and evidence, but at no point—even in the realm of my imagination—did I see her taking my side. She wouldn't. Ever. Andrew was a baby, harmless, clinging to her hip in the kitchen of her nightmare childhood. Even when he leered at me right in front of her, her blame was aimed at me.

Why were you in there?

The toilet flushed. Andrew zipped up and found a shirt, bemused at how I was balled up in the corner of the couch, nearly convulsing with my panties around my left ankle.

"You can stay as long as you want." He hovered over me until I turned. He patted my head. "You kill me with that hot/cold stuff, you know?" He let out a grunt as he tied up his hiking boots, found his keys, and started for the door.

After the car was gone I sat there, a wad of broken. The sunlight came and went, flashing on the walls through the passing clouds. Finally, later, whenever, I rose and left the carriage house a completely different person than the one who had entered.

In the shower I waited for a release that never came. I pushed away worries about pregnancy tests. STD's. I let the searing hot water bite my skin, pelt my head, and sting the scratches on my ribs. I scrubbed myself clean until it was too painful. Everywhere, even my face, swallowing the bitter suds of soap found in the pits of my mouth. Another urge struck.

I toweled off and dressed. Vengeance surged with my pulse, stronger than before, fueled by the burn between my legs. My head was unusually clear after the shower and now it was vivid and lucent as I marched into the garden shed where my nice, clean soapy smell evaporated into the odor of oil and grass, tools and motor oil. My eyes roamed, to the spade shovel, the rake, to the organic weed killer and spray bottles. It was all laid out before me. Bug Gone, window cleaner, motor oil, and behind it, a big yellow jug of antifreeze.

Back to the carriage house. Moving before I could think or recall the ghastly details of what just happened. Andrew's fridge held the usual take-out boxes and pizza crusts, yellow mustard packets and soy sauce. My ears stayed cocked for the sound of a car. He had half a twelve pack of some Oatmeal Stout left so I drank one to help with the trembling, the breathing. The living.

Andrew bought sweet tea by the gallon, and it just so happened he had two gallons of it sitting on the top shelf. I took both.

One wasn't opened, but he didn't strike me as a detail oriented guy. I couldn't help looking at the couch, to the dent of the cushions where we'd just been. My fingers had trouble doing much of anything, so getting the cap off of the antifreeze was a chore. I steadied myself with another stout and set my mind to the task. It wasn't much, maybe a teaspoon worth so he wouldn't notice. The twang of it hit my nose and I tossed one more capful into each gallon of tea and shook them up. I held the tea to the window to check for consistency, gave it another shake, and returned them to the fridge and got the hell out of there.

I called Vee and she picked up with a giggle. She was on the way to Richmond. She asked if I was okay, but in a way that was more, *please say yes because Spence's hand is sliding up my thigh and we're on the interstate and I'm having so much fun I don't have time for this right now.* I assured her it was no big deal. Friends did that for one another.

So I went home. To Dorchester Street.

Chapter 15

I waited until dusk, just to be safe, which meant stalking around Dunham and drifting through the soggy woods, keeping clear of joggers and resident campers. I was a jittery mess, breaking out with hives, a rash of sweat on my back, chills on my arms. Because I couldn't stop reliving it. I relived it over and over again.

Robbie still hadn't rented the house. I liked to think that somewhere in the back of his mind he didn't want to rent it out. It was a little after seven when I came down the street and saw it in the gray of dusk. Robbie would have a conniption if he saw how tall the grass was, thick and green from all the rain. But everything was quiet.

My shoes were wet and grassy on the floor so I wiped them down with paper towels. The cleaning supplies had been moved since my last visit, and all the water was gone from the fridge. Again it hit me how pretty soon someone else would be here, and they might not enjoy my random visits.

Even empty, the house enveloped me. Again the smells charged the chemicals in my brain, and no amount of scourging could ever rinse out the warm embrace I felt in its walls or the secrets the house promised to keep between us. I curled up in Mom's closet, took my pillow from my bag. I breathed the air Mom and I used to breath.

The antifreeze might not kill Andrew. And I wasn't sure how I felt about that. It should at least make him sick, maybe keep him away for a while, buy me some time until I came up with a better plan. Any plan.

The walls absorbed the pink sunset. Between crying spells, I looked over to where Mom was in her bed, a lump beside me. I wanted so badly to reach out and hug her. Touch her. I rocked back and forth, trying not to but biting the pillow and grabbing my sides until the scabs broke free and my shirt clung to the blood. A three-finger bruise was developing on my arm. I was falling apart.

No sleep. My back hurt from the hardwood floor. Same with my knees and elbows and other places that had nothing to do with the floor. Night fell over the windows and then I had no way of knowing what time it was. I didn't care. Outside, the street was calm and without the moon the darkness covered me like a blanket. Again my thoughts turned to Andrew and his tea. It was too late to go back on the plan. Not that I would. If remorse were clothes, I was a stark-naked lunatic.

But I was choking with dread. Sure it was my fault. I'd brought it on myself, but it was too disgusting to dwell on so I locked it down in my brain so I would never relive it for as long as I breathed. Finally, a fitful sleep took hold, and I drifted away staring at the ceiling, thinking about one of the last times Mom and I tried to do normal things.

We'd gone to the lake. I'll never forget the stares when Mom took her shirt off and exposed her pale, hollow body. Only made worse because my mom was one of those people born to be at the beach, who looked so natural in a swimsuit, tanned and bronzed and holding sunshine on her face like her own personal glow. I used to love when people told me I looked like her, but no one said that towards the end. By then her steps were halting. The cancer was a chain, and she was gaining a link every day.

That day at the lake there was this stupid little boy running around, swatting at butterflies and being a complete pain to everyone. When he saw us he stopped, his shoulders drooping and his eyes wide as he openly gawked at Mom. When he pointed, I planted my feet, wanting nothing more than to go kick him in the jaw. His mother took his hand and led him the other way, and I glared at them until he got his head back around. When they were gone I turned to Mom and saw that she was gawking too. At me.

It wasn't the first time I'd felt it, the searing hatred inside of me.

But that day at the lake was the first time Mom saw it. I shook with anger, and I jumped when her spindly fingers found my back. When she brought me back to her.

I woke up late, the sun bright and the room empty. The sound of Mr. Franklin singing to his plants. He had the squirrels tamed, and they'd scurry around his feet and beg for food. Mom used to call him the squirrel whisperer, and I chuckled to myself thinking about it. Our old neighbor had always been kind to us, even though he was half-screwed in the head. I peeked out and watched him for a while, thinking about happier times.

It was nearly ten by the time I got back to Dunham, which meant I still had a hike to Glenda's. I used my prepaid Visa card, the one for emergencies, stopping for coffee, looking pretty much like a girl who'd done some crying and slept on a floor. A girl who'd been through hell.

I created a story. I'd stayed at Vee's house and fell asleep. It wasn't great, but I wasn't able to put too much thought into it because I didn't actually care in the least. Not until I got to the house and saw Robbie out in the yard.

He stood, wiped the dirt from his hands then raised them with a stretch. "Hey there, Chloe."

"Good morning," I said to my uncle, the man who tip-toed around me like I was shattered glass. But after everything, I realized he was the closest thing I had to Mom, in human form, anyway, standing there with the morning shine in his fragile stare. It shook me to the bone thinking how he'd grown up with Mom, fought with her, teased her, defended her, and loved her. And now, biting my lip to stop it from quivering, all I wanted to do was launch into him and sob into his chest.

But what good would that do? It would crush the life out of him if he knew what had happened yesterday. He kicked a clump of weeds from his foot. "I got us some donuts," he said, with the makings of a smile.

I'd only thought about lying to Glenda. It was so much harder with Uncle Robbie. It was his face, the subtle gestures with his hands, so much like Mom it made me want to either slap him or hug him. But I wanted to give him a smile for his efforts, only that's when Glenda came zinging outside, ready to thrash the morning to shreds.

"Rob, I think we should put in the Clematis over—oh, Chloe, hi."

I glanced at the carriage house. With all my wondering about if Andrew was lying dead in his bed, the truck still being gone told me he was still among the living. Oh, well, there was still time to rush into his place and empty the tea.

But I didn't. I smiled at Glenda and hit the steps to go inside, ready to figure out what to do with the day. The last thing I saw was her hanging there, staring at Robbie, waiting for him to jump up and demand an explanation about where I'd been all night. But Robbie simply got back to his garden.

VEE STOPPED BY AFTER DINNER, still riding high from her state dinner, talking a million miles an hour about how she felt like a duchess, how she thought there might be a chance Spence might change his mind now and go to Georgetown, which we both knew was not happening, but when it came to Spence her thoughts went to smoke quicker than meth in a trailer park.

We hung out in the den because Glenda and Robbie were still at it in the yard, prepping things for the big garden spread in the *Dunham Weekly*. I nodded along at Vee's recap, but I could hardly think, keeping one ear out for Andrew's truck and the other for Glenda to come in and start her gushing with Vee. Of course Vee knew I wasn't listening to a word she was saying.

"Hey, what's wrong?"

"Nothing, it's just been a rough couple of days." I'd gone back and forth about telling her, but I just couldn't get the words out of my mouth.

"Is it Glenda?" She stood, batting her eyes and breaking into her

Glenda impression. She hopped and paced, bouncing around. "You know she means well."

I rolled my eyes, biting a smile. Vee continued bopping around the living room, bang-shaking away. "Oh, Vienna. I just love your hair, it's so kinky and frizzy. What do you put in it?"

Vee spun around on her heels. "Why thank you, Mrs. Vanderbrooke," she said, posing with a hand to her chin. "I believe it's called, um, African."

Pretty soon we were cracking up and giggling and it was almost like old times, just like when Mom would peek in on us or sometimes come and join us on the couch. Vee plopped down beside me, snatching the remote and hunting for something to watch. "So, you need to tell me what's up. Did something happen with Dylan?"

I sat up straight. "Did *he* say something did?"

A big smile spread across her face. "Is there something you want to tell me? Oh my, Chloe!"

I couldn't do this. I shook my head, tried to bury the flash of panic flooding through my face, but it only confirmed Vee's inaccurate suspicions. She slapped my arm. "When were you going to tell me?"

"Nothing happened, Vee. Not that anyway."

"Yeah right, you little hussy."

She was joking, but it reminded me of Andrew, pinning me down, his face smothering me. Vee's eyes went wide. "Chloe, what's... Hey come on, I'm joking."

"No, not that. It's nothing."

"Chloe, what?"

I pulled my hair back, let it fall, pulled it back again. "I just, I went back to my old place yesterday."

Vee's smile dropped with the remote. She bit her lip, set a hand on my knee. "Again? Hey, I know you don't want to hear this, but maybe you should talk to Oglesby about it."

I nodded. Funny how Glenda had sort of slacked off on my therapy. Maybe she thought I was cured, healed of the grief.

Vee stroked my hair. I let her have a pass on the shrink talk, because we'd been through so much together. Like two years ago when fat Collin Abbot used to call her an Oreo Cookie at summer camp and Vee would spend the whole night sobbing in her cot. Then one day I found Collin in the mess hall and told him how if he ever opened his mouth again around Vee I'd tell everybody about how his dad was having an affair with his dentist. Now people ask Vee if she's a model. And Collin Abbot was still fat.

Vee turned off the TV. "So, did you like, break in, or... I mean?"

I told her about the key. I kept it on my keychain now. I even told her I'd spent the night there but nothing about Andrew. Nothing about Andrew. Those words were life-changers, and so they stayed buried in a dark place. They slept like bats in my ribcage only to come fluttering alive at night. They made me think about Dylan, his face when I'd told him just a fraction of what was going on. So I didn't tell Vee. Even though we were best friends and she knew I had always been a little different. Just not *this* different.

I couldn't tell her about what had happened at the carriage house, the pond, my bedroom. How I've sort of tried to poison Andrew now and was doing nothing to remedy that situation. So I let her hold me. And she was holding me when the door swung open and Glenda tore through the house, singing at the top of her lungs.

I sat up and wiped my eyes and managed to get myself together by the time her eyes went atomic and her face bright with the hope of talking Pilates. And Vee obliged. I watched the two of them hit the floor.

And somehow, I was laughing.

Chapter 16

Last year, when Chris and I got together, I "overheard" Stacey Callahan and Olivia Morgan suggesting I was only at D.E.S. because my mom was getting it on with Mr. Suddith. They were sick puppies for sure, spreading rumors about his locked door at lunch or my mom's car being in the parking lot after dark. But so far, since my mother's sickness and death, they'd proven to possess at least a tiny morsel of basic decency.

But settling into the auditorium for the Cum Laude Society announcement, the statute of limitations had expired. Stacey and Olivia plopped down behind me, snorting and giggling as Mr. Suddith took the podium. It sucked because I'd felt a shiver of pride walking in, as Mr. Suddith had already given me a heads up I was one of the six juniors chosen. Yeah, me, Cum Laude. All I could think about was Mom. But those shivers turned to shivs with Stacey and Olivia cackling back there.

It started with them kicking my seat, snickering and whispering. My ears grew magma hot as Mr. Suddith began with his usual *diversity and embracing our differences* bit. I was about to lose it, because Mom would have been tearing up over such an honor, but those two halfwits wouldn't let it go.

Stacey (I knew it was her because she had a slight speech impediment being how she was mildly touched), whispered, "Embracing the help under the desk."

I set my jaw. Vee snatched my hand and squeezed so tight it hurt. My breath sputtered, fast and shallow. That they would do this, make a remark like that about my dead mother, only proved how heartless they were. I was about to whirl around and strangle whichever one I grabbed first when Vee stood and yanked me along with her.

She led the way as we shuffled out of aisles and into the lobby, heads turning and bodies swiveling at the movement just as Mr. Suddith mentioned my name, *Chloe Vanderbrooke.*

Applause.

Through the heavy doors, into the empty lobby, I doubled over, every heave and gasp sliding across the shine of the marble and tile. I set my hands on my knees while Vee patted my back like I did hers when she had to puke. Someone asked if we needed help, but Vee waved them off. At some point she helped me to my feet and we escaped outside where things were quiet with the assembly going on.

It felt like my lungs were wrestling, my heart cheering them on with its thumping. I tried to walk it off, pacing, sucking air and exhaling hot, wet rage.

Vee was calm as ever. "Don't, Chloe. Do not waste your tears on them."

I pressed my palms to my eyes. She was right, but it hurt, everything hurt. She suggested we go for a walk. And so we roamed around campus, Vee making dumb jokes she knew would get me laughing. Me crying and mumbling and finally venting. When we returned, the doors were open and kids were scattering about. I scanned the faces, looking for Stacey and Olivia in the mix, wishing I had a pair of brass knuckles. But I had a better weapon. I had Vienna Summerset.

Vee ordered me to stay put, shushing me when I protested. She sauntered over to them, kissing her hand as she strutted past the Bishop Mallory statue and slapping the old man's cheek. She was tall and confident with a near poetic bounce to her strides. It was like being on set at a movie location. Vienna was a star, and everyone watching her knew it.

Stacey looked up first. She and Olivia had sidled up to Steph and Maurice, two super-tall jock types from Romania. They turned and went slack-jawed at Vienna and those gorgeous greens turning up on them.

I wasn't close enough to make out what she said, something in Hungarian. It didn't matter. Steph and Maurice took another look at Stacey and Olivia and busted out laughing. Then, as Stacey ripened with rage and Olivia looked like she might get sick, the two boys followed Vee—her smile blooming like a primrose—like good little puppies back towards the hall. I fell in behind them, staring at the devastation left in Vee's wake.

"What did you say?"

Vee shook her head and smiled. She nodded to the boys as though letting them off leash. "I informed our friends about the searing effects of genital herpes."

Well, I couldn't help but feel better after that.

I didn't see Dylan until afternoon. Funny how he always used to be nearby, outside of class or catching me in stride on campus. Now he was clearly avoiding me. I found him all alone outside Kemper Hall, amongst the spoilage of old cherry blossoms, his face sour with consternation. He saw me coming towards him and simply looked the other way.

"Dylan, can we talk?"

"Sure, if that's what you want."

I shot him a look. "Okay, what does *that* mean?"

He snorted. "It means you won't tell me the truth."

I was still off balance, since the assembly, since the carriage house. Since Mom died. I took a breath. "I thought I did, at the pond."

He started along the path, gripping the straps of his backpack like he didn't really care whether I came along or not. I followed, wondering what was going on, or knowing what was going on but not ready to believe it. "Hey, are you going to talk to me or what?"

"Sure," he said, reaching out for a tree branch, his arm rippling with the movement. "Let's talk, Chloe. Let's talk about you and Andrew. Like, the way *he* talks to you."

His anger caught my steps. I stopped and he turned and faced me head on. "This is serious, to me. Is he touching you? Or, is he..." Dylan stopped and wiped his forehead, talking to the trees and shaking his head. "I can't even say it."

I got a hold of the rising panic inside of me. I rolled it up like a sail on the mast, wiping my hair from my face. "I've told you, he's creepy, but I can take care of myself. And he should be moving out soon, or...gone."

"Chloe. I don't know anymore."

"Don't know *what*?"

"About us."

It would have been easier had he just slapped my face. It would have hurt less than this shy little boy running off when I needed him the most. Serious *to him*? Like it wasn't to me? Where did he even get the nerve? Something ruptured inside of me. I wanted to claw his face, to kick him between the legs. Instead I just turned away, because I wasn't going to cry in front of him. I was done crying for the day. But I left him some parting words.

"You know what, Dylan? Screw you."

Chapter 17

I'd officially come undone. So I walked. From Cum Laude to truancy, it was all a joke. In truth, I'd known it was going to be awful when Mom died, but I never imagined things could slide to these depths. It made me want to break something. Andrew, and what happened in the carriage house. Stacey and Olivia. Dylan dumping me. All of it made me want to set the world on fire and watch it burn. Feed the flames with human flesh. I stomped along, ignoring traffic and everything around me, hiking up East Ridge.

A car slowed behind me. "You need a ride, Chlo?"

I jolt of terror hit me. Andrew leaned over the seat as the truck crawled along the side of the road, a tire rubbing the curb. The easygoing way in which he could smile and call me "Chlo" after what he'd done to me felt like steel wool scourging my neck.

"Go to hell."

"Come on, Chloe, don't be like that."

My knees locked, I had to jerk to a halt or fall flat on my face. "Be like what? I should go down to the police station."

I hated how I sounded like a little girl. How my voice squeaked because I was fighting back so many emotions. Or maybe just one huge, bursting-at-the-seams emotion. He sat there, enjoying it, leaning over as traffic passed. Normal people doing normal things, maybe. Or were there more Andrews out there in the stream of things, going along until they had their chance in the dark?

I made a show of looking left then right down the street. "I think it's right down the block, isn't it?"

He followed my gaze. A car honked behind him. "Chloe, I thought we...you know?"

I turned away while I could still function. I couldn't look at him. Death was preferable to this day. None of it seemed real. I started ahead but he drove beside me, talking. "You know, if you...do that. It will, it's going to get messy. I'll can tell you that."

"Yeah, for you. Maybe you'll have a nice roommate. One who strokes your hair in your jail cell." I stopped again, my nose burning. "You...raped me."

There, I'd said it out loud. Now I was about to collapse.

A car honked again. Andrew kept waving them on, unafraid. Unfazed. "Chloe, let's not go crazy here." He was grinning—*grinning* —his ugly smile like a rake clawing my back. "And that's not what happened, Chloe. You were in my place. Think about it, Chloe. Glenda won't believe you. Probably no one at school will believe you, and, even if they do, good luck with all your friends, being the girl who seduced an older man."

He kept saying my name. Chloe. Chloe. Like he knew me. I was a mess. A slobbering glaze of hate. It was all so incomprehensible. "What?"

Shrugging now. "I mean, you were in my house. I thought you were eighteen."

More honking. More cars passing. I shook my head. No, that's not what happened. I felt like running out in traffic, waving cars down so I could scream what really happened. Andrew was still waving for cars to pass us. He was so out in the open. When I managed to speak, my voice squeaked, a little girl whine again. "That's a complete lie. You'll go to jail and hopefully someone will do to you what you did to me!"

Another shrug. His smug grin. I scanned the ground for a rock to toss through his teeth while he kept talking. Between him and his sister, they never shut up.

"Think about the mess this will cause. You'd at least have to switch schools and it's a small town, people will talk. And, like I said about Glenda. But that's not what I want. We could just keep things..."

"Leave me alone! Just go home and drink your tea." With that, I heaved a book at his car. It hit the side door and maybe made a dent. His face dropped and his eyes hardened. Then he peeled away. I slung my bag too as he tore off up East Ridge, cars honking at me and yelling for me to get out of the road like it was my fault. *My fault.*

I shouldn't have said anything about the tea. But I snapped, wishing I could pour an entire container of antifreeze down his throat. Maybe buy two more for Stacey and Olivia. Maybe a fourth for Dylan.

My People-Who-Need-To-Get-Theirs list was running out of space. I had to take a break from this world of heartless people I wanted to strangle. From Andrew, who was right, because if Stacey and Olivia ever found out about any of this, my life was done, even more than it was already. I put my head down and kept going.

Coming up Madison Street, my nightmare continued as I spotted a tall, frail figure in the driveway. Papa Vanderbrooke, in his sweater, hands in his pockets, hobbling towards his Mercedes. He stopped and looked up, looked directly at me. I stood straight and still, glaring back at him.

He'd said my name at the funeral. "Chloe." And that tiny nod of acknowledgement was all I would get. The only word he'd ever spoken to me. Now, as we dueled in the shade of the trees, I held my chin high. I was inflamed, defiant, and ready to face him head on if that's what he wanted. But he turned away and got in his car. He backed out of the driveway and drove past me, his hands on the steering wheel, his eyes straight ahead.

Chapter 18

With Dylan hiding, Vee took things into her own hands. After a barrage of calls and texts, she eventually convinced me to join her and Spence and go to a party out in Esterly. I knew she was up to something, but with Glenda all in my situation about extracurriculars and skipping school, and the whole thing with Andrew, I was ready to take my chances. I needed to get out.

That didn't mean I had to make an effort. I didn't ask but simply walked out and waited on the steps without bothering to change out of the tank and shorts I'd thrown on after school. I told Robbie we were headed to a movie. He was out in the garden. I think Glenda wanted him to enforce some rules or ground me or something, but he said it was fine. Like I cared. I hopped into the car without a goodbye.

The day was still warm, but the leather seats in Spence's Audi were cool against my bare skin. Vee turned back to me, up to something, her face alive with mischief.

"Well, you look good enough to kiss, Chlo."

Spence adjusted the mirror. "By all means."

Vee slapped his arm then kissed his neck. The car swerved with their turbulence and I rolled my eyes. But I couldn't help feeling better, being out of the house. With the wind swirling and the music, it was the freest I'd felt in a while.

"So are you doing okay though, really?" Vee said it in a way only she could, going from fast and happy to slow and sincere with the arch of an eyebrow. I told her I was fine and reached for the bottle on the floorboard.

"What are we drinking tonight?" I eyed the fancy label. Probably something outrageous from the Nottaway's stash.

"That," Spence said, yelling over the wind and music, "is Denmark's finest vodka. Go ahead, test the waters."

"Really?"

"No, it's bottom shelf. Pure rotgut. But we're getting drunk and won't care after a couple shots, right?"

Fair enough. "Just take it straight?"

He smirked, his eyes swimming with anticipation in the mirror. Vee swung around. "No way, Chlo. Here." She handed me a cup with what looked like a slushy. "Here."

I'd only be doing Vee a favor, I thought, knowing how she couldn't handle her liquor. I sucked down a cold, headache-inducing pull of glorious grape. I can't say what came sooner, the brain freeze or the rush of liquor to my blood. I took another sip and smiled, closing my eyes and letting the wind sift through my hair.

"That a girl," Vee said and turned up the stereo. A Bruno Mars song played about love and honesty and all the stupidity fit to sing about.

I'm sure the party was just like a million others we'd been to, but I was three shades of spinning by the time we arrived. Suddenly the world was warm and wonderful and I wanted to float through the evening with my new vodka wings. But I stumbled getting my legs beneath me. Spence caught me by the arm and set me straight.

"Whoa there Chloe. At least let it get dark first."

I bit my smile. The day was vanishing but the night was getting a late start. Humid for spring, as though summer might steal it away all together. The McMansions were all the same, blocky and ugly, with garages as big as my old house on Dorchester.

Vee took my elbow and we started up the driveway. "So, now that you're feeling better…"

"Oh come on. What?" I turned to her and took a step back. Spence's palm braced my back. It felt like I was being forced to the town square for a public hanging.

"Dylan's here."

I spun free but Spence road-blocked me. Vee took my arm again.

I held steady to both of them while she kept talking. "Look, I don't know what's going on with the two of you, but shouldn't you at least talk about it?"

"No."

Spence took over. "Come on, Chlo, that dude is nuts about you."

I pulled away, stopped, ready to kick and scream and throw a fit. Up ahead the garage was open and we were close enough now to hear the usual party sounds. Jocks yelling at each other—deep, manly barks. Girls giggling. Two guys and a girl playing Bet Your Liver. A sloppy couple on the couch. Some loser climbing up on the roof without a shirt on. The cops would be here before ten.

"This is so not going to end well." I reached for Vee's cup, she pushed it forward and I took a deep, bolstering pull of mushy grape goodness. I wiped my chin. "Okay, whatever."

We trooped inside. Dylan was in the kitchen, talking to some ordinary looking guys about something dumb, for sure. He looked from me to Spence to Vee. He ran a hand through his hair in that stupid cute way of his. The vodka was not helping me stay angry with him. More the opposite.

Heads turned our way. Even with a buzz, it was always something to see Spence enter a party. People looked up, stopped talking. Almost like they were going to break out into applause.

Okay, Spence is here, the party can start.

I'd even seen it with adults. Last summer the cops came to bust a party and Spence stepped out and it was all nods and smiles and tell-your-father-I-said-hellos. Then they cleared us out without all the usual fuss about calling parents. I thought they might ask for an autograph. And he was still a month or two away from his eighteenth birthday.

Inevitably, Dylan came over to us. Because he had to, had to wade through the crowd and do some macho hand slapping with Spence Nottaway. Then he nodded to Vee, who crossed her arms tight to force the issue.

Dylan turned to me with the makings of a smile. "You okay?"

I stepped back, shocked, blinking in exasperation. A hand to my chest. "Why, of course I'm okay."

I leaned in close but stumbled just a teensy bit. My hair fell over my face. "Are *you* okay?"

He nodded, gestured to the bottle in Spence's hands. "Really?"

Spence uncapped it and took a swig. He tried to tough it out for approximately two seconds before he spat it out on the floor and flung himself toward the fridge where he yanked it open, found a beer and cracked it. He pressed it to his face, half of it falling to a foamy puddle on the floor. "Oh, that's bad."

The kitchen got crowded. Some idiots cranked up the trap music and we had a party. I was almost feeling good enough to dance when Dylan touched my arm. "So," he said, "outside?"

I shrugged and Vee basically shoved the two of us out the door. Through the garage and around to the side of the house we found a big trampoline. The sun had recently set and the horizon glowed.

"I didn't know you drank. I mean, liquor and stuff."

"I don't," I shrugged. "Not usually."

He laughed, like it was some inside joke he had with himself. Dylan had certainly come out of his shell, and I wasn't sure how I felt about it. I climbed up on the trampoline and attempted some clumsy jumps before realizing it was a terrible idea.

I fell to my back and lay there, letting the smear of clouds smother me. The world jiggled. Dylan plopped down, and when he took my hand, euphoria flushed through my limbs. I felt him looking at me. "So are you going to say anything? I mean besides 'screw you.' I think we've covered that."

I took a deep breath and closed my eyes. I'd almost let myself forget the whole reason we'd stopped talking. Now it all came back, falling through the cracks. Because of Andrew.

Euphoria gone. *Andrew's face on top of me, his grunting, his strong hands on my wrists. I lay there helpless.*

"Chloe?"

I could tell him right now. Try again and tell him everything.

About what really happened. It would feel incredible, to say it, let all the pollution out and start over. Maybe he would hold me and kiss the top of my head. Maybe he would know it wasn't my fault. How I was too ashamed to report it, broadcast it, announce it to the world. Afraid of the fallout, all of it, because it would be like it was happening again and again and again when I just wanted to let it erode. To fade away and wash back out into the sea.

It was asking a lot of a guy. A great guy, but still just a guy. A guy who might look at me like he had at the pond or at school the other day. A guy who might shake his head and roll off this trampoline and get far away from the crazy girl with all the drama.

So I curled into him, hard and close, my face brushing his warmth. Only a few strands of my hair between us. He started to say something, but I kissed him, the vodka knocking down the obstacles and pressure. He kissed me back and we fell into each other with the drunken sounds of the party inside. My smile pressed to his as we wiggled and bounced on the trampoline. Dylan surprised me as his hand fell to my waist and came up my shirt.

His breath hit my ear. I smelled the familiar clean traces of his deodorant. I let his hands roam along my hips and I fought the urge to squirm, scream, to run away as fast as I could. As far as I could. But Andrew eclipsed us. With his tile and tools, the reek of glue and grout, the harsh mint. I opened my eyes and saw Dylan, but Andrew was there too.

I sat up too fast. Dylan jumped away from me like I was a snake in his bed. "I'm sorry. Chloe, I'm sorry."

My head swam. "No," I shook my head, wanting to cry, then mad at myself because I was always about to cry. But there was something else going on. "No, it's not that, Dylan, it's not—"

"I thought, I just..."

I shook my head again, faster, because it wasn't him. Wasn't Andrew. It was the voices coming up the driveway—one deep and low, the other scratchy. Both voices clawed at my brain as four illuminated boxes swung with the strides of the herd.

Dimwits. Stacey and Olivia strutting up to the garage with two other girls I couldn't make out. Meanwhile, Dylan was still fumbling over an apology, so I kissed him again to keep him from talking.

Hushed whispers followed by giggles drifted to us, then the collisions of laughter. I pulled away from Dylan, who I'm sure was good and confused by my freakish behavior, so I gave him a smile and let my fingers fall from his chin to his chest and down to his belt. I whispered in his ear.

"I'll be right back, okay?"

"What?" he said, too loud. I shushed him again then slung myself from the trampoline, where the ground was hard and unabsorbing as I found my balance and crept over to the garage. It took a second to get my legs beneath me, but when I came to the corner, there they were, with Sara and Jill—unremarkable follower types—already cozied up with a group of guys. Something clicked in my head, and I darted down the driveway.

Spence never locked his car, and half the time didn't put his windows up. I guess when you're wealthy it doesn't occur to you to protect such disposable property as cars or phones or baseball equipment. And that's what I was banking on when I reached in the Audi and popped the trunk.

Four bats in his bag. Easton. Aluminum, different sizes and weights. I slid one from the other, my buzz fueling my quest to find what I hoped would give me the best pop. Some cars were filing in, so I gave it a minute until the parade of half-drunken kids meandered up the drive. Then it was all clear, the party was loud and the lights were on. And I was all alone in the driveway.

I found Stacey's empty Honda and tightened my fingers around the sandy grip of the bat. Eyeing the back window, I thought about her snickering behind me. My mother dies and she wants to laugh and add that to her little bully arsenal? Nope.

For two years I'd listened to her lies, watched these two idiots strut around and ruin other people's lives. Another glance around as a car passed by the wide road to another brick house. Cocked and ready, a sneaky grin found my face. I tightened my grip and took aim at the back window. Batter up.

A loud gasp froze me in place. "Chloe. Don't you dare!"

My eyes burned. Vee set her hands on her hips, her voice stern and clear of any drunkenness. "What do you think you're doing?"

I stood there with the bat, only seconds ago poised to strike, now getting heavy in my grasp. My lips trembled and my arms went tight, my mind caught between its own shame and rage.

"Chloe, put the bat down." She waved a hand at the car, her voice softer now, "Don't. Not for *them*. They're nobody."

The way she said, "nobody" so casually, so absolutely fact, it made me chuckle. Before I knew it she'd swooped in and engulfed me in a hug. The bat hit the driveway like a bell.

Spence was on it by the third bounce. "Holy crap, Chlo, not Big Red." He checked it for damage then turned to Stacey's Honda. He looked back to me and grinned. "Damn, Chlo."

My heart banged away. I looked up and saw another figure silhouetted by the lights of the house. Vee moved closer. She wiped my hair back with both hands, then set them on my shoulders, looking me head on. She laughed. "You're hardcore, girl. I swear."

Spence wiped his bat and set it in the trunk. He shut it and looked at us. "Okay, I'm done here. This party is busted and I hear there's herpes in the kitchen." He yelled up to the silhouette. "Yo, Dylan, you coming?"

I gave Vee a small smile and a shrug. "I was only going to tap it."

Dylan jogged down the driveway to us then looked back at the house. "Well, it's clear someone needs to keep an eye on Chloe, so, I'm in. Let's get out of here."

The headlights lit the trees as Spence took the winding road to the lake house, the music loud, the wind warm, as Dylan pulled me into his arms and Vee sang along with the radio.

Spence parked the car and killed the music. He turned back to me. "Is my car safe here, Chloe? Or are you still looking to break stuff?"

I laughed. Dylan did too. I took his face and kissed him again, holding onto him tightly because I was afraid one of us might run away.

"Okay, I guess not," Spence said and kissed Vee. They climbed out of the car, teasing and play fighting and grabbing at each other as they climbed the steps to the porch.

When it was just the two of us, Dylan pulled away from me, and I knew what he was going to say, so I blurted it out, "Look, I know you think I'm crazy but I don't want to talk about anything, okay? My mom or whatever. I just want you and me right now."

He pulled me in closer once again and smiled as he leaned his head back, holding a finger up. "One question though." He shook his head. "What exactly were you going to do, really? With that bat?"

I pushed his finger to my lips. "I guess we'll never know."

We kissed again, for a while, and Dylan was acting like a boy who'd forgotten his bible verses, until the lights came on and Vee clomped out on the porch with a beer, singing into the night. I kissed Dylan's neck then opened the door.

That was the last time. Of us. Of all of it. We drank without getting drunk or sick. All four of us happy, singing and talking and making fun of school and skanks and the world outside those woods. No one asked if I was okay or said anything about my bruises. Dylan kept his arm around me, his eyes on mine, and Vee and Spence never once fought.

It was like we knew it was all coming to an end. Spence was headed west and Dylan north come graduation. Vee and I would be seniors, but both of us were incapable of imagining it. Of getting closer to losing nights like this. It was warm yet cool. It was light, dark, and immovable. The songs spilled out of the house for only us. I didn't think about Mom. I let her rest in peace. I let her be dead for once without trying to drag her back into what was happening that moment. I'd join her one day soon enough. I'd tell her all about how great life could be for a night, with a cute boy who said all the right things, with friends who loved you unconditionally and without questions.

I soaked in it, stretching out into the minutes and filling the hours with my arms and hands in its warmth. I clutched Dylan, making sure he was still there with me. And he was, for that night at least.

Chapter 19

Doctor Oglesby tightened the screws. Our visit began like it normally did, breezing through our day-to-day. She gushed about her kids, how her young son was learning to ride a bike, how he was growing up so fast. *They do that, you know?*

I sat back and took it in, astonished with how she could listen to dodos all day and then come home with any sort of idea what a normal life was like.

She had a nice figure. I'd even guess she was kind of hot when she wasn't wearing drabby earth-tone suits and flats. I wondered when she had time to get to the gym and before I knew it, I was doing most of the talking—about Mom and even my dad. How I could always talk to Mom about anything, how she understood me, about how she was always so...*good.*

Dr. O said it was normal for me to put her on a pedestal, which ticked me off because that wasn't what I was doing. I mean, Mom wasn't perfect, she had her moods. She got cranky every once in a while. Even if it was more like Robbie's *awe shucks, that's a bummer* kind of cranky.

When it came to temperament, Mom and I were nothing alike. My anger had stamina, endurance, it was a well-oiled machine. It took on a life of its own. Like with the boy gawking at Mom at the lake, my anger stewed and simmered to a boil, bubbling over and leaving a mess you had to come back and clean up when things cooled down. My dad was a head case, so maybe that explained it, even when all I knew about him was that he was a good-looking drug addict with his own demons and depression. How he'd killed himself. And since Mom's death I felt an oddly intuitive connection to him.

Same for Papa Vanderbrooke. After I'd stared him down the other day, I asked Robbie about it. He'd come to talk about Grandma Millie, who was in the hospital with pneumonia. Maybe dying. You drop over to tell your son his mom might be dying and you still can't bring yourself to speak to your granddaughter out there on the street? That's some cold-blooded stuff, right there.

And this is what was in *my* blood, my genetic makeup. I told Doctor O this, too. I told her how it didn't matter how *good* my mother was, she was only a part of my family tree, the rest were real crab apples. They say love wins, but in my case, at least, hate had numbers in its favor.

It was a moment of weakness, opening up like that with Oglesby. But Andrew had knocked me off a cliff with his threats and consequences. And it was all starting to wear me down. I was tired of hiding and choosing, combing through my words. I wanted to tell her—someone, anyway—how *disgusting* I felt. How the best moments with Dylan were always followed by a crush of guilt. How he'd never ever want to touch me again if he found out the truth.

I didn't say it, though. I hardly even allowed myself to think about what Andrew had done. And with that at least, I was careful. After we talked about Mom, I spent most of our time venting about Stacey and Olivia and their bitchery. When I was leaving, Doctor O actually walked me out. She touched my shoulder and asked if she could see me again next week. Like I had a choice. But the more I thought about it, the whole hour had only been the setup. She'd buttered me up and next week she'd start picking locks and springing traps. Next week she'd get nothing.

In the waiting area, Glenda rocketed from her chair a crazy person, eyes picking me apart, looking for some sort of change now that I'd had sixty minutes of professional help. She checked with the receptionist, next Tuesday at five. Great.

Outside, the wind wreaked havoc on Glenda's bangs. She fought vigilantly, though, thrashing around, whipping her head until her sunglasses leaped off her face. She picked them up and shook her head back into them, muttering to herself through gritted teeth.

And I was the one in therapy.

The silent treatment was lifted. Glenda was off and chit-chatting again. I paid little attention until she mentioned something about Andrew camping on the parkway—which explained why the past few days had been so nice. No answer as to when he'd be back. Whenever it was, I'd be ready.

Things were splendidly uneventful for a while. With the cootie queens neutralized by the herpes rumors, school was bearable. Even Miss Shelby had backed off to the point I assumed there was a new cat in her life. Dylan and Vee and I went to Spence's game on Wednesday, where afterwards Dylan and I ditched Vee so we could go have some alone time at the house. Since the party we'd been doing so well, and the way he looked at me sometimes, it just made me laugh for no reason, probably because if I didn't, I would start crying.

But Thursday night came for me like I owed it something. It showed up at the doorstep like a big, hairy repo man, tapping a lead pipe onto the palm of his hand, laughing at me for thinking I could actually be anywhere near happiness.

I was studying for Calculus and in a pretty good groove. It was fundraiser night for Glenda and Robbie, but with Andrew out of the picture I'd been lulled into a slumber, and my guard was down and my eyes glazed.

I set the book on the side table. It was exactly 9:30. I figured they'd be home soon as Robbie had been yawning before they left. I knew these charity dinners were torture for him. It was clear he was itching to loosen his tie and veg out and watch TV. But I also knew Glenda would be a little buzzed, all razzed up and wanting to talk about the garden or the big feature at the house or something painfully insignificant, so I turned off the light in hopes she wouldn't try to come in and get chummy. Two minutes later I heard the heavy click of the main door downstairs.

A mega-volt shock pierced through my skull. Because Glenda and Robbie would have parked around back and come in through the kitchen door, which I'd locked. But Andrew only had a key to the front door—a horrifying little nugget I'd discovered when Glenda said her little bro might need to borrow milk or eggs or butter, and we might not be around to let him in.

I sat up and froze, staring at the door in the dark, willing my body to move and get up. Maybe I could wedge the chair under the doorknob. But my legs refused to work. I was afraid to make a sound, praying he *was* only getting milk or butter or eggs. The last thing I wanted to do was make noise, let him know I was upstairs in my bed.

A clink of dishes. A few quick sniffs and snorts. Mumbling. The door to the fridge rattled opened, then banged shut. A sloppy hum, offbeat and repugnant. The drawer crashed open. Utensils clattered around in his clumsy hands. Slammed shut.

"Hey, Chloe?"

A swallow scraped down my throat towards the storm in my stomach. For a few seconds my body was fastened to the bed. A step squeaked under the weight of his foot. A sloppy whisper hissed up the staircase and down the hall, under my door.

"Chloe."

Terror rattled my temples as he hit the steps. No. No. No. I got my feet under me, wobbling as the steps became stomps. I shoved my arm between the mattress and box spring, searching blind for the knife but nothing was there. Another swipe. It was gone.

On my feet, I grabbed the chair but Andrew beat me to the door. He lunged and we fell to the floor, me on my back with the chair on my chest, stealing my scream. It didn't take much for him to overpower me, my arms were rubber with fear. I blinked and he was up, hovering over me, letting me fight, gripping the chair and toying with me.

I tried to slide back but he crushed me again. "Get. Out," I managed.

The light came on and I saw the monster. Sweaty and panting, his eyes both wild and dead. He pounced, leering over me, still pressing the chair against my chest. His hat crooked and his t-shirt splotchy and stained, heaving with his stomach. A grin curled up his lips like it wasn't part of his face but some horror-show wax figure. The harder I squirmed the more he laughed, leaning over me, taunting me. "I know what you did, Chloe."

I wanted to kick him or hurl something at him but I was pinned down. And now, in the light, my throat closed altogether. Andrew had a knife of his own.

His cheeks twitched. A jagged wheeze rushed into my ear. Sniffling, blinking, his tongue swiped across his teeth. He was way gone, not with-it enough to worry about someone coming home. He admired the glint of the knife, one from Glenda's William Sonoma collection. I opened my mouth but managed only a whimper, like a puppy in a box. Andrew's smile widened. He leaned forward, setting his weight on the chair. On me.

"Yeah, I know what you did," he repeated, his voice high, almost girly. I blinked so hard it hurt, trying to reset the room. Had he tasted it? Seen it?

My thoughts were cut short when he slid the knife along my cheek, toying with my skin as tears flooded my vision. His face came close, smiling and proud. Then the weight was gone and I gasped for breath. Through the blurs and shadows I heard the chair crash against the dresser. Something heavy fell to the floor. He dragged me up by the neck. I wanted to fight but he was too strong, crushing me with one hand and enjoying it.

He tossed me onto the bed and the frame cracked under our weight. Before I could move he slapped a hand over my mouth, smothering me all over again.

I clawed at his arm. My calculus book smacked the floor. He choked me without fear, drooling and muttering, like he didn't care if I died. This time he was going to kill me. I had to fight. I broke through the panic and managed to get my leg free. I flung a knee into his ribs three then four then five times until he let go with a grunt.

His hand left my mouth. I gasped for air, like coming out of water. But only a heave or two before the edge of the knife found my throat.

This was it. My limbs went limp. The knife clicked against my windpipe, digging into my breaths. For some reason, under his weight, I thought about the marks it might leave, how I'd have thick, pinkish scars on my neck if I lived.

If I lived.

"You want it rough?" His voice was strange, high and cracking as though someone else was behind the empty eyes. The knife let up some. "Next time you might not want to leave the antifreeze cap on my counter you dumb little twit."

I shook my head, coughing and spitting. When I found my voice it was weak, shaky, like when you hear a 9-1-1 call on television and they have to add subtitles. "Glenda will be home..."

His hand fell to my chest, squeezing and rubbing. "We got plenty of time, Chloe."

My face burned from his breath. His slurred speech, the spittle on his lips and the bulging eyes with only a tiny dot bobbing in the gray. His smile was lopsided as he spoke. "I think it's time you ran away. Maybe we could both run away."

The flat part of the blade slid across my stomach, lower, tracing my pelvic bone. I couldn't stop trembling. He poked my legs with the tip, laughed when I jerked. Then back to my waistline.

Maybe he'd planned this whole thing out, with the camping—the fundraiser. Or maybe it was just blind, druggy luck and opportunity. My eyes blurred. My throat burned. He worked the blade back and forth, used his other hand to yank down my pants and rub my leg.

His breathing picked up, steady rasps, and I could feel his heart banging around in his chest. He was jacked, his jaw muscles working back and forth as he squeezed and pressed on me, grabbing between my legs, the knife toying with my skin. My body shut down with numbness as he unzipped his pants. I could let him do it, again, whatever he wanted, even kill me. Just get it all over with.

But I broke free from the numb. I couldn't do this again, I'd rather die. I closed my eyes and rolled into him, stifling my crying as I felt his grin on my face, his hands all over me, sliding down, groping, grabbing and pressing and getting into it. And when he let up to climb out of his pants, it gave me the opportunity I needed.

Ever since the kiss in the carriage house it had been headed here. So what were my options? To let him keep coming into my room? To force himself on top of me? Kill me and hide my corpse or whatever he had planned? People *would* think I ran away. And just as I'd underestimated him on that dreadful day on the couch, it was his turn to be surprised. So there, on the bed, with my mother's face in the frame on the dresser, watching as this monster drooled and fumbled around with himself, I found the warm, sweaty handle of the knife.

It took maybe two beats for him to catch his misstep. A groan left his throat. In a blink he realized the mistake he'd made coming into my room. It was on his lips as his mouth parted. In the flares shooting around in his eyes. A quick rundown of emotions danced across his face. Surprise, disbelief, hope, pleading, defeat.

All of it elapsed within two chirps of some clueless cricket outside. The time it took to tighten my squeeze around Glenda's kitchen knife handle. For me to pull it back—sliding my arm up over the smooth, Egyptian cotton sheets like silk on my skin—and thrust it into his stomach with a scream.

He reached for the knife as it tore into his side. Then for my arm. One last pathetic gesture, his fingers like a dead flower stalk brushing against my neck. I pulled the knife out and plunged it in him again. And again. Until his life spilled out into the bed, warm, onto me. His breaths collapsed and my screams sputtered. I couldn't tell what sounds were his or mine.

I still had the knife as I wiggled free. His body fell to the floor with a thump that seemed to finalize his death. And still, I couldn't let go of the handle, even as my body convulsed and I tripped on the chair and hit the floor, screaming out as I scrambled to my feet, slipped again, then lunged for the door. I was already vomiting as I tumbled down the steps. Away from Andrew. Away from the body in my room. I scrambled up again and ripped out of the house and onto the lawn.

My t-shirt clung to my stomach, soaked dark with blood. I pulled it over my head, warm and wet as it slid over my face, slick against the night as I flung it to the lawn. But there was more blood—so much of it—Andrew's blood slathered across my stomach, smeared down my legs. I fell to my knees, the knife back in my grip, stabbing it into the grass, hissing and spitting and tearing into the flesh of the earth. My breath caught in my throat. I gurgled, choked, felt my insides recoiling. I'd actually killed him.

I folded over and heaved again in the yard, spilling the charred contents from my stomach. My neck went limp and my head bowed. Exhaustion squeezed my limbs. The blood was cool on my skin now, sinking into my pores. My hands shivered as I wiped my hair back and tried to think, but my eyes watered and everything was smudged and blurred. I vomited again. Spit, blood, drool, tears. Dizzying lights and shadows. Warbled noises drifted up from downtown. My senses pummeled and misfired, from terror to rage, from rage to fatigue to nausea. Now it was morphing into something much grimmer.

I yanked the knife free from the dirt. It shook in my grip as I looked up at the night. The sour bile in my mouth burned as it slid back down my throat. There was nothing left. Nothing since the dirt on Mom's casket.

I set the knife to my wrist, ready to leave, ready to be done with all of it.

Chapter 20

A car drove up the hill, headlights leading the way as its tires stuttered over the cobblestones. I gripped the knife handle, the blade poised on my smeared skin, wondering what else I could do. Call for help? A neighbor? The police? Dylan?

The car passed before turning into a driveway a few houses down. The garage door rose. I picked myself up and stared at my uncle's house. The front door open, lights on inside. My head swam, my breaths worthless. For a moment I blamed Mom. I blamed cancer. I blamed myself for letting it go this far. But I shook it off. This was Andrew's fault. I wiped my forehead. The trouble now was with explaining it all.

I couldn't face it. The questions and consequences. The backlash. If I thought it was bad being the girl with the dead mother, the girl who'd been raped, how would it feel being the girl who killed a guy?

A siren screamed somewhere in the city. I spat the bile from my mouth and struggled to stand. I found my bloody shirt and started for the house. With each step, my panic receded, my vision sharpened, and the analytics set in. An urgent desire to fix a problem emerged from the smoldering wreckage of my brain. A challenge surfaced.

I set my mind to the details. Wash the knife. Wash the walls. Do something with the body. Step by step. But I had to freaking hurry.

I began with myself, with the strokes of Andrew's blood on my legs and midsection. I wiped myself down with an old towel, washing my face, dazed and staggering, but clearing as I worked my way back to my room. I wiped down the doorknob to the front door. Up the stair railings. Cleaned the vomit. Cleaned the walls. I backtracked and scrubbed and backtracked again until I stood in the doorway to my room, where self-defense had never looked so heinous.

Again, I focused on the problem. Data, metrics, analytics. That's all that remained. I needed a shower, obviously. And my underwear was somewhere under the bloody hump on the floor. Freakish, Andrew's body sitting there, collapsed and deflated. But there was no time to dwell on it.

A crunch of pea gravel stole my thoughts. Robbie and Glenda. Great. Twenty minutes ago they would have found me out in the yard, covered in blood and muttering to myself. But twenty minutes was an eternity ago, before a hardened callus formed on my brain. In that time, I'd been changed completely, and nothing I would ever see or feel again would compare. Ever. I'd made my decision. There was no turning back.

I pulled the wad of wet sheets and wrapped the body tight in the bedding. Andrew must have weighed around two hundred pounds, maybe less, so it was going to take some work. I hopped over to the door and shut it, catching a snatch of Glenda's voice, something about the build site for the new Boys and Girls club. I secured the chair under the knob.

Ten-forty-two. Glenda yelling down to Robbie as she came up the steps, her heels clicking and climbing. Then at my door. I'd turned off the light, which left me sitting on the floor in the dark beside her bloody pulp of a brother, wondering how I'd ever be able to pull this off.

Steps retreated down the hall. The toilet flushed and Glenda click-clacked out and the hall light went dark under my door. Downstairs, I heard Robbie rustling around, foraging for snacks. Probably tearing into a bag of flax-seed chips. More clacking in front of the door again. I covered a gasp when she tapped softly. "Chloe?"

Her voice still possessed a jovial energy from all the socializing. I held my breath. Held my thoughts. Held my quivering hands still. Another soft "Chloe?" before I heard her hand on the knob, sitting there. I thought about what would happened if she managed to open the door and found me sitting in the dark with her brother rolled up in her precious down comforter.

The knob went still. Glenda shuffled off, her heels clicking down to her room at the end of the hallway, mumbling some jazz number as she went to change clothes.

I spent the hours of eleven to one cleaning. As carefully as I could, a towel under the door so the lamp light wouldn't be seen by any nighttime wanderers. There wasn't much I could do, I'd have to ditch the sheets, the comforter, definitely flip the mattress until I could figure out a way to replace it. For now, I'd moved Andrew under the bed, which had kind of freaked me out when one of his ghoulish hands fell out of the bundle. Only hours ago that hand had been on my skin, holding a knife to my throat.

After a frantic shower, I snuck downstairs for more cleaning supplies and fresh sheets. Robbie and Glenda were down for the count. I washed the knife, scrubbing it until the sponge was in pieces, then set it back in the block. While Glenda would surely notice if her knife was misplaced, I was sort of hoping she wouldn't notice her brother was missing.

Chapter 21

Sometimes when I'm reading or studying, my mind will roam and explore different paths on its own, usually weaving stories of ridiculous circumstances. Most of the time I have to drop whatever it is I'm doing because I'm cracking up, laughing like a loon. So it was funny but not funny, how in the grimmest of circumstances, my mind chose to churn about with mundane, everyday thoughts.

Scrubbing the mattress with rubber gloves I caught myself wondering if my peach tank top was clean. Bundling up my bloody underwear, I realized I'd never gotten back my favorite pair of Toms Vee borrowed last month. Combing the floor, looking for signs of a struggle, I thought about Dylan and hoped he still wanted me to join him for orientation.

But still, in some faraway place in the back of my mind, as an unlatched shutter flapped in the winds of my gale-force migraine, I wondered whether I should just go down to the end of the hall and confess. But really, how would that go down?

Oh, hey, sorry to wake you guys up. Couldn't sleep. What's that? Oh yeah, funny story, while you guys were at your fundraiser, well, Glenda, your brother tried to rape me again. Huh? Oh yes, again. Gee, I didn't tell you? Silly me. Anyhooo, so he puts this knife to my throat and well, I kind of plugged it into his stomach a couple or eleven times. Yeah, it's quite the mess, sorry about the comforter, 'kay?

No, we were past that point. I curled up in the reading chair, my eyes stinging yet incapable of blinking, my hands reeking of bleach. What next? With Andrew, dead, rigor mortis setting in, underneath my bed. What next, indeed.

By six Robbie was up, with that morning cough of his. Birds

chirped outside. My eyes opened to the rising paleness at the window.

Dawn crept over the floor, revealing last night's terror, inching towards the body under the bed, to the heap of last night's clothes in the corner of the room. Prying myself from the chair, I was exhausted and possibly hallucinating, halfway expecting Andrew to scoot out and hop up to his feet, shake his head and say, "We need to talk, Chloe."

But there was no time for sleep. There was a mound of towels, heavy with blood. A gouge in the floor I didn't remember being there. A bucket of soapy water. Cleaning supplies. The sharp scent of bleach would forever remind me of death. I stood and opened the window, feeling the cool morning sweep in as I got dressed.

I headed downstairs to make an appearance. It had to be done. Even as the thought of school was unreal, like a movie or dream. Calculus was child's play after cleaning up a killing. But I had to go on. Be regular. Be routine.

I was pouring a bowl of cereal when Robbie came into the kitchen.

"Hey there, Chloe."

"Good morning," I said, way too cheery. I never said *good morning*. Everything felt out of place. I had to be normal, just another day and all. Robbie ho-hummed about his business, and I focused on gripping the spoon so it wouldn't rattle against the bowl. I needed to get it together. I could do this.

Robbie snatched the milk. My eyes swept the room. I'd Clorox wiped the counters and sink, but in the morning light everything seemed so...glaring. He plopped down with the iPad and started on his news, chewing and crunching and dribbling on his tie. This was where I'd usually give him a hard time, but I couldn't get the words out of my mouth.

Glenda rushed in through a cloud of old lady perfume, going berserk over a meeting she had with some fundraiser people. Luckily, she was running late. I told her I had a ride to school.

"Okay, great. I'll pick you up at the normal spot?" she asked, pouring coffee into a travel mug that read, STOP C443, which I'd bet my left arm had something to do with LGBTQ rights.

"I'm going to the baseball game."

A flick of the bangs before she smiled and kissed me on the head, sending me off the exit ramp of sanity. She was almost out the door when she stopped at the sink. I froze, thinking maybe she saw a speck of blood on my cheek or behind my ear. The room spun. What? What did she see?

"Oh, Andrew's home?"

I spooned out a single Cheerio, forcing the image of Andrew's eyes from my mind, how they wouldn't shut when he died. Robbie mumbled, "Uh huh" without looking up.

"I thought he was going to be at the parkway all week?"

More grunting from Robbie. I set the spoon down altogether. The Forerunner. It never crossed my mind. Glenda turned to me. "Chloe? Did Andrew come home last night?"

"I, um. I have no idea," I sighed. "I went to bed early. I wasn't feeling well."

I forced myself to shut up. Glenda stood at the door and stared at the truck like a freaking mannequin challenge as I clenched to keep from trembling. Finally, she shook it off, "Huh, okay, well I'll see you all tonight."

When she was gone, Robbie got up and rinsed his bowl. He turned back to me. "Just between the two of us, I'm ready to see old Andrew take off for good."

I nearly keeled over but caught myself. I stood slowly, got control of my voice so I sounded casual. "Yeah, me too. I'd love to live in the carriage house."

A few minutes later Robbie left for work and it was time to get busy. I gave it twenty minutes, so I could be sure no one forgot anything and came back. I was supposed to be at Dunham in five minutes, but that wasn't happening. There was too much to do.

I stood in the doorway to the bedroom, a canvas drop-cloth under my arms, working up my nerve. The first step was getting Andrew's body down the steps without staining the walls or floor. Luckily the little Persian rug in my room had been spared from the carnage. It would still need some steam cleaning, but details would have to wait. For now, I rolled it up to get it out of the way and spread the drop cloth. Two more deep breaths, and I reached under the bed and found a leg, again nearly expecting it to jerk or kick when I pulled him out.

He was stiff, his spindly fingers tight and creepy, bent at weird angles. I folded him back into the bloody pulp that was the sheet over his stomach. His skin was horrifyingly alive. I wrapped the comforter around him and rolled him onto the drop cloth. Seriously, how much blood did one dead loser hold?

A truckload for sure. I worked carefully, rolling his legs first then going back for his upper body. It felt like he'd died flexing, his muscles locked in place. Even in death he was fighting me. I couldn't look at him. I fitted a pillowcase over his head, but it only made things creepier. Finally, I got him all wrapped up. Time to transport the ghoul.

Clunk. Clunk. Clunk.

Down the steps we went, Andrew's head knocking and echoing around the old house. It reminded me of this eighties movie Mom and I had watched a few years ago, *Weekend at Bernie's,* where this old dude croaked and these two dorky guys slapped sunglasses on him and propped him up so they could throw house parties and still get laid. It worked for a while, everyone being too coked up to notice. But the way Glenda had stared out the window that morning, this wasn't so easy in real life.

I got Andrew to the kitchen without any leakage. I did a quick sweep of the neighborhood. An electric saw whined in the not-too-far distance, cutting through the morning peacefulness. Most of the old houses were under various stages of construction and rehab. The closest one, a dark Victorian, loomed over the carriage house with its countless windows and wrap-around porch. I was pretty sure it was still vacant, with all the bright orange notices clinging to the door and boards on the front windows. To the left there was tree cover and bushes. All clear.

The carriage house was unlocked. I shut down the rush of panic flooding my chest at being in there again. The smell of grout and tile reminded me of good old Andy. I found his keys on the coffee table beside his wallet, wondering if taking them was considered theft and if so, would it compound my crimes. We'd just finished a mock trial in Civics, and I'd crushed it as part of the prosecution team. But what I couldn't figure out was if I was even committing a crime. I mean, all I'd wanted was for him to stay away from me.

My driving skills were admittedly limited, but since my lessons with Dylan I had the basics down. Even still, the Forerunner was tricky, and getting it in place wasn't easy, lots of stop and go and sharp turns to get it backed up to the steps. Taking it easy so as not to gas or brake too hard and end up in the kitchen. Forward/back/forward/back, the gravel snapped and crunched as I got it close enough for what I had to do. I slid out and took another look around.

Getting the tailgate down was a chore. But once it fell I came back another foot and used a board I found in the shed to set it level from the tailgate to the porch so I could kind of roll the lump onboard, careful to keep things wrapped tight. I wiped my forehead, thinking how I should've been at Kemper Hall right then. Instead, I was using my knowledge of physics to hoist a body into a vehicle.

Andrew's legs didn't quite fit, so I had to climb in the back, put the seats down and yank and tug until I was sweating like Stacey and Olivia in chapel. Finally, I came back around to the rear where I pushed and shoved and cursed him for being so much trouble.

With his body stuffed in the car, I laid the board on top of him and went to find some rope, wiping my hands and feeling somewhat accomplished until I realized just how ridiculous that thought was.

Now for the next obstacle. What to actually do with his body.

Chapter 22

I called the school and told Miss Jonelly I was sick. Not quite a lie but plenty awkward with Andrew back there as Jonelly chattered on, even congratulating me on Cum Laude. She was awfully proud of me, she kept saying, as I mentally backtracked through the house, searching for missteps.

The clock on the dash read 8:20. First bell rang in my ears. I pictured Miss Shelby, her flabby arms up on her desk, ready to ask for our accounts. Oh, wouldn't I have a great one for tomorrow. In the Forerunner, I adjusted the mirrors and studied the red gouges across my neck. Yikes. Maybe I could flatter Glenda with a scarf of my own. I gripped the wheel. Focus. One problem at a time.

"Okay, Andrew, where do you want to go?" I whispered, setting the lever to the R.

It was a tough start. I couldn't get the stupid seat to go up and had to perch myself on the edge. After some clunky maneuvering, I got the truck turned and crept out of the driveway where I waited until the street was absolutely clear before I summoned the courage to pull out.

The Toyota lunged forward. I smashed the brakes. Big breath. I had to get it under control before I plowed over a mailbox or clipped a parked car. Slowly, I rolled towards the intersection, getting acquainted with the steering and pedals. The car was sluggish compared to Dylan's truck. Nothing was the same. And it smelled of sweat and feet and I tried not to think of everything at once. Of skipping school, driving down the road, Andrew's Gatorade sloshing around in the passenger seat, his corpse sloshing around in the back.

For some reason Holcomb Pond came to mind. It beat digging a grave.

I eased the truck down the hill, ready to take a nice and easy right turn. After that it would be a straight shot for a while, between traffic lights and watching for cops. I did the best I could, considering, and things were going okay as I crept down the clunky cobblestone street, until a shiny blue truck came hauling up the other way.

Dylan. What was he doing? My heart leaped in my throat. I slid down in my seat as I hit the gas, trying not to look his way. His truck passed and I couldn't tell if he'd seen me or not, but then yes, he must have. A flash of brake lights in the rearview. His truck came to a complete stop in the road. Not good. We'd only just patched things up and if he saw me driving Andrew's car it was going to take more than a little explaining on my part.

I hit the gas and swung out, nearly getting sideswiped by a bus. A horn blasted and I mashed down on the gas. The Forerunner revved, and I barreled up the road. A couple of miles, stop and go. All was well until I missed the turn and had to pull off and get turned around and wait for yet another light to change.

The Forerunner swung wide and hopped the curb. The red light took forever, giving me all sorts of time to worry. Eyes wide, on the edge of the seat, my hair in a messy ponytail, I must have looked twelve. All it took was for one cop to see me and I was done. I gripped the wheel, hardly listening to the hicks on the local wakeup show joke and haw about an upcoming chili cook-off.

Green light. I coaxed the truck out without ramming the minivan in front of me. Again, I took it slow, only I took it too slow. Some jerk behind me honked for me to get going as I looked for the turn. Inconspicuous I was not.

The Forerunner swallowed the little road. I nearly clipped several cars on the way to the woods. The steering wheel was wet from my palms by the time I made it over the cattle guard, leaving a dusty cloud behind me. I braked to a jerky stop at the pond and stepped out to take a look at things. The dew in the tall grass glistened, steam rising from the pond. It was weird being outside at this time of the morning, the sun higher in the sky and the clouds breaking apart, making room for the day.

Andrew had said no one ever came down here, but I wasn't so sure. I shut the door quietly and walked along the bank. Bullfrogs and crickets clicked in the grass as I tried to find a good place to—wow, I couldn't believe what I was doing. A frog plopped into the water, and I leaped back and nearly screamed. My nerves felt like a split end and the lack of sleep was catching up with me.

Dumping a body into a scummy pond was definitely more of a nighttime job, but I didn't have the luxury. I considered the overturned boat on the bank. It looked far too big and heavy for me to flip over and actually use. A raft of ducks paddled by the bank. The whir of morning commuters hummed in the distance. I sucked down a breath, because, again, wow.

I shook off my doubts. It was too late to backtrack. A small rickety dock looked like the best place but also the most obvious. A steep embankment on the far end might be the spot.

Back behind the steering wheel, I eased the Forerunner backwards towards the bank. It was tricky, and I came in at an angle. When I tried to straighten it out, the tires spun in the mud. I hadn't been thinking too much about the tire tracks or forensic evidence, just that it would suck having to explain how Andrew's car got submerged in a secluded pond on a school day.

The tailgate gave me a hard time again. I put the key in and turned but only the window came down. I turned the key the other way and the door locked. The handle was no help at all so I lugged out the plywood and the paver blocks and rope from the back seat then crawled over his disgusting dead body so I could lift the handle and kick and kick and kick the door from the inside until it gave.

I found some work gloves in the back. Then, eyes closed, I gripped his lifeless ankles with both hands. The worst part was unraveling him so I could stuff his wallet in his back pocket. He was soup from waist to armpits, and I nearly heaved. Left or right pocket,

I didn't know. I cursed myself for not noticing. I guessed right and got it over with, then I wrapped him back up.

What a difference a year made. Well, almost a year anyway. Last summer Mom and I were mapping out her death, planning my life. She'd been so optimistic for me. It was like she looked at me with her heavy eyelids and saw someone else. She never would have guessed it would come to this.

Andrew hit the ground like a bag of sand. It was ten after nine and Environmental Science class was looming. I dragged the body around to the edge. The going got heavy in the marsh near the pond. I tried to keep him out of the muck, but it had been raining and the tall grass wasn't helping. My shoes were soaked to the socks and the tarp kept spilling open, revealing all the gruesomeness inside the comforter. I told myself it was sand. Just sand, nothing else, as I got around to the bank.

It was slick and the roots were no help. The comforter snagged on a post, leaving a trail of thread and feathers as I got him to the edge. A comedy of horrors was what it was.

But what choice did I have? None, now, and so I focused on breathing—thanks Doctor O!—as I went back for the pavers. It was humid and buggy. I swiped my hair back, my shirt sticking to my back as I worked. I unloaded the pavers one by one, got them over to the bank and stuffed them in the comforter. I tied the whole bloody bundle up like a package and tried to figure the best way to go about this.

Everything I did was based off TV shows and movies. *Law & Order* stuff. My only hope was that if they ever found Andrew, his body would be too disfigured to tell he'd been stabbed a whole bunch of times for trying to rape and kill a sixteen-year-old girl.

In the end I just kind of slid him in, getting in up to my knees. I found a branch and shoved him off. A blur of beige and bubbles under the surface, floating through the leaves. Whatever Andrew's life, his death was a mere disturbance of sand and twigs, sinking into the murky depths of a sad little pond. My bare feet sunk into the squish of the muck and I tried not to think about water moccasins as I watched the bubbles purr to the surface. It was entirely too close to the edge. Hopefully, people would obey those PRIVATE PROPERTY signs pinned to the trees.

After the last ripple spread to the shore, I squished and squashed my way back to the car. Wet and muddy but so far successful, I turned the key. Nothing. I held my breath and turned the key again, then again, but nothing happened. I was nearly hyperventilating when I realized I'd left the car in reverse. Lucky for me it hadn't rolled off and into the pond. I shoved the gear lever into park and turned the key again. Presto.

Chapter 23

So much to do. For starters, I needed a new comforter. Glenda would notice that kind of stuff. With that in mind I made one more stop with the truck, wrapped a towel around my waist, and became a Walmart shopper. I'd have to find a way to explain the $100 charge on the Visa, but I had an inkling of an idea involving lady parts and accidents and enough tears to make Uncle Robbie clear the room.

Mistakes were rampant. From the broad day body dump with the muddy embankment leading up to the botched launch of Andrew into the pond, it was certainly a mess. However, putting a knife into Andrew was not a mistake but survival. Retribution even. It was either his body or mine coming out of the room, so that wasn't the issue. The issue was explaining it.

Mistakes or not, it was chance and timing that blew up in my face. I mean Dylan. What had he been doing in the neighborhood that morning? Up until then I'd thought about ditching the Forerunner, but how? Where? And now that Dylan had spotted me driving it, I was stuck. It would need some serious cleaning though.

Around lunch time he sent a text. Where are you?

I sent one back. Sick

There was no time for him at the moment. First the room. I needed to bleach it, scrub it, polish it. Air it out so Glenda wouldn't start with the nose twitching.

It wasn't perfect but I needed to work things over in my mind. I could handle people. I knew how to shut down and close them out. It was all the blood that worried me. Blood was everywhere, spreading and staining. Screaming for attention.

I was scrubbing the bathroom when Dylan showed up. I'd sort of expected it, though, and as I watched him from the window, eyeing the house, especially the truck, I peeled off my gloves, trying to gather myself as I ran down the steps and met him on the front porch. The house was still airing out. I couldn't say I looked my best. My hair was stringy, stuck to my scalp, and I was wearing one of Mom's old oversized t-shirts and loose-fitting shorts. But it was a sick-day, right?

"Hey," I said, catching my breath.

"Hey." He looked to my ratty clothes. My hair. I thought he might lean in for a kiss but he didn't. I kept my voice upbeat.

"No practice today?"

"No, skipped."

He leaned back, hands on the railing, his gaze over my shoulder, checking out the house like it was the first time he'd seen it. I clasped my hands together; they hadn't stopped trembling all day and I assumed they would keep on for the rest of my life. The cleaning had given me something to do with them, but now, standing idly, they were a quavering confession.

Some middle school kids hiked up the street, under the shade, laughing and joking and being silly and stupid without worry. One of the boys waved to me, a flash of the hands before his friends started up with the giggles again. I waved back and Dylan looked over his shoulder, then right back to me.

"What were you doing this morning?"

My breath caught in my throat. "What do you mean?"

He squinted in the afternoon sun. I turned to the driveway, to his truck that was partially blocking the Forerunner. I needed to move it like two feet closer to the carriage house, exactly where it had been parked. I had to be exact with everything. My eyes swept over it, making sure nothing else looked out of place. Back to Dylan.

"Oh, you mean—"

"This morning," he said again, sharp and clear, like I was dense. His stare clung to me, and I tried to hold his eyes but couldn't. "I saw you driving," he motioned to the Toyota. "That."

"Oh, yeah, well I was just practicing." There was mud on the fenders. Too much mud. I had to hose it off, but not too clean, Andrew didn't keep it clean.

Dylan exploded. "Practicing? In *his* car? Skipping school?"

I started at his voice, forced myself to look at him. He turned away. The sun was bright, a sky with no clouds. Such a perfect day to lay a blanket out at the park, let him kiss that spot on my neck that gave me chills. I tried to come up with something, anything to say. Trey Carter and the hippies rumbled past in his old boxy Volvo, blasting some jam band, probably going to smoke up.

"Yeah," I said, switching tactics. "What were *you* doing?"

"I was coming by to check on you. To give you a ride to school. I waited at the house. You never came back."

The way he said it, his tone, I gave it back to him. "So what, I wanted to drive so I drove. Not sure why it's such a big deal."

"I thought you were sick."

"You know what? I'm done." I turned for the door when he called out.

"Did you spend the day with him?"

"Who?" I gave him my nastiest eye roll. "Seriously, Dylan. No, he's not even here. He's...camping or something." I presented myself, rolling a hand over my shirt. "I spent the day on the couch, relaxing. You going to go tell Jonelly?"

It came out sharp and harsh. I reached out for him and he snorted. Fine, I had plenty to do. "Look, are we finished here?"

He stared at the ground with pursed lips, almost pouting. But when his eyes came back they softened. Maybe he thought I meant us being done for good but that wasn't it. I only wanted his little interrogation to be over.

He shook his head. "Is there something I should know, Chloe?"

"What? No."

A flash of rust colored blood-clouds on the mattress. My hands tingling from bleach. Pinkish and burning from being scrubbed raw. I couldn't sort through the blur of emotions, I had only chores: clean up the blood, replace the blanket. Return the other knife. Dump the body. No time to think about Dylan. About us. Besides, the look on his face wasn't something I could hide or clean or even change. I didn't want things to be like this. Not now or ever. But there wasn't anything I could do at the moment.

And then he leaned in closer. "What's going on with your neck?"

"Huh?" My hand shot to my neck like I was choking. "Oh," I laughed, rolling my eyes. "I was wrestling with Vee and my shirt kind of rubbed against it. Looks worse than it is."

His eyes narrowed as he studied it closer. I lowered my chin.

"Wrestling? Is that how you got those bruises on your arm, too?"

I pulled back. "Yeah. Hey look, I've got to get back inside."

"Yeah, okay." He started for the truck. My hand lingered on the small rope-like welts on my neck. I turned back to the house, hoping against everything we could patch this up later, even as he never looked back as he got in his truck, backed out, and sped off.

I wasn't sure when to expect Glenda, but it was after four when I found a few drops on the carpet and went to work on those. I'd steam-cleaned the rug, rinsed out the containers, flushed pinkish water down the toilet and scrubbed it down with a toothbrush. The stairs looked good, almost too good. I traced and retraced my steps to the shed. I'd just gotten out of the shower and was thinking about what to do with the Forerunner when I heard Glenda's keys hit the counter.

"Chloe, you here?"

"Yeah." I rushed down the steps. She had two canvas bags at her sides, overflowing with organic goodies.

"Oh, hey. Could you help with the groceries? I bought that Greek yogurt you liked so much."

"Oh, thanks."

Her gaze found the scarf around my neck and she lit up. "Oh, I *love* that scarf on you."

"Oh, yeah, I hope you don't mind me wearing it," I smiled. It was cake, making her happy. A few smiles, some nice words, and she was good to go for a while. I clicked my heels and hopped out to get the groceries.

By the time I returned, she'd changed into her yoga pants and was sipping a glass of wine. A good sign, wine made Glenda bearable. Until she had too much.

"So how was school?"

"I didn't go," I said, opting for the Band-Aid approach. Best to yank it off and get it over with. She set the wine down and looked me over.

"Are you feeling okay?"

"Yeah, just this morning, I got sick and," I stopped, realizing she might think I meant morning sickness. "I mean, you know, going to the bathroom."

"Oh." She gave me a stern look. "Well, did you at least let Robbie know?"

"No, it was after he left so I just called Miss Jonelly. I might need a note, though." I grinned. You know, just two girls and their secrets.

A sip of wine. She was right on the brink of a lecture when her phone buzzed on the counter. Two seconds later she was swept into the world of real estate.

"I told Janet the house would sell...that area...oh yes, well the broker said..."

Usually I would have cleared out of there in a hurry, but today I needed to stick around, see how this was going to play out. Two things worried me. Well, a million things worried me, but front and center was Andrew's truck. I'd wiped down the steering wheel and door handles like they do on TV, but I needed to detail the back, get the mud off the fenders. Still, the worst part of it was that Andrew never went anywhere without the truck. That had already caught Glenda's attention this morning.

So much had been left to the unknown. The overlooked. I'd been rushed today, so I'm sure I'd missed something. My eyes scanned the kitchen floor.

"...but you know, honey, the rates the way they are right now..."

Glenda wandered into the living room, setting her wineglass on the mantel so her hand was free to flail. With my foot, I swiped at what could be a scab of dried blood on the kitchen floor. When she turned around again, I grabbed a Clorox wipe and rubbed it clean. She never missed a beat.

Uncle Robbie arrived home after a while and relieved me from hearing the most mind-numbing work story ever told. I nearly bit a hole in my cheek when Glenda went for the William Sonoma knife to chop some vegetables, thinking how absolutely disgusting yet fascinating it was to watch her waving it about, talking about Janet and houses and interest rates and other bloopity-blah. I was sure Robbie had tuned out.

Uncle Robbie did more neck exercises and jaw clenching as Glenda droned on about work, friends, and a litany of first-world problems. Nothing was too mundane: an exceptionally long traffic light, a shade of paint, an open house that was canceled due to all the gentrification protests. Sometimes Robbie gripped the countertops so hard his forearms bulged, and I would have gotten a kick out of it had I not been preoccupied.

Glenda popped the cork on a new bottle of wine. I wandered off and climbed the steps, the scarf itching my neck. I hoped I hadn't missed anything in my sweep of the house. In my bedroom, I went over everything again, scrubbing until my hands were red and splotchy, prepping myself for the questions sure to come my way. I also came up with an escape plan.

Chapter 24

I choked down rubbery wheat-pasta spaghetti as Glenda gave us the update on Grandma Millie. She was doing better, recovering slowly but hopefully she'd be able to go home soon. Glenda, the saint she was, had stopped by with flowers. She thought it would be nice if we all dropped in to see her.

My jaw fell. Robbie stepped in with an excuse for me, so I didn't have to actually tell Glenda I would rather swallow Drano than go visit a woman who'd never so much as picked up a phone to speak to me. And that's when Glenda took a hairpin turn and got back on her favorite topic: Andrew's car.

Again, best to let Robbie deal with her in that calm way of his. His slow blink of the eyes, the quick wipe of the face, a sip of water when all he really wanted was a few seconds of silence. Glenda, however, being completely clueless to Robbie's discomfort, seemed to be very much aware of mine. She kept eyeing my scarf as though she knew it was some shield, never missing a breath as she prattled on.

"It's just weird. I thought he was back from camping. The Forerunner's here, the kayaks are around back."

I took a lesson from Robbie and sipped some water before saying anything, figuring my biggest risk would be appearing too eager to answer. But she was full tilt tonight, pushing back suddenly, scooting her chair like her heart was exploding. "Maybe I should go check on things," she said, setting her fork down. She wiped her face and got up, sending tremors through the white wine in her glass. "It's not like him to miss a free meal."

Uncle Robbie set a hand on her arm. "I don't know, hon, maybe he's getting some rest."

Her energy shook me. You could practically hear her crackling, buzzing like a live power line. I set my glass down, improvising, trying to plug a new twist. "Actually, I think I remember him saying something about riding up with friends."

"Friends? Here in Dunham? Riding up? *Where?*"

Her *bam-bam-bam* questions stunned me. She sat down on the edge of her chair, eyes wild, pinning me to my seat. I half expected her to take me by the shoulders and shake the answers out of me. I should have kept quiet, but she'd rattled me with getting up like that. I looked at Robbie and tried to relax.

Why not let her go up there? Nothing was out of place, it was the same slacker paradise it had always been. I took a breath. "No, it was just, last weekend I guess, before he took off he said something about riding up. Something with the truck, I don't know."

Wow, I couldn't keep my mouth shut. Glenda hadn't blinked in minutes.

"The truck? The Forerunner?"

Like Frankenstein's pug, the way she leered, half-cocked, repeating everything I said in the form of a question. It was like the practice wall at the tennis courts. I'd hit a forehand and back it came, a streaking yellow ball zooming at my face.

"That's all I know, really, Glenda, I wasn't really paying attention." I rose from my chair and gathered my utensils and plate, then Robbie's because he'd set his silverware and napkin on it and was rubbing his temples. In the kitchen, I placed them on the counter and nearly collapsed. I mean, Andrew was almost thirty, couldn't she just cut it some slack?

Now I'd set her off. She was in there yapping at Robbie about the parkway and Andrew's friends and that stupid Forerunner, refusing to let it go. She marched into the kitchen, the plates clattering with each step until she shot out the side door. I turned back as Robbie limped in, slumping and beat. I eyed him carefully to see how he was going to play it. He joined me at the sink and we stared out the window. "I don't know where he went, but I'd love for him to stay gone. I'll even have the car towed to a garage for him."

Through the window we watched Glenda stride to the door, bound and determined, arms swinging wildly. I looked up at Robbie, and what I found in his eyes was not love, or even a faint admiration for his wife of ten or so years. Then he turned to me.

"I got an offer on the house." He rinsed a plate then went searching for a towel. I handed him the decorative one with the puppies even though Glenda refused to let him have a dog. "Dorchester," he said, as though it needed clarifying.

He toweled off his hands. The light went on in the carriage house, and I winced just thinking about being in there. I looked to Robbie. "I didn't know it was for sale."

"It's not. Glenda put out some feelers. Just an offer, is all."

Was he asking for my permission to sell it? Did he know about me sneaking inside? If he did, he didn't look upset about it. I shrugged. "Oh, okay."

He glanced at the towel, balled up in his hands. When he hung it back on the stove it slipped off the handle and fell. We both just stared at it. "I just wanted to let you know. I haven't decided what to do with it just yet. I just," he took a giant breath. "I just wanted to see what you thought about it, I guess."

I picked up the towel, shrugged. "Well, I mean, it's your house so I guess if you want to sell it you should."

He nodded, the strain showing on his face as he turned back to the carriage house. "I'm not in a rush. Glenda wants to sell."

Of course she did. And now she was on my trail. My story wasn't great, and I hadn't helped things by improvising on the fly. I should have said something that morning. Maybe I could tell her I heard something outside on Thursday night. Yeah, I remembered peeking out my window and seeing a couple of tall, gangly, hippy types. Come to think of it, I'd seen Andrew grab some things and take off.

I left Robbie in the kitchen to contemplate his life. His sick mother and his freak show wife. I had my own problems. Mainly the fact that I was going to need a new mattress or a getaway plan. Soon.

❧

By Sunday Glenda was certifiable. While Robbie was at the hospital visiting his mother, she worked the phones. She called Andrew's old employer and left messages, pacing as she waited for someone to return her calls. From what I'd learned through Glenda and Robbie's conversations, Andrew was a drifter and never stuck around long enough to get tied down with responsibility.

Glenda claimed her brother was a creative type, a free-spirit world traveler, he was even working on a screenplay. Robbie held up his hands in surrender. Fine, whatever you want to call him, he'd said with a laugh. This inflamed Glenda to the point Robbie was well on his way to sleeping in the carriage house if he wasn't careful. Then again, that might have been his goal all along.

Next, Glenda called Renee, the ex-girlfriend who hadn't seen or heard from him in months and oh, by the way, Andrew owed her $300. Glenda tried a few old friends back in Roanoke, acquaintances in Maryland and so on, but nobody had heard from Andrew.

On Monday, Robbie offered me a ride to school. Dylan wasn't going to show up, not after the way he'd stomped off Friday. He hadn't even returned my calls or texts. And Glenda was still in bed where she would be for a while. She'd taken to Ambien and wine like bread and water. I wasn't complaining.

Something was on my uncle's mind as we rode without talking, the top down on the Jeep so the wind drowned out the radio— something more than Millie Vanderbrooke's pending release. And as we pulled onto East Ridge Boulevard and came to one of those many stoplights, Robbie tapped the wheel and looked over to me, squinting into the morning sunlight. "So, I've decided not to sell the house."

I smiled back at him. His face was defiant. Proud. A little like Mom's. "What about Glenda?"

His smile widened. "She'll get over it."

Maybe he could sense my attachment to the house. Maybe he had his own reasons altogether. Either way, we both sat up a little straighter, victorious in the bright, promising sun. Robbie fiddled with his hands, his eyes steering his head in my direction. "Have you uh, have you been by there...since?"

I glanced at him then looked away. "Yeah."

"Really?" His eyes grew with his smile, such a Mom-like expression it caught my breath.

"Just drove by it with Dylan," I lied.

"Oh. Well, I'm not going to sell it, but I will have to rent it out soon. Maybe if you want, we can go inside before, just to, I don't know, maybe not."

This was my uncle, the one from the beach. The guy with the tattoo. I smiled. "I'd like that."

"Cool," he said, then, "So, you like Dylan? I mean, he's okay?"

"Yeah," I shrugged, thinking of the Dylan I knew before all this happened. "He is."

The light turned green. We started again up the road, the wind between us, blanketing us, hitting our smiles like a breath of fresh air before the day managed to steal them away.

At school, Vienna hit me with the third degree about skipping, which was funny because being up Spence's butt she hadn't bothered to call all weekend. I told her I wasn't feeling school. Then she hit me with the question of the day, "So what's up with you and Dylan?"

My irritation faded. Vee's hair was pulled back tight, so her eyes seemed to pierce through the morning sunrays. You couldn't look at her without falling in love—even when she was being annoying as ever. I shook my head. "I don't know, nothing really."

"Spence talked to Dylan—he said you've been acting weird lately. I told him it wasn't an act."

"Ha, hilarious," I said, and she started laughing. I was so jealous of her right then. To be so playful and cheery, carefree. It almost didn't seem real.

"Well, whatever it is, fix it. Because Spence is having a thing on Friday."

I sighed. "Yeah, I don't know."

Vee shook her head. "Don't get moody on me, Chloe V. If you can skip school, you can come out and have some fun."

Have some fun. As though it were possible. One thing was for sure, though. The Dylan situation had to be fixed, but delicately because he was a delicate boy. At lunch I caught him in the dining hall, looking over the sandwich wraps with a meticulous eye. I watched him for a minute, thinking, *now here's a guy who could get away with murder. If he killed someone there would be no loose ends, no tracks, no evidence. This boy is thorough.*

When he glanced up and noticed me, he looked especially handsome in a button down and chinos. It went well with all of his seriousness. I moved in and bumped his arm with my shoulder. "So, you come here often?"

No smile or laugh. He turned and regarded me as though I were some day old, pasty chicken salad. I dropped my shoulders. "Come on Dylan, what's the deal?"

"What's the *deal*? Seriously, Chloe?"

I looked around, unprepared for his tone. It was so...mean. I tried to keep it light. "Okay, sheesh. I mean, is this still about the truck?"

He snorted, like I was a child who could not fully understand the implications of adult problems. His eyes narrowed, squinted in disgust, aimed at his leather shoes. Some giggly kids cut in front of us and we backed away, trying not to appear like we were in the middle of breaking up.

I tried not to look like a girl about to burst into tears at this fine institution that took in kids from all over the world. Mostly white, buttoned-down-privileged kids but some brown and others darker still, all wearing identical sports coats and ties, khakis. Each student had their own form of hardship. From Ivy League let down to villages without clean drinking water. To those in passing I must have looked like just another blonde, a simple rich girl in a spat with her cute little boyfriend. Not a bastard child with a dead mother. Not a girl trying her best to avoid a murder rap.

But even with all the debris orbiting my life, I never expected Dylan Kowalski to lean close to my ear, to part his lips and utter the words, "What I need to know, Chloe, is if you're screwing him."

A sound escaped my throat. My jaw hung open like a broken desk drawer. Only a few weeks ago he was too shy to ask me to a dance. Now, his voice was so cold I shivered, prickles of sweat beading up on the back of my neck as a blinding, white-hot rage hit my temples. I took a step back.

"Okay, first, I cannot believe you'd say that to me."

He tried to cover his surprise with smugness, turning to the windows, shaking his head like *he* was the victim. I gave him a chance to take it back. "Dylan, you didn't mean that, did you?"

Across the hall, Spence and Vee walked in like the royal court. I almost expected Spence to toss up a wave to the crowd, for the press swarm. Dylan came back to me, returning back from some trip in his head, backtracking now. "If he really did those things to you, and if you didn't want him to, it seems to me you would tell someone. Have him arrested or something. But no. You're out joyriding in his truck?"

My head shook left to right. I reached out again, my emotions swaying too fast to digest. "It's not like that, Dylan. Besides, it's not as easy as you think."

"What's not, telling the cops that he's... I can't even say it. Or is it consensual?"

I was about to heave a chair at him when Spence and Vienna waltzed over to us. Spence smiled, pointing to the sandwiches in the glass container, loud and showy. "Dude, stay away from the tuna." Vee took one look at us and whispered into his ear. He nodded, smiling again. "Okay, we'll see you two at our table," walking backwards and waving a finger, "No tuna."

I hardly saw them, or anything else. The clatter of trays and plates, easy laughter and hums of conversation. Food seemed as trivial as school. All of it, it was so fake I had to escape before I screamed. I turned to Dylan. "I really thought you were different. I mean, all this time, you've been playing me like this nice guy, and..."

I couldn't do it. I spun off and started for the hallway, against the flow of traffic breezing in, laughing and smiling. And he just stood there.

Outside my tears drowned the day. My breath came jagged and quick, too fast to catch as I took the steps down to the path, to the trees, picking up speed until I was running so Vee couldn't come out and try to tell me it was okay. Nothing in this world was okay. I raced through the woods, stumbling on fallen branches and rocks, not hearing the whistles and cheers until it opened up at the soccer fields where a practice match was underway. I skirted the fields and kept running to Dorchester.

The lawn had been mowed. Around back some weeds had been pulled and there were some empty buckets and a tarp. I entered without caring who saw me. Everything echoed in the empty house.

"Mom."

Out loud again. It was strange but comforting within those walls where I'd called her name so many times before. Part of me, somewhere, expected to hear movement in the back room. To hear her voice.

"Yes, sweetie?"

Her face wrinkled with concern. Her arms stretched out to take me in.

"Mom, I need you."

I barreled ahead, my wet face smashing into healthy breasts. Full of blood and fat and life. Her arms came around me tight and she stroked my head as I sobbed. "Mom, he would have killed me."

"I know, sweetie. It's safe now."

My chin quivered. My eyes closed. They opened to the ceiling fan in the kitchen, as I lay with my back on the floor, catching the breeze on my face. Mom at the sink with the dishes where I used to rush in and find her, without a clue of how incredibly wonderful life was at that very breath. I closed my eyes and there she was, right in front of me, drawn on my eyelids. I willed myself to keep her there, to hear her, smell her, to feel her touch on my face.

The sun filled the house. The floor was warm against my chills but cool on my cheek, still wet with tears and sweat. I wanted to lie there forever, in that shell with my mother, away from my current life, away from the world, away from everything and everyone and all the awful things they did to me.

Chapter 25

It was after four when I got to Madison Street. A forty-minute hike helped me piece together what to do next. Nobody was home, Glenda must have gone to work after all, but it still startled me to see Andrew's truck in the driveway. Even as fish food he could still get a rise out of me.

I was sure Jonelly had called Glenda about me skipping, so I was going to have to whip up something about a bad day dealing with Mom. But a new fear surfaced on the way home. Dylan could go to the police.

With that in mind, when I got to my room, I tossed clothes into a duffle bag. Shoes, some food, even a Swiss army knife on the dresser seemed like something to pack. I had to be prepared.

The tremors returned to my core, rattling in my chest, scraping my breath until I was lightheaded. But I couldn't sit on my bed—my bed was soiled, haunted. Andrew still had a hold of me, entering my thoughts as well as my dreams. Groping and touching with ice-block hands.

Outside I heard the bite of gravel under tires. I stood, peeked out and saw Dylan's truck. Again. Too many things were happening at once. What did he want from me? I couldn't deal with it, his hot and cold routine. I ran down the steps, stopping on the last one.

I jumped as he banged on the door. I backed away as he cupped his hands and peered in the windows. Then he turned for the walkway. I ran to the kitchen, watching as he stalked out to the driveway, past the Forerunner to the carriage house where he started banging on *that* door.

What was he was doing? Why did he keep showing up? It was

bad enough with Glenda making calls and searching the place, now Dylan was out there being Mr. Macho. I stepped out the kitchen door to the small porch where I'd rolled Andrew's body into his own car.

"Dylan?"

He swung around like a lunatic, eyes darting, his hair sweaty and kinked. I rushed down the steps, across the tiny pebbles stabbing the bottoms of my bare feet. Dylan got back to the door and the pounding, knocking one of Glenda's plants from the window ledge.

I threw my hands up. "What are you doing?"

He stood heaving, his arms at his sides and his fists balled tight, staring at the shards of the pot like it was human flesh. I grabbed his arm but then stepped back. For a second I thought he might hit me.

"Dylan."

He turned back to the door. "Is he in there?"

"Who, Andrew? No, he's not in there."

"I think he is." A nod to the main house. "Or is he in there with you?"

"What? Dylan, please," I said, surprised at the curl in my voice. "He's out of town or something."

"No he isn't," he yelled, banging at the door again. "Come out here, you coward!"

He was so puffed up and red-faced, his chest pulsing in his t-shirt. Sure, I'd seen him in a speedo, and my hands had pretty much been all over him, but standing there, in the shadow of his raging, was like being next to an engine. Then he went ape.

First, he tried the knob again, like maybe it would suddenly decide to unlock itself. When it didn't, he took a step back and kicked it. On the third kick the wooden frame splintered and the door swung open.

I was stunned, too helpless to do anything but stand to the side as Dylan rushed in like SWAT, head swiveling and panting in the midst of the shoddy construction. I came up behind him and took his hand, for my own sake. In the stale room, smelling of grout and caulk, I needed his hand as I faced the couch. As I faced hell.

Clothes strewn all over the floor. Trash and beer cans, some tools and sawdust. Dylan turned back to me, all heat and anger and crazy. I held his hand up and kissed it.

"You believe me now?"

"He's in the house, isn't he?"

I tossed his hand aside. "Dylan, please. Please, just…"

He's dead. I almost said it. *I took care of it.* But Dylan brushed past me and marched back outside to his truck. I looked back at the door, split at the frame and hanging by a single hinge. Meanwhile Dylan was stomping off for the kitchen with a crowbar in his hands. I had to get him under control. He was mad, huffing around, talking to the house.

"Where are you? Come out and face me!"

"Dylan, you're acting insane."

"Yeah, me? I'm not the one sleeping with some old dude."

"Wow. I'm not sleeping with *anyone.* What is wrong with you? Did you lose another bet or something?"

He paced the living room, looking up the steps like he was trying to decide whether or not to charge upstairs, tracking mud all over the rug. I could only watch, barefoot and invisible as Dylan argued with the voices in his head. And just when I thought he couldn't act any more like a spaz, he plowed into the couch and sunk his head into the pillows where he grabbed at his hair, rocking on his side, mumbling. Boy, I could sure pick 'em.

I gave him a minute to get himself together before I crept over to the couch, figuring my only hope was to soothe him into being rational. "Dylan, no one's here but us."

He wheeled around, still heaving, panting, but crashing now. "But his truck?"

"That's what I've been trying to tell you. Andrew left with some guys a few nights ago. They went out to the parkway. Camping or who knows what. He left his truck. That's why I took it out for a drive," I said, feeling the pieces click into place. He searched my face and I smiled, watching the softness return to his eyes, the relief spread over him.

"Really?"

"Yes. I figured I'd have a little fun with the truck. That's why I was so freaked out when you saw me. I didn't want anyone to find out."

"So, he's really not here?"

"No, you goofball." I nudged him. I wasn't thrilled with those things he'd said to me, but we'd get there. I leaned towards him and kissed his lips, tangy with sweat as he kissed me back. We were well on our way to making up when a car door shut outside.

"Um, that's Glenda," I said, standing up. Dylan slid the crowbar under the sofa and stood beside me just as she walked in and set something down en route to the kitchen, her stupid fake smile etched in place.

"Oh. Hello, Dylan."

"Hi, Mrs. Vanderbrooke."

Her smile broadened with Dylan's manners. It disappeared when she turned to me. "Chloe, can I have a word with you in the kitchen, dear?"

I smiled at Dylan, rolling my eyes as I slid my hand across his forearm. He fixed his hair, flattened his jeans.

"What's going on, Chloe? With school. Miss Jonelly called again and said—"

"I know, I'm sorry. Again, my stomach." I looked down, tugged my hair over my neck. She grimaced.

"Do you need to see a doctor?"

"I don't think so, no. I'll be fine tomorrow."

She took a breath. Her phone buzzed, but in a world-class exhibit of self-control, she didn't take the call. "Sorry," she said, wiping her face and glancing out the window. "I'm just anxious about Andrew. It's not like him to head up to the mountains without his car, or his kayaks. Something's going on."

For the love of everything, woman. What is it with your brother?

"I'm sure he's fine," I said, but then, before I could stop myself, "He's a grown man."

Her eyes flashed. A flicker of rage. "I'm aware he's a *grown man*, Chloe, he's also my brother. And no one has seen him for over a week. Except you."

Her tone cut through our façade. Up until then I'd only seen the annoying side of Aunt Glenda. But there, in a glint, I saw something cold, familiar. Something Andrew. Then it was gone.

"Okay, well, school tomorrow. I'll write you a note, okay?"

"Sure."

I slunk off towards the living room. It was only a matter of time before she noticed the door. "And Chloe?" she called me back with an edge of authority. "No more boys in the house when we're not around, okay?"

Boys, as though there was a line forming outside. "Yeah, okay."

Dylan had himself somewhat pieced together by the time I got back to the couch. "Well uh, I need to get back to school. We've got practice."

"Okay, I'll walk you out."

Glenda was on the phone in the kitchen. *So then they wanted to look at the place on Westover...* Dylan tucked the crowbar in his pants and we slid past her. She covered the phone with her hand. "So good to see you, Dylan, bye."

Outside, Dylan brushed back his hair, his face still flushed and his shirt damp. He turned to me. "I don't know what... I'm really sorry about the door. It's just that every time I think of him touching you, it makes me crazy."

I slid closer to him. "Look, all of that's over now. He's never going to touch me again."

Dylan gave me a look. I watched the struggle on his face as he fought to deal with right or wrong, caught in the gray smear between the two. He wanted to help me, but I thought part of him wanted to blame me, too. He shook his head. "How do you know that?"

"Trust me, okay?"

Dylan looked over at the door, and I felt him melt into me, almost. Suddenly he jerked away. "Aw man. You know what, I've got to go tell Mrs. Vanderbrooke about the door. Tell her I'll fix it."

I grabbed him before he could get away, enjoying the feel of his stomach and my quick spark of brilliance. "No, I'll take care of it, okay?"

"Huh, no. I need to tell her—"

"Tell her you just fell into it?" I wasn't sure why I was laughing, maybe I was losing it. The door was destroyed, hanging by splinters, but it just might be a little piece of perfect. "Look, I don't want to tell her you kicked the door in, okay? I don't need all of that in my life."

Poor Dylan. Not charging in there and taking full responsibility went against everything he stood for, or something. He looked at me again. "Are you sure?"

"Yes, please, let me take care of that." I nuzzled in closer, feeling his warmth. His strength.

"Okay."

Dylan looking at me with such promise in his eyes, it was almost too much. When he leaned down and kissed me I felt everything dissolve. I could hardly let him go.

"So is that a crowbar in your pocket, or?"

We were cracking up when I reached up and pulled his face into mine for another soft, salty kiss after all the craziness. I stepped back and he turned for his truck, both of us cheesing as he backed out and got turned around.

When I turned back for the house, I found Glenda in the kitchen window, staring past me to the carriage house door, hanging open for the world to see. It was a look I'd seen before. On her brother's face just before I killed him.

Chapter 26

Things got crazy, fast. When I walked inside, Glenda was on the phone with the police department, going on about a break-in. Two squad cars arrived in minutes, poking around, asking questions, nodding as Glenda blubbered on, going headshake crazy in the driveway. I hung back at the kitchen door, watching the scene as though it were all fake, until Glenda came for me.

She asked what I'd seen, which was nothing. I told her that but she kept badgering me until even the cops seemed a little uncomfortable with all of Glenda's flailing and crying, her dramatic calisthenics. Personally, I thought she could use a quick tasing.

After about an hour of note-taking, the badges made their escape. Nothing was missing, besides one adult male. Robbie arrived as they were retreating, slumping towards the house like he'd rather take a flogging than deal with this.

For me, though, the broken door twist could go either way. It could put a new scent on the trail. Andrew had some bad people looking for him, people coming after him. And that's exactly how Robbie saw it too, when the next morning I heard him and Glenda going at in the kitchen.

I crouched on the steps to listen, peeking through the banister to where Glenda paced. Robbie hovered over a cereal bowl, studying his iPad.

"It's like they don't even care someone kicked in our door."

Robbie set his spoon down. He wasn't happy about the door, but in a different way. "Someone looking for Andy. There's not much they can do at this point."

"It's *Andrew*," Glenda corrected, snatching her own spoon off the counter. I thought for a second she was going to bite it clean off. "And that's bullshit."

Glenda's cursing was sharp, pronounced, pointed at Robbie. He sighed, glancing up from the iPad. "Come on, Glenda. Didn't he owe people money? Not exactly stockbrokers, either. Now he's got them coming around here."

She glowered, her face melting with anger. There was little question she was coming unhinged. "No, Robbie. And none of this makes sense. The door, the truck. He wouldn't just leave like this and not say anything." She went to work on a fingernail, gnawing like a rodent. "I don't like it. It seems strange to me. You know his favorite hat is in the back of the truck? When have you ever seen him without that hat? Something's happened, I know it."

My stomach dropped. I bit the inside of my cheek. For all my cleaning I still hadn't gotten to the back of the Forerunner. I put it on my to-do-right-freaking-soon list. Meanwhile, Uncle Robbie seemed bored with the whole topic, getting back to his breakfast.

"Chloe said he rode with some guys."

"No. No, it doesn't add up. And Chloe..."

Again Uncle Robbie set his spoon down, exasperated. "Chloe what? What do you think happened, exactly, Glenda?"

"I don't know, something. Something's going on."

"With who? Andrew? Is he still, you know, doing coke?"

Glenda stopped with a squeak, slammed the spoon to the granite, and pivoted to her husband, livid. Disgusted. "No, Robbie. He went to rehab. I hardly think this is the time to bring *that* up."

"Actually, it seems perfectly reasonable. The door's busted in because he probably short-changed someone. What's next, they'll come in here?"

Go Robbie. You tell her. The coke thing didn't surprise me, either, not after the other night. And it fit nicely with the busted door. With that, I slid off the wall and moseyed into the kitchen. Both of them turned to me, like a couple of boxers between rounds.

"Good morning," Glenda said like a total snob. "So look who's going to school today."

Robbie slid the box of Cheerios to me. A simple gesture, but one that made it clear whose side he was on. And yeah, sides had been drawn, that much revealed itself on the way to school. Dylan had a student council meeting. Robbie had a meeting. I was stuck with Glenda, who'd been adamant about taking me.

If happy Glenda was unbearable, bitchy Glenda was torture. She cursed at other drivers, tapped on the wheel, fished out gum from her purse, and was otherwise miserable.

"You want me to drive?" I said, after she nearly took us into a city bus. We were at the light and she was fiddling with the stereo, changing the station every five seconds.

"Huh? Oh, no I'm fine. Besides, you don't even have your license."

"I was kidding,"

No fake laugh or giggle. No more "honey" or "sweetie." Her red-rimmed eyes bulged with intensity, tired and wired at the same time. The light changed and we charged ahead. Glenda was in straight screw-it mode, digging in her purse, jamming a smoke in her mouth. I chuckled when she let down her window and spit out her gum. She lit up in the car.

"Old habit," she said, and I shrugged. She blew a stream of smoke out the cracked window, but it must have worked to soothe her frayed nerves because after a drag or two she relaxed.

She turned to me with a squint. "So, did your mother never push you to get your learner's permit? I mean before...everything?"

I turned to her, but she only stared straight ahead. I let my window all the way down, for air. "Um, not really, she was dying, remember?"

"Oh, no, I didn't mean...it's just how, you know, just seems the two of you spent all your free time shut inside the house. But I suppose with her depression and all."

My toes jammed into my shoe. A surge of anger hit, and this time I couldn't take my eyes off her. "What are you trying to say?"

Glenda shook her head, nearly smirking as she puffed on her smoke. "Well, you know, how she battled depression most of her life. And you know, the suicide attempt."

Mom lay in bed with the shades drawn against the heat of the day. The day she told me about the cancer. A tingle shot down my neck, jetting through my arms as she took my hand and pressed my fingers into the flesh of her left breast. It was hard, like a marble in there. I'd jerked my hand away, the bumps on my arms trapping the chill as I shivered, waiting for her to say it was nothing. To say something. But her face was gray, like skim milk in a dirty ash tray. She was crippled by the horror of what was happening inside of her.

I was livid my mother never told me about the biopsy—or the results. About aggressive cancer cells and stages and lymph nodes. All of it flashed to mind as Glenda now turned to me, as though she were peering in on these most intimate thoughts.

I shook my head, so stunned by this sudden yet casual assault I could hardly string together words. "She never, no she didn't."

"Oh, sweetie, I'm," she put a hand to her chest, exhaling smoke from the side of her mouth, filling the car with the exhaust from her words. There was a sheen of satisfaction in her eyes. "I didn't mean to... I thought, well, I thought she would have talked to you about it."

My gaze fell to the steering wheel. I could reach over and yank it towards me. Maybe we'd go up on two wheels, plow into the brick wall at the edge of campus. That would be one way to end this conversation. Instead, I sat there, ticking with anger.

Glenda hummed along and pulled the car to the sidewalk. Before the car came to a stop, I had the door open and flung myself out. I whipped my hair back, leaned towards the window, all set and ready to tell her where to go. But I never got the chance. She simply drove away.

Chapter 27

R obbie had some guys come out to fix the door on Friday. Glenda immediately flipped because she *needed* to take pictures for her Missing Person's report. Finding Andrew was Glenda's new cause in life. She only spoke to Robbie or me when she needed info about a date or a timeline.

Dylan picked me up that evening, pulling up next to the filthy Forerunner—the spun-up mud from Holcomb pond advertising my little secret. Dylan still wanted to pay for the door and the labor (he actually said labor) and so I leaned over to shut him up about it. Glenda watched from the window like a creeper.

At Spence's lake house, we passed a line of shiny cars, looking for a spot. Dylan glanced over at me and smiled. "You okay?"

Okay. No. Sleep came in tiny fits during the night, always ruptured by nightmares. I couldn't stop shaking, and I was puking up everything I ate. "Sure."

"You sure?"

"Yeah," I said, sliding closer. "Are you okay?"

He pulled off the road and played with the keys. Some kids laughed and whooped as they stumbled past us, ready to tear into the night. I curled under Dylan's arm, feeling safe in his clean smell, his sport deodorant and crisp laundry detergent. I closed my eyes and soaked him in. The feel of his chest. My face in his neck. His bare arm pressing against my shoulder. Such a simple thing, but I could have stayed there forever.

But forever was a blink. Dylan sat up and I pulled away. "I guess we'd better get down there."

We found Vienna and Spence on the back deck, in the thick of things.

"Hey, losers," Vienna said, pulling me in for a squeeze. She was well into a bottle of Boone's Farm. Her breath reeked like rotten fruit salad. Dylan made his way over to the guys, where Spence had the fireplace going just as the sun fell into the trees. Vienna handed me the bottle.

"Here's to Cum Laude, you big nerd."

I took a sip. It was tangy sweet with a slight burn. The evening sun cut through the tree branches, glittering on the lake as the music and laughter intertwined with the smoke from the fire on the patio. Another sip to fight back the darkness in the woods. And one more because I enjoyed the burn on my throat. A fourth as I hoped to scrape off the smell of blood and bleach and lemon that never left my nose.

More cars, the rest of the baseball team, judging by all the bass thumping. Private school kids, basic boys, each indistinguishable from the next, spilling out, punching each other, acting street with their Volvo's and Mini Coopers, talking slang they'd picked up from Youtube. Later, when they got a nice buzz going, they'd talk trash about public school kids. The drink was dangerous. I handed the bottle back to Vee. She poured some in a cup.

The fire raged, because drunk boys liked to feed fires. They liked to snort and piss and spit and see who could snort the loudest and piss farthest and spit the most. The more people I was around the more alone I felt. I needed to get away.

I stumbled down the path towards the lake, the wine sloshing in my Solo cup. I set off to the right, towards a secluded dock where I could hear the party but not have to be a part of it. I stared into the black sheet of water, thinking about bubbles. About sinking. About evidence.

I wasn't ready for this, coming here. I'd scrubbed the underside of my mattress all over again, until all that was left of Andrew was a brownish cloud. But it may as well have still been his body under my bed at night. The nightmares wouldn't stop. The sound of the door handle jiggling, the visions of Andrew with the knife. Only now sometimes Glenda had the knife and she was stabbing me.

A frog gurgled from somewhere beneath the dock. Vee must have gained control of the music because a Lauren Daigle song barreled into the night. Then came heavy footsteps in the dark, twigs snapping. I turned around to find Dylan.

"There you are."

He sat beside me. His leg touching mine. I took his hand and felt him looking me over but not asking the dreaded question: *Are you okay?*

I only wanted to feel pretty, wanted him to touch me again. To look at me the way he had at the baseball games. The marks on my neck had faded some, the bruises now a faint yellow. But my insides were scarred and ugly, grotesque even. I'd never be the same. I leaned into him and tried to reel in my emotions, but the wine flushed the tears to my eyes.

"Chloe, is everything okay?"

And there it was. I dabbed my eyes. "Yes, I'm just really happy." My tongue was a slug, lips numb. My mind worked fine in my head but everything took a minute to get the message. "Kiss me."

He leaned over and his lips found mine. A real kiss that captured the summer. I grabbed his face and kissed him harder, willing the warmth to return between us. Until he snorted and pulled away. "Whoa, Chloe, easy now."

"Sorry, I just…"

He looked down to my empty cup. "How much have you had?"

"I don't know." I didn't want to talk about it—about anything. I was so tired of talking and lying, filtering my words and thoughts, bending them to people's liking so I wouldn't reveal secrets. I held my thumb and forefinger maybe an inch apart. "This much maybe?"

He laughed. "Okay, just don't get wasted."

"Nope, not getting wasted."

Vee, however, *was* getting wasted. We heard her coming from a mile away, dragging and rustling and plodding towards our little dock. We rose and walked over to her so she didn't fall face first into the lake.

"All right, people," she said, her hand missing her hip so she had to sidestep to stay upright. "Why are you social distancing?"

Dylan held his arms out over the dock, which sent her into a song.

"Sittin' by the dock of the bay, watching the time... roll awaaaaay!"

She attempted to whistle and it was like watching a little kid chew a wad of gum. Dylan and I giggled. Vee pouted. "Stop, I can't whistle when I'm smiling. Hang on."

We spent the next ten minutes watching a girl who could quote Socrates try to whistle. Finally, Dylan and I took her by the arms and the three of us hiked up through the darkness towards the noise.

It was down to maybe ten of us when the inevitable happened. The party moved towards the water, and Spence was trying to play guitar when I spotted Vee hunched over by the bank like a cat with a hairball. I touched Dylan's arm and let him know I needed to help her out. He rolled his eyes.

"Hey, Vee."

"Huughgahhh. Can't talk right now."

I knelt down beside her and rubbed her back. Again. At least this time we weren't stuck in a bathroom. It was nice out and the katydids pulsed in the dark between the trees.

"I can't believe...how..."

I turned my head as she puked some more. I made sure she didn't face plant but otherwise let her do her thing. The stars were out and the moon was a big glowing ball in the sky.

"Oh, Chloe." Vee smacked her forehead. "Don't ever let me drink this much again."

"You said that last time."

"Shut up."

I helped her to the other dock, the same one as before, off to the side and away from things. I lay down beside her and we were both on our backs. She grabbed my arm, like she was scared I was going to leave her.

"Tell me a story," Vee said, wiping her face and turning to me. There, on our backs, our feet pointed to the water and our faces to the stars as a spread of luminescent moonlight covered the lake, I thought how she was the closest thing I'd ever had to a sister. And lying there with her, holding her hand, it was easy just to start talking.

"Okay, well, there once was a girl named Vienna. She was awfully comfortable with her sexuality. In fact, she slept with everyone in the school."

Vee slapped my arm, arched her back, and scooted closer to me. "Hey, no, a real story."

"I thought that one was pretty real. She kept trying to drink but didn't have the stomach for it..."

"I hate you." She rolled onto her side, using her folded arm for a pillow. Her knotted hair fell over her eyes, her breaths like a wino and her face like a little girl. "And Spence is the only one, like, ever."

"I know, I know."

With that settled she reached for my hand. "Tell me a scary story. I used to love scary stories when we camped."

"Did you get wasted like this in Girl Scouts too?"

"Aww Chloe, please?"

I looked over to the bank where I could see the fire, Spence working out the logistics of a Ben Harper tune, only the chirr of nature mingling with drunk laughter. Vee wouldn't be long getting passed out. I took a breath of damp air, my voice hardly more than a whisper.

"Okay, well, there once was a man, an evil man who liked to hurt girls. He'd wait until it was late at night, when everyone else was asleep..."

She wiggled her shoulders, settling in for a ghost story. "Okay, a big, bad man," she said, eyes and ears eager for more. "A cute man?"

"No, not cute. An ugly, disgusting man. He traveled around, always on the prowl, looking for families with girls so he could have his way. But he always disappeared before anyone could catch him."

An explosion of laughter from the boys, baseball talk. Vee blinked a few times, nuzzled her head in her arm. "Go on."

"Well, it just so happened, that one day the man chose the wrong girl. He tried to force her to do things, even when she told him to stop, begged him to stop..."

I paused, my heart thumping with the night. Vienna let out a grunt as she faded, still with a grip on my hand. I continued, my voice lower, just over the crickets. "So one night he entered the girl's bedroom, just like he had done before. And the girl said no, again, like she always did, and it made him angry. He didn't like being told no, so he put a knife to her neck."

Up at the house, a car cranked up and peeled out, leaving things quiet again on the water. Vee was out, her face like a painting against the night.

"So she pretended it was fine, and she let him touch her, but this time, when he slid his hands underneath her clothes, she took the knife and plunged it into his guts. The man gurgled and moaned, but she stabbed him again, and again. Until the blood and the life drained out of him, onto her arms and her stomach. But she didn't care, she was happy. She was free."

Vee's snoring hit its stride. I trembled, my heart drumming in my ears. "So she loaded him into his truck and dumped his body in Holcomb pond, where he sits rotting and waterlogged on this very night, where he can never hurt her again. The end."

I took her hand and kissed it, set it at her side and wiped my brow. She was a goner for the night, and I needed to get her inside. But I was crackling with energy after saying the words out loud, buzzing and jittery, without a clue of what to do with myself. I got to my feet, turned my head, and nearly fell off the dock into the lake.

A gasp and a scream collided in my throat. A figure stood at the edge of the dock. A few steps and he came into focus. I staggered backward, holding my breath as I found Dylan, only a few feet away, staring back at me like I was a creature from the lake.

Chapter 28

He didn't make a move, not a step back or towards me. His face was a stone. His eyes wide and unblinking. I managed to inch towards him.

"Oh, hey." I tried to laugh it off, but only a nervous cackle sputtered from my throat. I really did sound like a creature from the lake.

When I closed the gap between us, he backed away. "Chloe. Is it, is that true?"

"Is what true?"

"Did you *kill* him? The pond near your house? The pond...the one with me?"

"What? *No!*" I stammered, more shocked at him saying it than anything else. At how fast he'd put it all together. I looked back at Vee. "Oh, that? Dylan, come on, I was telling a scary story until she passed out."

I could make out his features now. The moonlight playing on his cheeks, the twist on his lips as he rolled his head back, side to side before he spoke. "The truck. That morning. Chloe, you..."

"Dylan," I said, taking another step to him. "Are *you* drunk?"

He shook his head. "I don't drink."

His eyes pinned me back. I shivered, rubbing my arms. Dylan stood before me, judging me, making no effort to reach for me or soften his icepick gaze. I had to fix this.

"So, let me get this straight," I said in my best you're-out-of-your-mind voice. "You're basically accusing me of not just killing Andrew but tossing him into a pond." I brushed past him. "Really Dylan, you overestimate me."

But he hadn't overestimated me. He'd seen me for what I was. And it was going to take some convincing to talk him out of it, to explain how ridiculous it all sounded. And I tried, as we stood there for a while, ten, twenty minutes maybe, until Spence came over to scoop up Vee, still passed out on the dock. Only then did Dylan let me near him. Let me put my arms around his waist. He hugged me back, limply, like I was something dangerous and needed to be watched carefully. But I managed to convince him. At least I thought so.

Later, after Vee was put in bed and all tucked in, Dylan and I hung out by the fire, pretending not to study each other as everyone laughed with Spence and the rest of the late-nighters. But every time I looked over at Dylan he was staring out at the pond, where we'd shared that moonlit canoe ride not so long ago.

I told myself it would all be fine. What choice did I have?

I BLINKED to life in a bed, looking at the pictures on the walls. The Nottaways' troves from every corner of the world. The Hamptons. Nova Scotia. Prague. New Zealand. Over the doorway was a fishing rod that probably belonged to Hemmingway, maybe a Roosevelt. A butterfly net over the desk. It was like waking up to a Smithsonian display.

Everything was still. Outside, some birds squabbled in a tree. My clothes smelled like campfire. My legs were riddled with bites and welts. My head rang. I checked my phone and saw it was after nine. Two missed calls from Glenda.

Dylan was gone. I rolled out of bed and crept down the steps to the deck, then farther down to the dock at the water. I figured Vee would be down for a while. The damage from the night was scattered along the embankment. Beer cans, wine bottles, solo cups, a bikini top, some plastic plates. But the early day was nice, the sun was strong and golden, fighting through the trees to get to the water.

I was about to start walking when someone called from the lake. I turned to find Spence gliding across the water on a kayak, his effortless strokes hardly causing a ripple in the water. He hopped out and tied up, all seize-the-day style.

"Hey, Chlo."

"Hey," I said, looking him over. I guess at some point in his life Spence had decided not to be a typical trust fund brat. He had the youthful smile of a kid with a firm grip on things. His eyes were sharp and focused. He didn't seem the least bit hungover or even breathing heavy from the effort.

He set the paddle on the bench, nodded my way. "How you feeling?"

"Good," I said. Which was true. As good as I could feel considering my boyfriend overheard me confessing a murder.

"I wish I could say the same for Vee. She's comatose. I was just coming in to check on her."

"Oh, good luck." For a moment we just stood there. Spence looked up towards the house.

"Hey, uh, so Dylan took off."

"Yeah, I noticed."

He wiped something from his leg as the breeze swept through his hair. Spence always had this comfortable command of things. I thought he'd make a successful politician, leader, or CEO one day. Whatever put him in front of people so they would do what he wanted.

He kicked some trash to the side, motioned for me to go up the steps first. "Look, he's just... I don't want to get in your business, that's between the two of you. But, whatever it is, I can see he's hurting. Bad. That's my boy, you know?"

Charming or not, I wasn't about to get into this with him. And Spence was quick enough to pick up on that. "But I'll tell you what. Let me go check on Vee, and I'll give you a ride home, if you want?"

Back in the kitchen, he swept a hand towards the built-in refrigerator. "Help yourself to whatever you want. I think there's bagels, some fruit or whatever," he called over his shoulder as he bounded up the steps.

I couldn't eat. Bits and pieces of last night were coming back with a punch. Me telling Dylan he was being unreasonable. How I'd made up the story only to mess with Vienna. Him looking at me like I was a crazy person, which, the way things were going, I couldn't exactly argue the point.

Spence returned wearing a gray V-neck and pink shorts. He jiggled his keys, shook his head. "For such a pretty girl, she snores like a chainsaw."

"That's my Vee."

I climbed into his Audi. Spence made a few jokes about the baseball bats in the trunk. Again, I wondered what my few friends really thought about me—the girl whose mom died. There were so many versions of me. Around Dylan I felt strong and in control. Around Spence I was self-conscious, unqualified. Around Robbie I could be loose and ready to laugh, and with Glenda I was careful, vengeful, waiting for a misstep so I could pounce.

Even with Vee I'd been distant lately. Truth was, since Mom died I'd been a chameleon, wearing and shedding different personas to fit my company. It was like my true identity was trapped inside a pitch-black coffin with my mother.

A blast of sun hit my face as we pulled out. Spence tapped along the wheel, fiddling with the stereo until sports talk droned underneath the wind. He glanced over at me, all smiles and sunglasses. "Chloe, you gotta understand, about Dylan. He's a great guy, really, I've known him for years but, he's hella shy, you know?"

"Yeah," I said, wondering where this was headed. "That's what I like about him. But lately he hasn't been so shy. Just mad."

Spence shook his head. sandy blond hair danced and settled perfectly. I could see why Vee—and every other girl—was crazy about him, but he was too perfect for my taste. I liked a flaw here and there, someone who blushed. Someone like I used to know. Spence turned his head to me, back to the road, and finally back to me again. "No, I mean, you're his first girlfriend. Like, first, first."

"Okay," I shrugged, eyebrows arched. I mean, I already knew he was a virgin.

Spence smiled, set the sunglasses up on his head. "I guess what I mean is, well, the guy is sensitive. And again, I know this isn't my place, but let me just say this so we can be done with it." He looked to me again as we flew past a truck and dipped back to the right side of the road. "Don't mess with him, all right? He's too good a guy, you know that. I mean, I know he might be quiet and shy and all, but he's a good dude. So if you're, I don't know, just let him down easy. There, I said it, I'm done."

"Look, Spence. I'm not breaking up with Dylan."

He nodded. While I could respect what he was doing for a friend, that's not what was happening. A thousand words came to mind, and I wanted to tell Spence how there was no other guy, that I would never—didn't want to—wasn't thinking about dumping Dylan. Instead I looked away and let it all drown in the wind.

We talked light the rest of the way. School, Vienna, even baseball, until we got downtown. The day was coming in bright, umbrellas bloomed along the sidewalk at the outdoor café. Servers out with brooms and dustpans in anticipation of Saturday brunch. Spence turned left and my seat vibrated as we cut up the old cobblestone street, past the row of thick oak trees, where an unmarked yet very obvious police cruiser sat near the curb in front of the house.

I stifled a gasp. Spence looked at me as he pulled into the driveway. "This one, right?"

I nodded, but no sound escaped the narrowing passage of my throat. A dark car with antennas and government tags. This looked legit, not like last time, with the two dopey cops outside, shucking through all Glenda's noise. We needed to turn around, zoom back the way we came. Spence had the means to aid and abet, I could live at the lake house—maybe he could get set me up in a ski lodge along the

Rockies. Anything but walk into the house and face whatever awaited me. I was about to go to jail.

As Spence pulled in the driveway, Uncle Robbie came around from the garden shed. He wore gloves like a goof and hoisted a shovel, like he might be setting out to dig my grave. Instead, he smiled.

"Hey guys," he said, nodding to the house. "I had to get out of there." He looked at me. "Glenda filed a Missing Person's report. Not sure why they didn't handle this downtown. Something about the Forerunner."

Whatever relief I found with Uncle Robbie's smile was confounded by the new development with Andrew's car. "The Forerunner?" I managed. My voice shook. Spence craned to see over Robbie's shoulder, thoroughly interested with the scene in a boy sort of way.

"Well," Robbie started, his face registering that it wasn't Dylan in the car but another boy. He noticed the dirty, high-end Audi. I did what I could with introductions, considering.

"Uncle Robbie, this is Spence Nottaway. Spence, Uncle Robbie."

I may as well have said Kennedy, the way the Nottaway name hit Uncle Robbie. He stiffened, removed a glove and thrust his hand past me. "Nice to meet you. I, uh, think we handled an account for your family a few years back."

"A pleasure, sir." Spence said and I rolled my eyes, but without much gusto being how there were detectives in the house. You know, detecting stuff.

I got things back on track. "So, what's up with Andrew's car?"

Robbie took his eyes off his cash cow. Suddenly all the casualness was gone. "Oh, well, I'm sure it's nothing. Glenda found his phone in the seat or something."

My blood turned to slush. I managed a glance at Spence, still trying to get a look at things. "Well, thanks for the ride."

"No problem. Hey, let me know if you need anything, okay?"

"Yeah, thanks."

Spence backed out and gave us a wave. Robbie smiled and

saluted, still holding the shovel like a farmer. The Audi zipped down the street and out of sight.

Uncle Robbie shook his head. "You certainly know how to make friends, Chloe."

"Vienna's boyfriend," I said, staring at the Forerunner. The hat. The phone. Plus there had to be blood back there. Deep breaths. It was all piling up.

Robbie stretched the glove over his hand. "This is all too dramatic for me. I almost want to tell the detectives the guy is probably on a bender somewhere, you know?"

The front door opened and there stood Glenda, her two detectives in tow. They stepped out on the porch. Robbie muttered something under his breath and got to work on the flower beds.

"Chloe, oh good, you're here. Could you come inside please?"

Chapter 29

They didn't seem like detectives, at least not like the ones I'd seen on TV or in the movies. Or maybe they did but I was too freaked to notice. Detective Kramer was a chick. Nearly pretty, Latino, with thick brown curls, a blue sweater over a collared shirt, dark jeans and decent shoes. Right off the bat she tried to lower my guard, insisting I call her Detective Sarah.

The other one was trouble. Martin, he said with a nod, his eyes fixed on mine.

Detective Kramer, or Sarah rather, got the ball rolling, assuring me they were only trying to find Andrew. Nothing more. Since I was the last one to see him since he'd left, they simply wanted to know if I had anything to add.

Glenda fiddled with the coffee maker. Detective Sarah declined a beverage while Detective Martin took precise, measured sips from his Diet Dr. Pepper, each time twisting the cap back on tight as a wrench. He was on the short side, his shirt crammed into his pants against its will. Sarah asked about school.

"It's fine." I fed them a quick smile. "I'm ready for summer."

Detective Sarah nodded. "I'll bet." She took a seat at the table and motioned for me to do the same. Glenda poured coffee—the last thing on the planet she needed—and joined the party.

"Don't let her fool you," she said, inserting herself. "Chloe is an excellent student. Only a junior and already Cum Laude Society. We're awfully proud," she added, as though she'd been my personal tutor. And her tone, sweeter than saccharin.

Detective Sarah's gaze brightened. "Wow, that's wonderful."

I closed my eyes with a sheepish grin. "Thanks."

Weirdly, my chats with Doctor O had sort of prepped me for this. I gathered my nerves, wrapped them tight, tossed back my hair so I could help everybody realize good old Andrew was probably somewhere in Mexico with plenty of booze and blow. But Glenda, sitting beside me, buzzing with details, made it hard to focus. Something was up. Something a bit more ominous than a Missing Person's report. I eyed the notepads, the subtle glances, Andrew's phone sitting between us like a hand grenade.

With pleasantries out of the way, Detective Sarah dove in. "Okay, Chloe, so when did you last see Andrew Lankford?"

Things turned formal fast. I cleared my throat and went to work, careful to keep things as vague as possible. "Well, I think it was last week. Heard him, really. His truck in the driveway, some car doors shutting. A car pulled off and it was quiet again."

"And this was Thursday, the eighteenth?"

I shrugged. "Yes, I think so." I turned to Glenda. "When you guys were at the fund raiser thingy."

Glenda brightened, eyes flickering. Even distraught and moody, coping with her brother's "disappearance," I was banking that she'd be willing to yap about herself. She hit the ground running. "Oh, Robbie and myself, we're on the board. We do fundraising balls and dinners every Thursday night at the Glimmerdale. It's been a smashing success, I think we've had some officers attend, even Mayor Adams."

Detective Sarah let her go on for a moment, until Detective Martin leaned forward, edging his way into the conversation. He clicked his pen and cocked his head to the left, popping and cracking into action, settling on his ample haunches. "Chloe, are you and Andrew close?"

Boom like that. He came out firing. I tried to mask my raging panic. Glenda's lips trembled and her eyes bugged. She looked like a pet store fish in a baggy.

"Close?" I asked. Monosyllables were all I could handle.

Detective Martin sat back, resettled his legs in the chair. I didn't care for him. He struck me as a man who enjoyed rainy days. A guy not much in the mood for a joke. A man with no interest in a romantic comedy, or a movie in general. His voice was a mechanical drone—a drone that matched the robotic hand reaching for the phone sitting in the shadow beneath his chin.

He pressed the button on the phone—Andrew's phone. It glowed to life on the detective's pocked face. He made a few casual swipes and Detective Sarah's mouth went tight. Then he turned the screen to me, so I could see a photo of my own stupid face staring back.

"It's just that, well, this," he turned the phone from me to him, me to him again. "It strikes me as a playful relationship."

A noise escaped Glenda's mouth. I stared at my dumb flirty face. Head cocked down, hair up, a few strands falling over my eyes. Challenging eyes. Daring eyes. Teasing eyes that said all that needed to be said. My cute little nose wrinkled and my tongue pinched ever so gently between my teeth.

It was only my face, from that day in the carriage house. Nothing dirty or incriminating. Yet it was in so many ways.

"Chloe," Glenda whispered in condemnation. Mercifully, Detective Martin set the phone down. I held my head in place, even when all I wanted to do was bang it on the table. Wow, Andrew. Ever heard of a passcode? I stared back at the detective's face, studied how the cluster of blackheads around his nose matched the stubble on his chin. Something inside of me waned, but I caught it. I held the wall up. I blinked it all away with a shrug.

"I was just having fun."

"Again, Chloe," Detective Sarah said, reaching out to me. "This isn't about you. We're only trying to locate Mr. Lankford."

His knife was on my throat! Pressing down, cutting into me! And after what he'd done in the carriage house. What did they want from me? I pulled my hand away. "Why does it feel like I'm a suspect?"

"You're not, Chloe. We have no suspects. We're not saying a crime has been committed. We just need to know if he confided in you, told you anything we should know."

Glenda poured it on thick, sobbing now. Detective Martin was unaffected by it all. Bored, staring at me like I was a slab of meat behind the glass. That's when Robbie came in through the kitchen door.

He took one look around and shot a furious glare at Glenda. "What's going on?"

Robbie was ticked. No pleasantries, no hiding the irritation in his voice. I guess it was one thing having Glenda sulk around the house, but he was through with the detectives lurking around the place.

Detective Sarah turned to Glenda, who snapped out of the tears but remained victimized. Now it was my turn for the drama. I blinked into some tears, making it clear I was getting roughed up by the detectives sitting in his kitchen. Robbie shook his head.

"Okay, this is over. We're done. If you need anything else, we'll be happy to come to the station. With my lawyer."

Glenda shot him a glossy glare, one you didn't need to be a detective to know there would soon be more going on between them in the courtroom than the bedroom.

Detective Sarah rose. "We'll be on our way. Thank you for your time, Mr. Vanderbrooke." She gave me a small smile, then turned to Glenda. "We will let you know about the vehicle."

Glenda nodded slowly. I tried to hold my eyes in my skull. So much for cleaning out the Forerunner. Not with Glenda hawking my every move. And even if I had wiped it down there was bound to be hair, blood, certainly *something* that would show up in a lab. Maybe the mud would lead them to the body for all I knew. Not good.

Detective Sarah gave us one last compassionate smile. "Thank you for your time, Mrs. Vanderbrooke. And thank you, Chloe, I know this might seem a bit much for your Saturday morning."

Yeah, like I had a life anymore. Detective Martin twisted his bottle cap into submission. He studied my face like there would be a test on it back at the station. "We'll be in touch," he added, scraping the chair on the tile floor as he skootched it back under the table. Robbie set a stare on him as he walked out.

When they were gone Robbie lit into Glenda, who lashed back about her missing brother. Things got heated. I headed upstairs where I found my brand-new comforter balled up in the corner of the room. My duffle bag open, like someone had rifled through it.

I guess Glenda didn't need a search warrant.

Chapter 30

I watched from the bedroom window as a flatbed tow truck backed into the driveway. Some bulky maneuvering, the truck *beep-beeping* into place, and Andrew's Forerunner was hoisted onto a bed and hauled off and carried down the cobblestone road with a rumble of gears and the grind of brakes. Off it went, to be combed for tiny, microscopic evidence.

Things were moving along for a Missing Person's report. All thanks to Glenda, who stood outside smoking a cigarette, doing her best to play the role of a battered woman on a Lifetime series. It was only a matter of time now.

I fell back into the chair that had become my bed. Before I could get comfortable, the footsteps came. Glenda opened the door without knocking, her MacBook open, the screen washing her face with a ghoulish glow. "Chloe, you spent a hundred dollars on a comforter?"

"I meant to tell you. I took the other one to the lake, at Spence's, and it got ruined."

Refusing to be blindsided again, I'd come up with an excuse for the blanket when that little curmudgeon Martin had left, right before I'd found Glenda had ransacked the room.

"And why wouldn't you tell me?"

This woman was taking notes from the detectives. I shot her a look of pity. "You've been so stressed. I didn't want to worry you with it. I'm sorry, I can pay you back."

She eyed the MacBook, scanning my Visa account. Looking over every cent I'd spent and where it had happened before she spun off and away. At least our charade was over.

When I came downstairs, she pounced. "You took my comforter *to the lake?*"

Robbie sat seething at the window, arms folded and muttering his disgust with the whole thing. It didn't help how the tow truck had ripped up the grass and had torn his mulch beds to shit—his words.

Glenda's lips pressed together like a tightrope. The façade crumbling one bang-shake at a time. Now the house was quiet and eerie. The dinner table resembled a hotline call center. The MacBook, cellphone, post-it notes, and legal pads filled with scrawling. No more jazz, no more humming and strumming, only the rhythmic thump of our collected heartbeats, like a clock on the wall.

For the rest of the day I called Dylan, leaving messages, asking him to call me back. On Sunday, I started on the texts. Each one more desperate than the last. The house was closing in on me, the empty driveway a reminder that the Forerunner was confessing its secrets. Blood droplets, hair follicles, mud and dirt and who knew what other kind of damnation lurked in its fibers. On top of everything else there was Glenda's pacing and phone calls, Robbie's silent anger, and behind my eyelids was the constant image of Dylan's face in the shadows at the lake.

So I called again.

WHEN DYLAN DIDN'T SHOW up for school on Monday, I spent an hour in a bathroom stall. He'd already blocked my number, as though I were a stalker. The shakes returned worse than ever, rattling my hands to the wrists so I could hardly latch the stall door when I heard people entering. My breaths were shallow and useless as I rocked back and forth, wishing I could fix things with Dylan without telling him the truth.

When Vee caught up with me in the courtyard later I jumped. She looked me over carefully. "Okay, so what did you do to that boy?"

"What?"

"*What?* Dylan. Spence said he's gone into hiding." Vee lowered her voice and leaned close. She wiped a strand of hair from my face. "What happened, Chlo? And what's up with you?"

"Nothing happened. He just, I don't know what his deal is, Vee. He blocked my number."

"What? Oh." She looked around, towards the building. "Why would he do that?"

"I don't know, but..." My words trailed off. I didn't know what to say or how to begin. I'd always been fine on my own, until Dylan. The way he was avoiding me made me feel desperate. Vee eyed me up and down, searching for answers, when a Frisbee landed at our feet.

Two boys—obviously freshmen, stood awkwardly, arms dangling, as though trying to figure out who was going to walk over and make the first move. Vee picked up the Frisbee and smiled. "Hey, come here. Both of you."

The boys exchanged looks. Shy and giggling, their loose shirts hanging off their shoulders. One was Asian, with glasses and a red tie. The other was blond, the type that in two years would be strutting around the grounds with the same smug look most of these kids took on by the time they were upperclassmen. Maybe it was taught or maybe it was inherited. Nature or nurture, either way it was a given.

"Who threw it?" Vee asked. Their eyes fell to their feet. The blond one snuck a peek at Vee's legs before his eyes swept across my chest. Usually I enjoyed messing with the little boys, but I was too much of a basket-case to fully participate. Finally, the blond one stepped forward. "Sorry, Vienna."

Vee smiled. "Darn right you are." She leaned closer, and the boy's eyes went wide. "Watch it."

Vigorous nods. Such good pups, happy just to have been in the same breathing space as the great Vienna Somerset. I'd miss this, I thought, even as we had our senior year ahead of us, it was all gone. At least for me.

"Cute," Vee said, watching them hustle off. I tried to smile and nod along, but everyday life failed to hold my interest. School, class, friends and the future, all of it had vanished, replaced by a sinking dread in my stomach.

I was in Miss Shelby's class when they came. Shelby was going over Robert Frost's *Home Burial*.

...And living people, and things they understand.
But the world's evil. I won't have grief so
If I can change it. Oh, I won't, I won't!

Mr. Suddith appeared at the door. I straightened, searched his face for shame or disappointment, anger, as Miss Shelby stopped the poem, stiffened, then hurried over to him, patting down her frumpy clothes like she did whenever someone important came around. She told us to read the text while keeping an eye for themes of work ethic and abandonment. I did neither.

Hyperventilating without drawing attention takes skill. Complete self-control. A tight grip on the desk, full, deep breaths, yet steady and sturdy, as to appear relaxed to my peers and adequately counteract the fight or flight reflex running rampant through my veins when Miss Shelby leaned her flabby face into the doorway and said, "Chloe, could you gather your things and come this way."

Heads turned to me. Nothing shocking though, they probably thought I had some prestigious duty to fulfill. A luncheon with the board. Volunteer work with FEMA. An interview with a recruiter. They didn't know. Not yet they didn't.

My legs lifted me out of the chair. My hands collected my things. I made an effort to keep my face pleasant. Pleasant was better than sullen. I wanted them to remember me that way. It was what I wanted to impress upon them before I was arrested for murder.

Miss Shelby put a hand on my back. "Mr. Suddith would like to speak with you," she said, stating the obvious. My eyes couldn't meet his gaze. I avoided the tight scowl carved into his features. I felt the betrayal and confusion lurking under his graying eyebrows. But so far, no officers or detectives. Not yet, anyway.

Miss Shelby lingered for a moment, until Mr. Suddith dismissed her with a curt nod. "That will be all, Hannah, thank you."

Hannah. Well, I never would have guessed it. Then again, I'd never put much thought into her name. Hannah nodded and glanced at me once again. I waited for her to say something like, *I always knew it would come down to something like this*, but instead she turned and ducked back into her hole.

"This way, Chloe."

His silence killed me as our steps clicked through the hall, slapping the brick pathway outside as we crossed the corridor along trimmed grass, under the statues and landmarks. When we reached the admin building, Mr. Suddith stopped and put a hand to the rail.

"I hope you don't mind me pulling you from class, Chloe. Miss Jonelly says you've missed some time recently." He turned to face me. "I have some of your mother's things in the office, supplies and desk items and whatnot. I also wanted to check in with you personally."

I exhaled a breath I didn't know I was holding. I turned my head. My eyes welled. I knew how much Mom meant to him. Everything he was doing for me was out of respect to her. The way his voice shook as he took my shoulder, giving it a gentle squeeze as he led me into the office where I'd sat with Mom so many times.

My mom had sobbed like a baby when she'd gotten the job. Then all over again when I enrolled. All because of Mr. Suddith, a man who would never seek or take credit for all he's done for us.

He escorted me into the room, where there was no Detective Kramer, no trap to spring. He motioned to a chair and eased into his own behind the desk.

He gave me a moment to get myself together. Then he took a breath. "I um, we thought you might want to have a look, take what you want," he said, motioning to a box sitting on the other chair. "We would have done it sooner, but we wanted to give you some time, and well, I've been tied up with appointments and board meetings."

It didn't appear I was going to be hauled off in a squad car. At least not today. Mr. Suddith watched me carefully, shifted, then rose from his chair. He walked over and gently closed the door behind me. I turned to the box. Desk pictures in small frames. Mom with hair. She and Mr. Suddith at a ceremony. Mom and other well-dressed, bow-tied old people. Mom and me under a tree, her arms draped over my shoulders. The two of us looking out at something not in the frame. I took the picture out and held it close. Mr. Suddith took his seat and picked up a pen.

"Chloe, how are you doing?"

I looked to him, holding back the well of tears. His gaze settled over me, friendly, paternal even. "As a friend, Chloe. This has nothing to do with school. Obviously, your grades..." he waved a hand over the desk. "Well, congratulations. I missed you at the announcements the other day." His gaze fell to the picture. "You know, your induction. Leigh...your mother would be proud."

I wiped my eyes. "Thank you," I said, staring at the frame. "I miss her, more than I thought I would." My voice broke. Another rush of tears. If he only knew.

He slid a box of tissues my way. Outside, over his shoulder, the trees wiggled with the breeze. Mr. Suddith gave me time. He was good at that sort of thing, treating me as an equal. Just two people chatting.

He motioned to Mom's box. "A lot of it is just office stuff, I didn't know what you'd want so we left it all for you." He shook his head. "Don't feel obligated to keep everything."

My attention turned back to the box. A notepad filled with Mom's neat cursive. Appointments and motivational stuff. A notebook with some sketches. Markers. Highlighters. Salt and pepper shakers. A change pouch. I wanted it all, every paperclip.

"Our new assistant," he said quietly, "Miss Joiner, is a nice lady, but she's got big shoes to fill. Your mother was one of a kind. And I see a lot of her in you."

I'd always liked him. Sure, Mr. Suddith looked like any of the other old stiffs on the campus, with the jacket and tie, khakis and tasseled loafers, but there was something rebellious behind his lively eyes. He drove an ancient Land Rover that broke down all the time. He had two sons, one of them in the Peace Corp and the other was a tour guide at Yosemite or Yellowstone, I could never remember which. Mom told me once she'd received a call from the free clinic downtown, from a frazzled case worker who wished to thank Mr. Suddith personally for his generous donation. Something like eight grand. He'd never mentioned it. Never got all fancied up on Thursdays like Glenda to shout at the world all the good he was doing.

Now he was eyeing me with a look I hoped was interest and not suspicion. "You know, I've proposed a scholarship in her name."

My eyes snapped up. "What...*really*?"

He nodded. Clasping his fingers. "Just a proposal. For working mothers. I'm still crunching numbers."

The bell knocked from the tower. Mr. Suddith turned in his chair. "Well, I know you've got to get back," he said. "I just wanted to see how you were getting along."

I was dazed. The scholarship, how incredibly sweet this man was. But all that came out was, "I can keep the box, though?"

"Oh, yes of course," he gestured to it with one hand. "It's all yours."

I picked up the box, cherishing every pen and thumbtack. I turned to thank Mr. Suddith, who hopped up to get the door for me. "Oh, there was one other thing," he said, leaving the door shut and his hand on the doorknob. My stomach rolled. "A detective called me this morning. Asking about you."

A flash of heat on my neck. Mr. Suddith looked at the box. When he looked up, his eyes were glossy. "Nothing too invasive. About attendance, disciplinary issues. I told her you were a model student."

I forced myself to nod. Swallow. Breathe. "I, um, I don't..."

He shrugged. "Not sure what it was all about. Like I said, just wanted to make sure everything is okay."

I nodded, the box like concrete in my arms. "Everything's...okay."

Mr. Suddith nodded. "Very well. Enjoy the day, Chloe."

I walked out of the office, clutching Mom's old things. Miss Joiner gave me a sad smile that was so much a part of my life these days. Outside, I looked back to the window and Mr. Suddith raised his hand. I nodded and walked towards Kemper Hall.

The box clattered as I hit the trails, teetering on another meltdown. Missing Persons? Nope. If detectives were calling the school, it sure sounded more like they had a person of interest. I could only imagine what Glenda had told them about the comforter, about Andrew and me in the carriage house. Now they had the phone and the Forerunner. The hat. DNA. All they needed was a body. And Dylan could help them out with that.

I stood in the empty house. Heaving. Imagining Mom. Imagining us. I took out each picture and set it on the counter. Mom's calendar showed a dentist appointment she never made. Two fillings, I remembered her joking about it. "Cancer of the teeth," she'd called it. I wish it had been so easy. That they could have taken out her cavities and mixed the cement in the machine and filled her breasts. I took the calendar and pinned it in her closet. I arranged her pens and markers neatly along the floor. Tacked up her corkboard with all her little sayings and quotes and sketches. I tried my best to put her back in the house.

When my phone buzzed I was on the floor in Mom's room, staring at the ceiling and zoning out, trying not to think about anything at all. I scrambled to see if it was Dylan. It was Glenda, so I let it go to voicemail. Later, I checked it.

Chloe. You need to come to the house right away. There's something... I just got a message from school and...you need to get home now...

Chapter 31

The sun had dipped behind the trees by the time Uncle Robbie's jeep pulled into the parking lot at D.E.S. I'd hiked back to the school to avoid additional questions, but I figured there weren't detectives waiting when Robbie didn't ask where I'd been or what was going on with all the skipping school recently. He only asked if I was hungry.

Whatever Glenda's urgency, we stopped at Frank's. Mom and I used to go all the time, sitting at the indoor picnic tables with the worn, vinyl cloths. Frank's was always packed, its giant, sopping cheeseburgers and home cut fries were the best in town.

Robbie ordered the works. I got mine plain. I breathed in the thick, delicious aroma of grease in the air. We split a basket of fries and settled in behind a family with two spazzy little boys. I welcomed the noise, it helped us get over all of the awkwardness between us, because in there with Robbie, there was no way I could think of anything but Mom.

I bit my lip. "Uncle Robbie, have you been back to the cemetery? Since..."

He shook his head. Fat, maroon bags under his eyes, a few days' worth of stubble settling in on his face. But his little grin was real. "No, but why don't we go one weekend? Just us."

"Okay."

We picked through our basket, sipping our drinks and talking in spurts. Neither of us wanted to go home. We didn't talk about Glenda or Andrew, but our careful discussion about Mom eventually found its way to Papa Vanderbrooke—how his stubbornness remained even now, with his family falling apart.

Robbie tore into his burger. He wiped the ketchup from his lip. "You know, I was so mad at him for so long. That he could just turn his back on his own daughter, but what got me even more upset was how he could turn his back on you. It's like, fine, you're angry with Leigh, whatever, but your granddaughter?"

I told Robbie how we'd faced off the other day, and Robbie shook his head. "Maybe one day he'll regret all of this, but I wouldn't hold my breath. We didn't break any new ground when I went to check on Mom." He took a deep breath. "I'm just so done with it, with him. That he can't realize what he threw away with your mother. Even now, with her gone."

I gave him a little grin of my own. "Soooo, the stubbornness comes from that side of the family, huh?"

He wiped his face and sighed. "Well, yeah."

Suddenly it felt I could ask him anything in there, like we were hidden under the music and the chatter, buried in the thick grease from the kitchen. So I spit it out before I lost my nerve. "Did you ever meet my dad?"

Uncle Robbie looked up from his plate, surprise giving way to a nod of acknowledgement. Like he knew this question would come one day. We'd never talked about it, or much of anything serious for that matter. Even planning my own mother's death it was usually never more than music and movies. But now, as he leaned back with a stretch, it was clear something had shifted between us. "Yeah, a few times."

"Not a fan, huh?"

"Look, I'll say this, he convinced Leigh to run off to Jamaica, to spend two years with him. And they made you. So, I guess I can't hate the guy too much."

"But then he ditched Mom. While she was pregnant."

He dug into the basket, pointed a fry at me. "There's that."

I finished off my burger. But there was one more thing I had to ask him, looking him right in the eyes. "Did she really try to kill herself?"

Uncle Robbie winced. His lips moving for a second without sound. "Chloe, who—" He stopped himself, his voice lowering with his gaze. "Glenda."

"Did she?"

Robbie's eyes glistened, mirroring the lights above our heads. He studied me for a second, then, like deciding I was old enough to hear it, took a deep breath and dove in. "I'm going to be honest, Chloe. That guy beat the crap out of her. All the time. You know how she loved to paint? He told her she wasn't any good, said she was wasting her time. Sound familiar? He controlled her, Chloe. He beat her while she was pregnant with you. Then he shot himself and it was all over."

He took a look around, his voice lower now, "She should have been happy, she deserved that. But he was...it was...well, then she came home to her own father who didn't want her."

"Or me."

"Yeah."

"So, what happened? Did she—"

He shook his head, closing it off. "It doesn't matter, Chloe. She loved you so much. She loved you more than she loved herself. That's what matters." He went to say something else but stopped.

"What?"

"Well, it's just that, for a while your mother was so worried about how, that all the men in your life—in her life—were, less than ideal. She wanted me to be around, to be like a role model or something. Guess I failed there."

When we got back to the house, Robbie parked where Andrew's car had been, the empty spot a reminder how it was only a matter of time before everything came crashing down. He killed the engine and we sat staring at the door. Collecting our breaths.

Robbie turned to me. "Chloe, I'm just going to say something, okay?" He took another deep breath, lips parting and closing, fighting with how to say whatever he had to say. "I don't know what exactly is going on. People are acting strange. But, I..." He paused again, arranging his words. "I'm just going to tell you. Glenda and I might not make it through this time. I don't know, part of me just wants..." He looked at his hands, as though the answer had sifted through his fingers. I turned to face him, silently urging him to finish.

"If there's anything you need from me," he said finally. "I'll do it, okay. I don't always show it; I don't know...but, I love you, Chloe, okay? So anything. Anything at all."

I nodded, closed my eyes, and held back tears as we sat there in his car with that between us. With Mom between us.

"Okay," he said to himself and opened the door.

"Hey," I said, before he could get out, before we went in the house and he crawled into his shell again. He turned back with tired eyes, lines in his face, his thin hair retreating back. I gave him the best smile I had.

"You're a pretty decent role model."

<h1 style="text-align:center">Chapter 32</h1>

It was time to leave. And it wasn't much trouble, not with Glenda nestled in her nightly Ambien coma, or Robbie in the den, passed out on the couch under the glow of the television. I drifted down the steps, out the kitchen door, and down the driveway.

The talk about Mom sat heavy on my shoulders, bearing down with Andrew and Glenda and my deadbeat dad. But even with all of that, it was Dylan who had me crazy. I couldn't sit up there in my room, wondering. I needed to walk, to see about things for myself. I had to see him face to face and hear what he had to say. What he had planned. Because the image of him on that dock at Spence's house was stamped into my memory. I needed a new lasting impression.

I hit Main Street, towards the café. The terrace was busy with people drinking and laughing the way only drunk people did. I had no money for an Uber so I was going to have to hitch. I slowed my steps, scanning potential targets for a ride.

It came easy.

I've been warned so many times about the dangers of hitchhiking and strangers. But what was there to fear anymore? Chances were, anyone I found wouldn't be nearly as dangerous as Andrew was, and look how things turned out for him.

My ride turned out to be a harmless, pudgy slob who liked to scream drunkenly over death metal and sneak peeks at my legs. Four miles later I stepped out on the side of the road and thanked him for the ride. Considering his car smelled like pork rinds and dank weed, the fresh air was like a gift on my face.

I watched the taillights float away until all was quiet. Then I cut over a street, where most of the houses looked the same. My legs were still vibrating from the blast of music on the seats. I checked my phone, 11:13.

I hiked to the Willow Creek subdivision without much of a plan. Thinking of Dylan had me catching my breath. Chris and I had ups and downs but I'd never once felt such a crushing worry like this, even when he hooked up with the dimwits. I'd simply walked away, knowing boys came and went. But Dylan was different.

My brain couldn't handle the thought of him moving on. Of him with some cheery Christian girl at youth group. One that would help his mom bake cookies, who had both parents, siblings, and wore sweaters to hide her breasts.

Out front I stared at his house. Not a single car had passed since I'd entered the neighborhood. A few houses up, a dog barked from the backyard. Crickets. Just an all-American night in Willow Creek.

Dylan's light was on in his room just above the garage. I'd been up there once, just to peek in because Mrs. Kowalski was chaperoning our time, making sure our relationship remained in the boundaries of the Good Book. Another quick survey of the street, and I skulked up to the side of the house.

My heart thumped as I searched for a ladder or anything that could give me a boost, knowing from my time with Glenda that a homeowners' association would frown on such a thing.

I had to improvise. I found a mountain bike and rolled it to the side of the garage, a dog yapping somewhere down the street. I leaned the bike against the house. I climbed up, testing the seat with my foot before putting all my weight on it. Even on the seat, I was more than a foot short, but I could reach the gutter.

I was up to a hundred and five pounds, last I checked, so I wasn't sure what exactly was going to happen. The downspout creaked but held. On my toes, I tried to swing my way up onto the roof.

To anyone out for a late-night stroll, I could only guess how it looked, some stalker chick determined to catapult herself up on the garage of the Kowalski's place. Finally, I managed to get one foot up on the gutter, my head facing pavement and my knee rubbing raw against the shingles, I swung and clawed my way onto the roof. I felt like a beast.

Now what? Before, it had all been about getting to the house. Sneaking out. Finding a ride. Hiking to Dylan's street. But on the roof, I was left with only moonlit improvisation.

I wiped myself off and tapped on the window. I actually considered my appearance. I fixed my hair, smoothing it back behind my ears, then adjusted my top. My knee was scraped up pretty bad, but all was forgotten when a figure came clomping over to the window.

Dylan's eyes bugged when he saw me. He looked over his shoulder then back to open the window (unlocked, I noted). No smile or even relief. "Chloe, what? What are you doing?" He basically hissed at me.

"I needed to see you. You won't answer the phone. You didn't even come to school today." My voice came out high, like a little girl. Desperation leaked from my nostrils, permeated the pores of my skin. He was driving me to the brink with that blank stare, the way he could end things like this.

Behind him lay his phone, glowing with text messages he refused to answer. Like a punch to the gut. Maybe he was chatting with someone, seeing someone else already. I reached out. "Are you breaking up with me?"

His gaze fell to my scuffed-up knee. My tears came without warning, leaking freely, plopping on my leg like a surprise rain shower.

Dylan let out a big sigh. "Chloe. No. I mean, I just need some time to think."

My brain couldn't take anymore. "What did I do?" I reached for him again, gripping his forearm, pressing my nails into the skin, trying to take a piece of him with me. He took my hand and stepped out to the roof, like a cat being coaxed from beneath a car. I thought he might sit beside me, take me in his arms and we might work on fixing things. Instead he sat a body width away and turned to me, but not fully.

We sat that way for a while. When he spoke, it was evenly, carefully. "Chloe. What you said at the lake, to Vee, when you didn't know I was there..."

"Oh come on, Dylan." I turned to the neighborhood, rolled out like a prop. Like we were sitting on a balcony with a night scene drawn out before us. All over again I had to convince him that I didn't do it, or, I had to do it. But I couldn't bring myself to tell him everything.

"I was telling her a story," I said, leaning towards him. "A story. A silly, stupid, scary camping story like we used to tell at camp."

He let that sit between us for a while. "It sounded more like...like a confession."

The shingles were gritty, rough beneath my hands when I pressed my palms to them. It was all I could do to keep my arms from wobbling. My lungs from collapsing in fear. I felt his head turn to me again and when I thought it was safe, I wiped my eyes to avoid breaking down altogether.

"What happened, Chloe? What happened with Andrew?"

I sniffled. "Nothing."

"So, if I went to the police about it, they wouldn't find a body in Holcomb Pond?"

I shook my head. Dylan continued asking questions, bearing down on me. The street was so quiet, the night so wide and endless above our heads. I thought I could say it and it would float up there into infinity. I could tell him and still keep it a secret. I could have him, and the rest of it would go away.

"I went in the carriage house. I don't know why. But I was going to do *something*." I shook my head. "Something stupid. I don't know, spit on his toothbrush or something dumb. But then he came home and he just..."

"Just what?"

"He forced me, Dylan," I said, my voice like a rusty hinge. The tears washing everything out. I took Dylan's hand because I couldn't go back to the memory without him.

He squeezed my hand. "What do you mean?"

Why did he have to know so bad? It strangled me. I could hardly say his name. "Dylan." A whisper like a hot coal in my throat. The stars blurred and stretched as I shook my head, trying to make him see how hard this was for me. "Please."

I lost his grip. He sat straight up, rigid. A cold wall that deflected my pain. Colder still when he looked at me flat. "I did some searching, Chloe. Andrew Lankford's been reported missing."

Waves of panic shot from my limbs. I pulled my knees up and set my head between them.

"Chloe, I mean, did you...?"

I bit my bottom lip. Mom was dead and living with Glenda was hell. Where else was there to go? My grandparents hated even the *idea* of me. How could I ask Vee to let me live there? Or go to a home? *A home.* I'd been down the road of possibilities so many times it was like I'd already lived every scenario. Setting out on my own with a waitressing job, living in a trailer like my mother had for a while. Heading west. Go north or south or wherever. To an island.

Or I could spit it out. Let it happen. Let it all end. I could finally answer all the questions raining down on me. *What happened, Chloe? Did you really kill him? Where is Andrew?*

I couldn't take it anymore. I set my head up, wiping my nose. "What would you have done, Dylan?" I said, through a thick glob of tears. "In your perfect little world, what is the *right* thing to do when someone overpowers you and takes what they want?"

His eyes were wide now, darting back to his bedroom window. "You go to the police."

"You do, huh?" I nodded, a blast of heat rising in my chest, fighting through my voice. "And that's it," I shrugged. "You go to the police and everyone in this town talks about what a slut you are or what really happened. Your own *boyfriend* doesn't believe you. People read about it like it's entertainment, a trial where every day you have to relive it over and over again. Then the sorry loser sister takes his side, probably because she's more whacked in the head than he was. And there's nowhere to go anyway because your mom is dead. Do you understand? Dead!"

He held up his hands, tossing another glance to the window. "Chloe, please, my parents."

I couldn't believe him. "Right, parents. The neighbors." I spat the words, flinging my arms around. "This, all of it. This perfect life. And then I come along... all I wanted was for us to be together."

He straightened himself out, his chest swelling with his breath. He seemed to be working something out in his head. He spread his arms out, palms up. "Chloe, you can't run from this."

I stared at him through the steam in my eyes. The same boy who'd been too nervous to ask me out. Who had come to my house to pick me up with all of his stand-up manners. Now I thought he might restrain me. Have me arrested.

This was a mistake, coming here. I got to my feet. Dylan watched me like I was a fugitive. I got to the edge and turned back to him. "This is when I need you the most."

His head turned and he stared me right in the eye. "Did you kill him?"

It was the third time he'd asked. I guess he really wanted to know. More than anything else. I looked up to the stars, then down to a weak little boy.

"What do you think?"

His mouth parted. I crouched, finding my way down, hearing his shoes scraping the shingles as I lowered myself from the gutter. I found the bike seat but misjudged my footing and slipped. Dylan reached out for me but it was too late, I hit the ground and my ankle popped. I yelped as a blast of pain shot up my calf, I rolled onto my back, squeezing my eyes and writhing in pain.

"Chloe."

The porch lights snapped on. I got to my feet, limping off as Mrs. Kowalski stepped out on the front porch. The last thing I saw was Dylan, still up on the roof, against the glow of his window.

Chapter 33

It was 12:15 and I was going home, to Dorchester, where the quickest route was through school. I hobbled along East Ridge, an explosion of pain with each step as I limped down the strip, looking to cut over to Dunham. I didn't have the capacity to hitch, or hardly breathe for that matter.

Mainly drunks on the road this late, so there was some honking and whistles, but I kept my head down and limped ahead. I didn't wipe the tears, didn't stop to examine my ankle throbbing for attention. I set one foot in front of the next, while my mind raced ahead. Somehow I'd made it worse with Dylan. How he'd all but blamed me for everything. How Mrs. Kowalski had probably called the police. Suddenly school and Glenda, even Andrew's Forerunner, mattered less and less in comparison to how badly it hurt that Dylan refused to believe me.

I rubbed my arms, banged them against my sides, fighting the urge to jump out into the street and let the next truck take care of everything. Maybe then I'd see Mom, alive and well in a frosting of clouds. She'd take me in her arms and tell me the real story of what had happened. I could ask her why she tried to take her own life when mine was only beginning.

I set off to the side streets, my ankle screaming, hindering my steps. A few wrong turns before I came out on the wooded backend of the Dunham campus, away from the dorm buildings, where the lights along the path cast a glow against the stone and brick buildings, the windows shiny and black, save for the auxiliary lights in the stairwells of the newer buildings.

Mom sure thought she'd rescued my future bringing me here. I spat on the ground. What future? A cell? I prowled along the shadows, around the edges of the fine institution, realizing this visit was hardly different than any other. Truth be told, I'd always known I didn't belong at Dunham Episcopal.

I curled along the path, sinking deeper into the woods where spring had thickened into summer. The critters whirred and chirped in the darkness pulsing at my sides. Down the hill, the blanket of trees thinned out, and I emerged at the lacrosse fields where Chris and I used to go to be alone. Where I'd lost my virginity under a starry sky a year ago.

I turned my head to that same, indifferent sky, thinking how I'd believed that night was magical, my metamorphosis, celestial even. Now, I turned away, about to retch. It never dawned on me it was one of the oldest, clumsiest activities of mankind. Something animals did between napping and licking themselves.

Any magic from the night was gone, replaced by the horror of Andrew. The way he'd smothered and absorbed me. How I couldn't get his smell from my nose. How his hands had crushed my wrist, then my throat, until I thought it would snap.

My phone buzzed as I arrived at Dorchester Street.

Please understand.

I opened the door and went for the fridge as though I'd never moved away. I didn't want to turn the lights on, so I used the fridge light and dampened a paper towel under the sink faucet to clean up my knee. My ankle needed ice.

You can get through this.

With the water still running, I leaned over, letting it wash over my face, taking down greedy gulps until I nearly choked. I wiped my hair back. More messages from poor Dylan, fighting hard with his morals.

When I shut the fridge the house went dark, but I knew my way around darkness. I hobbled to Mom's room where I fell into the closet, my breathing still heavy from the hike to the house. I found Mom's phone charger in the box from school. There was no point in responding to Dylan, little good it would do. There was nothing to do but wait. To wait for them to come.

I watched my favorite video. The one where I'm holding the phone and Mom is painting my nails. My muffled giggles kept brushing against the speaker because she kept tickling my feet. She told me to hold still only to tickle me again. My knees knocked together, shaking the video on the screen because I kept cracking up. In the background the news was on, a hurricane was smashing into the Bahamas.

I paused the video just as Mom peeked around my knees. Her hair to one side, her eyes wide and gorgeous with her smile. For a while I only stared at her lovely face. Before cancer and illness and death dinners. Or maybe the cancer was in there, dormant and hidden, waiting to strike. Finally, I pressed play again.

"Are you recording me?"

"Uh huh."

"Oh," she said, all dramatic-like, flicking her hair back. "Welcome to Leigh's Spa and Salon." She held my foot up. "Today we will be working on this, uh, atrocity."

"Hey."

She smelled my foot and fake gagged, looked back to the camera. "Oh, I mean, this um, lovely foot. I will be applying a file here to these nails," she said, her hand waving over my foot, "which, as you can clearly see have been neglected for some time. After a soak, a rinse, we will apply a cuticle cream and finally a base coat..."

"A what?"

My laughter came so easy. It belonged to a girl without pain or loss. I stopped and started the video again. I watched it a second time, pausing again where Mom peeked out. I stared at her eyes, bawling uncontrollably. Then I continued to torture myself.

"The base coat, my love. It will take some work, but it is Sunday and with you being my only customer, well, I do think with time and effort we can get this to resemble a foot once again. Shall we try?"

The video ended and my memory took over. Mom scrubbed my

feet that day, gave me the cucumber eye treatment and a hot towel wrap. It was my reward for making Dean's List. She used to do that, come up with little pamper days, as we called them, anytime I managed straight A's or aced a test. Now I was Cum Laude and my feet looked like roadkill.

I scrolled through pictures after that, moving to the void where Mom's bed once lay. Where we'd snuggled and talked about the future. Mom stroking my hair until I fell asleep or got annoyed and went to my own bed.

Then I was back in the closet, not sleeping but completely comfortable with Mom's sweatshirt for a pillow, her scent in my nose and the fresh image of her face in my mind. The rest of my world was on fire, but I was safely tucked away in a cocoon.

MY STOMACH JOSTLED me awake and my ankle took over from there. The sun crashed into the blinds. Mr. Franklin was up and at it next door, singing Broadway tunes to the squirrels in his garden. I slid over to the window and peeked out, watching for a while as he tended to his pots and compost. I remembered how I used to climb up into the tree that straddled our yards, laughing as he'd sing and hum like he was onstage. I used to think it was the strangest thing I'd ever seen. Now, in the early morning sun, all was still, and I found comfort in his voice.

He moved a bit slower, his face a little more wilted, but he still had it. Even as it had only been months since I'd been gone. Now, hearing him in the morning took me back to another time. His humming made me feel safe.

I found a granola bar in Mom's box and washed it down with water from the faucet. It made for an okay breakfast. My ankle was stiff and hot. Puffy. I hobbled around, found my phone, and when I turned it on, the texts and voicemails came dinging and chiming in. Oh, and I was late for school, like that mattered.

The day was bright and clean, like life was taking a slow blink of the eye so I could catch up, enjoy a few last moments of solitude. The birds outside, the cars drifting by the street. Chunks of granola hit the floor. A car slid to a stop outside.

Running wasn't an option, not with my ankle. And I'm not sure I would have anyway. I didn't know how it would play out, but I wasn't stupid, dots had been connected, T's crossed. All of my mistakes had backed me into a corner. The phone, the hat, the Forerunner, the rooftop confession.

Now Dylan's texts made sense. He'd done the right thing, made amends for the door he'd kicked in. Maybe the authorities were scraping together a team to drag the small pond. They'd I.D. the body, considering Andrew's wallet was in his back pocket. Meanwhile, Detectives Martin and Sarah would have no trouble putting together a case. They'd take it to Glenda and everything would bust at the seams. Yes, life had blinked. Now it was staring me in the face.

As I walked out of Mom's room, I didn't fear what was coming for me, only that the whole school would know what happened in the carriage house. In the bedroom. I hated that everyone would hear secondhand all the sordid details of that night. Whatever Andrew had taken from me that awful day, the authorities would take all over again. It was enough to make me want to die. It made me consider other options. Options my mother once considered.

I stopped before the kitchen. My eyes swept the house, stopping at the kitchen counter. There were cleaning chemicals, a dull knife. I remembered seeing a belt in the closet. Quite a number of other ways to escape what was on its way for me. I slid down the wall to the floor with Mom's picture. I broke the frame and held a shard of glass between two fingers.

A car door thunked, followed by another one. I pulled myself to the window and watched. No SWAT teams or police dogs, no platoons hauling up a battering ram. Detective Sarah and Uncle Robbie, approaching slowly. The unrelenting sunshine.

The detective's head swept from one side of the house to the next. I wondered what in her training had prepared her for this moment. A moment that had crushed Uncle Robbie. His shoulders drooped, his gait wobbly. Even in the trenches with Glenda he'd never looked so rough.

Uncle Robbie rattled his keys. But the door was unlocked and swung open, brushing the floor with a familiar sweep. Detective Sarah removed her glasses and openly flinched when she saw me. Her eyes widened and instinctively she started for the gun at her hip but stopped upon recognition. Her mouth opened then shut, her shoulders dropped with a sigh.

Robbie let out a cry, brushing past her, falling to my side, his shoes squeaking on the puddle of melted ice. His voice pinched between relief and panic. "Chloe. Please, Chloe."

He pulled me to him with such force Mom's broken picture fell from my lap. His whole body shuddered as the shards of glass slid like ice across the floor. He convulsed into agony as he squeezed me so tight I lost my breath. When he released me his face was slathered in tears.

In the midst of it all, Detective Sarah eyed the kitchen. Her gaze swept the archway between the two bedrooms. She surveyed the small house quickly and expertly, before her face contorted with confusion. At last she appraised the living room, but made no immediate gesture to arrest me.

Robbie was hysterical. "Oh Chloe, what happened? What did he do to you?"

Detective Sarah holstered her gun and shook her head. She wiped her eyes and squeezed the bridge of her nose. "Mr. Vanderbrooke, please. I'm...please...call your attorney."

Robbie didn't hear, not through his sobs, tears spilling from his eyes, sliding down on the floor beside me, as he made no effort to wipe his face. I turned away, to Detective Sarah.

"I guess you're here for me?"

Her head tilted. Her mouth parted. She nodded, then, turning around, "Is there anyone else in the house?"

I gestured to the shattered picture frame. Sarah closed her eyes. Slowly. When they opened again they were weary, beaten, like she'd lost a fight in her head. "It's okay, now Chloe. But Chloe, I have to..." She sighed again. "I'm going to have to transport you downtown."

Uncle Robbie wiped his face again. "Oh no. No, no, no, no. Oh, Chloe."

He just kept saying it. Over and over again.

Chapter 34

I pieced together the rest of the day. Robbie carrying me out to the car. The ride to the police station. How no one said too much. Then, I lost gaps of time and was only somewhat aware of what was happening and what it meant. I caught some attorney talk, Sarah speaking to me in soft tones. Uncle Robbie nearly being detained at my booking. Radios squawking when officers passed.

My ankle was a balloon. Blue and black but sprained, not broken. They had it taped and Sarah never left us, at some point stroking my hair while she tried to help Robbie. I was glad it was her and not Martin. She told an officer something about hating her job that day. It was hard to tell if I was a victim or a suspect. If I was a patient or maybe somewhere in the middle of it all.

Regardless, the next day I found myself on a cold chair in an interrogation room. Uncle Robbie looked terrible. I told him I'd answer any questions. All of it. Same for the detectives. I had nothing to hide anymore, fire away. Still, Detective Sarah advised us to wait. Everything moved at lightning speed yet crawled at the same time.

I regained focus, slowly. The fog cleared and my ankle stiffened, and I realized there would be no more hiding. Uncle Robbie was still a mess as he explained how Glenda had lost her mind, gone ballistic on police officers and had to be restrained. She'd finally got that tasing.

But I found little consolation in Glenda's breakdown. I thought about Dylan. How he'd turned on me. I wondered if he'd gone straight inside and alerted the police. Or maybe it was Mrs. Kowalski, saying *I told you about that girl*, looking at Dylan's dad, both of them knowing their boy had brushed wings with Satan herself. Together, they made the call, reading scripture afterwards to rinse the residue of sin from his hands. Something like that anyway.

My attorney arrived and wasted no time. Mr. Lawrence Wainwright was a salt and pepper type who looked like he taught Civics at Dunham. I liked him okay, even if it was obvious he was in over his head. But who was I to talk?

"Here's our problem," he said, talking more to Robbie than me. So far he'd avoided looking directly at me, like I was easier to defend if things didn't get personal. Fair enough, he was a big guy who took up the whole chair and didn't mince words.

He shifted to get his foot up on his knee. "Self-defense may hold up, but we have the issue of the body in the pond. Not exactly something we can brush under the rug. And those pictures," he said, eventually peeking over to me. "They will definitely try to make this a consensual thing."

Robbie shot out of his seat. "She's sixteen!"

"Certainly," Lawrence said, throwing his hands up. "Hey, I'm just telling you what we're up against."

Robbie wasn't going to make it. Not like this. Not when he was tugging on his already thinning hair, swiping at his face. Like I'd told Detective Sarah, it was okay, I'd just tell them I was guilty. But Robbie was bent on getting me out of there right that second. Time stood still. We sat in the freezing cold room for hours and hours while I told them everything. And it took forever because Lawrence kept interrupting, making me go back and repeat what I'd already said twice.

Later, Robbie finally sat down, smacking the table. "Look, I don't give a damn about the body. Andrew was scum. The man raped her. Raped a sixteen-year-old girl. He put a knife to her neck! How is this even a case?"

Wainwright nodded. "Agreed. I'm just telling you how this works. We have some other things going on, too. The press has a hold of this story. Local, for now, but I have a feeling it's too sensational to keep that way."

Robbie, up and pacing again, "You've got to be kidding me."

Sensational. I guess Wainwright owed me one for his big break. And he warmed up to me in that regard, talking to me, asking me questions in that southern gentleman way of his, at least when I wasn't zoning out. Otherwise he and Robbie discussed evidence, prosecution, mandatory waivers—while I only thought about Dylan. How he'd looked that night on his roof, those things he'd said to me.

Mr. Wainwright plodded on. "I'll try to get a gag order, but it's going to be nearly impossible for this not to go national."

For a while we all sat there, to the point I could've drawn by memory the pattern of the carpet in that closet of a room. I studied the grooves and scratches in table, the worn chairs, even the purplish gleam of the camera lens sitting in the corner, watching us at all times.

Wainwright wiggled a loafer, waved his hand to me. "Look, we have a young white girl—blonde, pretty, extremely intelligent, you name it. That right there gets the media all hot and bothered, so, things could go either way. I can get sympathy, with her mother's death and all...but the body in the pond." He paused to click his teeth, he did it all the time and it annoyed me to no end. "It's a problem."

Another pause, this one for dramatic effect. He smacked his leg with a grunt. "So, let's focus first on the transfer hearing..."

I spaced out as he went on about competence, maturity, social and emotional capacity, cognitive judgment and reverse waivers and so on. What he meant was that I could be charged with murder. As an adult. And here I'd been worried about exams.

"Judge Wesley is fair enough, but honestly your fate rests in Doctor Shelling's hands, so, we'll see. We could be okay, should be, I just want to keep a level head, Robbie."

Wainwright worked something out, though. The next day, inexplicably, I was transferred to Cleary Juvenile Correction Center —a place best defined as the antithesis of Dunham Episcopal School. Oaks and Ivy traded for kudzu and razor wire, nothing but brown and yellow fields of dry grass and dust. In the haze sat an ugly brick sprawl of a building, complete with guards and watchtowers, bars on the windows.

Mostly black and brown girls on the inside. But it wasn't quite the dumpster dive you always see on TV. I mean, it was no five-star hotel or anything, and most of the kids I came across were hollowed out, empty sockets where eyes had been and straight lines where smiles had been long deserted. But I was isolated. I guess privilege and sensationalism kept me safely tucked out of harm's way.

What I worried about most were the thoughts in my head.

Chapter 35

I spent two days in a concrete room, staring at a bench that was bolted to the floor. A steel toilet. The urine-yellow paint of the cinderblock. Day and night strung together like one long florescent dream. My thoughts soared and plummeted, my memories took me to the hospital. The day Mom died.

Her final moments were spent in a beige tomb—a room only hours away from being cleaned and refilled. It smelled of death and flowers, with a priest lingering outside the door, ready to jump me with scripture the first chance he could get.

Mom and I spent all night cuddling together as people came and went, peeking in, their voices low with prayers. When we were alone, I hugged her so tight I thought I might be able to squeeze her back to life. And I thought maybe I had when she started suddenly and gasped.

"Do you hear that, sweetie? Can you hear it?"

I nodded. "Yes, Mom. I hear it."

She relaxed, her head settling back to her pillow. With a crease of her lips she was gone, and my dim glimmer of hope expired—sealed away under closed eyes, even as her gentle smile remained on her lips.

I'll never know what she heard. But I'm sure it was beautiful.

DOCTOR NANCY SHELLING was a tiny woman with kind hazel eyes and a mouth so small it looked incapable of more than a whisper. But I was wrong, she was quite the spitfire. Then again, what did I expect, this was prison. Lawrence (he told me to call him Lawrence), said she was fair. How fair was crucial, because whatever she got out of this little interview would stick.

We dove into the muck. The biggest difference between her and the other counselors, therapists, and doctors I'd seen before was how the shackles were off (so to speak). No more filters or games. We were past any need to spar or dance around the issues, it was all out there on the cheap industrial table between us. Mom. Andrew. Dunham. Glenda. Rape. Murder. Body ditching. All tagged and ready for sorting like a bargain bin yard sale.

So how messed up was I, anyway? Honestly, it was refreshing, almost, sitting in a drab, poorly lit room with nothing but the truth.

Robbie was having issues, though. He'd taken a leave of absence from work and after the split with Glenda he'd moved out of a house he loved like a child. He was living at Dorchester—draining his savings to pay for my lawyer and his impending separation. Yeah, it dawned on me I'd ruined his life, but he waved off my apologies like they were pesky gnats, ready to dump whatever was left of the shrinking Vanderbrooke legacy into this fight.

Was it self-defense? Lawrence said we weren't there yet. He spoke of indictments, bail, comparable cases, while Robbie spent his visits pacing, like there was an easier solution to all of this and he was determined to find it. Coffee and crying, it was pretty much his routine these days.

In truth, I was a little tired of all my uncle's wailing. Some days it was all he did, and I found myself wishing he'd leave so I could get back to my cell. I loved him more than anything, but we had to get past the wishing, the would've/could'ves. All the sobbing and moaning wasn't much help.

We had to face it.

Chapter 36

"Our biggest problem is the body, Chloe."

Oh how Lawrence loved to talk about Andrew's dead body. As though I needed to be reminded of why I was there. I could tell he was getting frustrated with what he perceived as a lack of interest from my end. But as I tried to explain, I'd done so much thinking about all of it already. I was over it.

He shed his jacket and his pit stains were righteous. "I know we have self-defense here. It's awful, what you've been through. I really don't think any jury or judge could convict. But," he sighed here, and I almost got the feeling he was grandstanding solely for me and Robbie's benefit. "The fact that you planned it out. Took the body to the pond, wrapped it up and..."

Robbie peeked at me sideways whenever Andrew's body came up, just like he flinched when words like *corpse* or *mutilation* were brought into play. I could tell it unnerved him. My capacity, for lack of a better term. That said, I never mentioned how I'd already known I was capable of it before the act. I mean, yeah, it was self-defense, but also with a Papa Vanderbrooke dash of rage and vengeance—a combination that had been stirring around in me all along. But no one ever asked me about that.

And I was tired of sitting there listening to Lawrence's orating while struggling to look like I cared the tiniest bit.

"They might try all sorts of things," he said, prattling on, "illegal disposal, obstruction, theft, you name it."

"Theft?" I objected. "Hey, I put the wallet back."

Lawrence shot me a stern look. I gave it back to him.

"Chloe," he said, eyeing the door, kneeling down in front of me, trying to force feed me the dire urgency of the situation. "This, this isn't a joke, honey. Your life is at stake here."

His shaky jowls reminded me of an evangelical preacher, the ones on TV who hit you with the red-faced shouting when you're still groggy on a Sunday morning. The ones so over the top you think it has to be a joke.

I crossed my arms. "So his body, I'm guessing it was in rough shape when they pulled it out?"

Lawrence looked to my uncle, exasperated, but Robbie wasn't taking calls. He'd retreated into himself. "Well, I haven't seen the body, but I'm sure the prosecution could bring it up."

I crossed my arms. "Good."

Lawrence stood tall, knees popping and sighing. "No Chloe, not good. You need to keep your mouth shut in the courtroom. You need to stare at the floor. And you need to keep that eff-you glare outta your eyes."

I turned to Robbie, cut a smile at Lawrence. I didn't know he had it in him, the old gruff. He wiped his forehead, composed himself. And while I took pride in the fact I could get a trial lawyer so worked up, it didn't exactly speak volumes to his temperament.

We took five, regrouped. Later, Lawrence tried again. "I can't say for sure what's going to happen. In a perfect world, a man who would do something like that would go to jail where he wouldn't be able to hurt anyone else."

I unfolded my arms, grabbed the seat of my chair on both sides and stared down the big bad lawyer. "Well in that case, I'd say justice went above and beyond. Because he didn't belong in jail, he belonged—"

Robbie leaped up and threw his chair. "Dammit Chloe, you have to show remorse for this to work. Okay? You can't go in there and smirk at the judge. You can't dare them to charge you with murder. Do you want to spend five or ten, twenty years here? In prison?"

Lawrence the lawyer stood still and silent. A guard peeked in to see what the fuss was all about. Jolted by my uncle's sudden anger, I stared straight ahead, stung by the slap of his words on my face. Robbie set his palms against the wall, shaking his head. In the corner of my eyes I could still see his chest heaving and the tears flooding. I knew he blamed himself for what had happened to me under his roof. That he'd somehow failed his sister. But this wasn't his fault.

I turned my head slowly to him, speaking softly but clearly. "I'm not sorry he's dead. Okay? I'm not. The knife, the one I...used? He brought it into the room. *He* put it to my neck and told me he would kill me. He was *going* to kill me. So I don't care what the judge or prosecutor or what *Glenda* has to say about it, he's dead for that reason alone."

The room struggled to hold our anger. Lawrence, looking like he could use some Pepto-Bismol, nodded, slicking back his hair. "Okay, let's just, let's take a break, okay?"

"Fine."

Isolation. The days strung together. When I did get outside I spent the time staring out at the nothingness surrounding the prison. If I looked out there long enough the chain link and razor wire meshed and blended in with the backdrop of woods and I imagined it was summer camp. The cover of the trees was a natural preserve and not a thin strip of cushion from the expressway. The guard towers were observation decks and the blue sky stretched for miles without end. To the sun, it made no difference, being out there or in here.

Time embraced me. It threw me along like a feather in the breeze, tickling my senses with its precious seconds and minutes. I thought a lot about Dylan, both in memory and fantasy. When Robbie said he'd called several times, asking how it was going, what he could do to help, a flush of warmth filled my chest. I knew I could forgive him for going to the police. In a way, I already had.

I read the newspaper. It left my fingertips smudged like they'd been when I was booked. Dunham Episcopal graduation wasn't far off—two weeks away. I pictured Spence and Dylan in their gowns, owning the day. The baseball team made it to the state playoffs, where Spence managed a homerun in a close loss. I thought about his bet with Dylan, the night with his bat at the party. I cherished the night at the lake house. But I couldn't dwell on that, not now, not in here. It might kill me.

Yet still, my thoughts clung to Dylan. When I pictured him with a new girlfriend, holding hands or kissing in the truck, looking at her the way he used to look at me, I wanted to slam my head into the cinderblocks. Instead, I stayed in my memories. I relived them in my cell.

Lawrence had been right. My case was getting attention. A few details had surfaced about the gruesome murder on Madison Street. The press had withheld my name but not Robbie and Glenda's, so even those dimwits Stacey and Olivia would have figured it out by now.

I thought of Mom at the lake. Healthy and radiant, her effortless strokes in the water. Hard as I tried, I could never keep up, never manage to match her long strides. I remembered her at school, how during my freshman year I ran into the Admin building crying, begging for her to let me go back to a normal school, screaming about the dress code and strict rules. She'd stood her ground. It was exactly what I needed. I'd been so mad at her, told her I hated her, told her I never wanted to see her again.

Our brief stop at her funeral reception. More Mom stories. How nearly everyone from school had shown up. From cafeteria workers to board members. It was a beautiful thing, seeing Juan and the facilities guys rubbing elbows with all those suits, and now I wished I could have allowed myself to enjoy it.

At one point I'd snuck out back for a while, in search of fresh air and hoping someone would share a flask. They didn't. Instead we shot the breeze. They all had stories about Mom, from funny little anecdotes to heart-wrenching tales of courage that had me blinking back tears and biting my lip.

After a while I had to get back, but before I left, I turned to Juan, one of the maintenance guys who had nodded his condolences. *"Ella está en el cielo?"*

He closed his eyes and smiled. *"Sin duda."*

Those memories kept me afloat. And then, two days later, the night before my bail hearing, we huddled up in our little war room.

Lawrence was confident. "So how do you think you did?" he asked. Remarkably, Mom's former boss, Mr. Suddith, worked some channels so I could take my final exams from Cleary. Honestly, I'll never know how he pulled it off.

I shrugged. "Okay, I suppose."

Never one to divulge, he crossed his legs and suppressed a smile. "Sure you did."

Robbie had at least shaved, but there was no fixing the bags beneath his downtrodden eyes. He needed to sleep for a week, between his eyes and his gaunt cheeks he looked sixty. But he was determined. That good old Vanderbrooke stubbornness, I guess.

Holding back tears, he set a hand on my shoulder. "I went to the house the other day, to get some things. Your mother's phone, like you wanted."

"Thank you," I whispered.

"Glenda wants to put the house up for sale," he waved his hands, "the Madison Street house." He rolled his hands. "After all of this is over."

"I'm sure it will fly off the market."

He grimaced, and I thought about him fussing over a piece of trim, painting, all his painstaking work. Now it was known as the Madison Massacre House.

"I'm sorry."

He shook his head. "No, it's fine. I just want to... I just want out."

We sat there for a moment. Lawrence went through some notes. Robbie sat up. "Chloe. There's other stuff. Glenda. She's flipped out, telling the prosecution that," he shook his head, "that Andrew was trying to work things out with Renee." He shrugged. "And you couldn't handle it."

I looked to Lawrence, who was peering over his glasses. "Well *that's* bull—"

Robbie held up his hands. "I know," he said. "And we," he turned to Lawrence, "we don't think it will be an issue. It's obvious she's delusional. Besides, the mattress is evidence alone he entered your room to begin with. I'm only telling you now in case it comes up in court."

"So will Glenda be there?"

Robbie nodded. "I imagine she will. They can't stop her from coming, and this thing, it's consumed her, Chloe. It's consumed all of us."

We looked at the floor. Our conversations started off okay but then sputtered and broke into long gaps of silence. Quick spurts of words before we returned to our corners to regroup. Finally, Robbie smiled at me, touched my hand. Something was up. Lawrence was into his bag of tricks again.

"Chloe, I have something I want you to see," he said, as though the jury were present.

Wonderful, here we go with the motivational quotes. Instead he pulled out a sheet of paper and handed it to me. A photocopy of a letter. I recognized Mr. Douglas Suddith's letterhead. Addressed to the judge. My breath caught as I read on.

About how *proud he was* of me. How I'd become such a remarkable girl. About how my grades spoke for themselves, how I'd managed to breeze through exams while awaiting trial. The tears were streaming down my cheeks when I got to the part about how I was welcome to return and continue my path to Harvard (he actually wrote Harvard, too). Finally, the praise turned somber as I read on, about how I was the one who'd been failed, that he should have seen the signs of abuse. I was a puddle after that.

"The judge will read this?"

"Already has. I submitted it yesterday. "

"What does it mean?"

He shrugged. "Well, it doesn't hurt."

Robbie rubbed my back. For the first time in a while there was some daylight in my uncle's eyes.

"What?"

"Nothing."

I cocked my head. "No, what is it?"

"It's just, I know how this sounds, but Leigh would be proud."

I fell back in my seat. "Yeah. I'm so sure."

Chapter 37

No one told me Judge Wesley was a woman. Or how I hardly looked like an adult in my baggy jumpsuit. That the courtroom would be packed with friends and enough character witnesses to convince the man upstairs I was a decent human being and not the Murderess of Madison Street.

Miss Shelby—Miss Hannah Shelby of all people—gave a most glowing account of her star pupil. I covered my face when she read two of my dubious accounts to the judge, holding my face tight and wondering if such a thing constituted perjury. She went on about my grades and Cum Laude, how she'd never seen such perseverance from a student who'd been through such stress. Wow, you never really knew, huh?

Doctor Oglesby painted the picture of an emotionally scarred girl. She described how I'd lost the only person I'd ever trusted in this world and was trying to fill a gaping hole left by a father who'd abandoned her and grandparents who'd never offered even the faintest wisp of affection. Ouch.

It was of Nancy Shelling's opinion I'd been so traumatized by Andrew Lankford that in my state of panic, after defending myself in my own bed—*objection!*—I'd been so disjointed from reality I could not be held responsible for tossing his mangled body in the pond. Short, sweet, and pretty damn accurate, Nancy. Well done.

Detective Sarah continued with this narrative. How she'd found me at Mom's house, curled in a ball, swollen and bruised, sitting in a puddle of vomit. How I was shaking and mumbling to myself. How I'd sweat through my clothes and wet myself and cut myself with the glass from the picture frame in my hand. She'd never seen such a case in her ten years as a detective. It was, in her professional opinion, quite obvious, my signs of abuse. *Objection!*

It was the second or third objection when all order broke loose. It began with Glenda's gasp. She'd completely lost it and had to be removed from the courtroom, kicking and screaming and pointing at me, making threats. I kept my face straight ahead, thinking how I could live the rest of my life in jail if it meant never having to hear her voice again.

When the smoke cleared there was Robbie. Mom's brother. He'd lost his wife and house, but still had the place on Dorchester and agreed to take full custody and do whatever the court advised in accordance with my bail. My role model had scraped together twenty-five large and hadn't blinked since the beginning. He got up there and let the tears fly. How he'd failed me. How he'd failed his sister. How he should have seen it coming and would've killed the bastard himself. Before I knew it, I was crying.

Then it was over. A day that began with razor wire and hopelessness, ended with freedom when I was released on bail. With restrictions, obviously.

It was a circus. Robbie shielded the cameras that had descended on Dunham's courthouse steps. *The Times. The Reporter, The Gazette, The Washington Post,* and freaking *CNN*. They came for a shot of the little murderess. I never wanted to be famous, but Lawrence had cornered me earlier with a good lecture about how I should look after bail was set. Not that he was taking his own advice. He was yapping it up, soaking up all of this sudden free publicity.

The sun was out and it was summertime hot. Lawrence went on to the press about the proceedings, how he thought there'd be no indictment and the prosecution would scurry off to lick their wounds and offer a plea. Maybe probation. If things went well I'd return to Dunham and things would, might, begin to get back to normal.

For now, I was going home.

<h1 style="text-align:center">Chapter 38</h1>

We pulled down Dorchester, emotions racing like the wind through my hair. But the wind felt fuller, stronger, and I hoped my emotions would catch up. Robbie had cleaned up the yard. He had big plans for Mom's garden. We were going on about anything except what had just happened. I figured one day I'd tell him how grateful I was for everything he'd done, but for now, I just needed him to prattle on about mulching the front yard and pruning the crepe myrtle near the street.

A car sat out front. Spence's Audi. Two figures leaned against it. My heart reminded me where it was in my chest as Robbie slowed down and looked to me. "I uh, I told your friends it would be okay to meet us."

"What?"

I bolted upright. A small terror flashing through my limbs. Spence and Vee breaking apart. Spence with his shades on and smiling. Vee, shielding the sun in her eyes, almost hopping in place. I looked back at Robbie, who shrugged. "Okay?"

I nodded, slowly, feeling the guilt for ignoring my best friend's letters. We pulled to the curb, and I hardly had the door opened when she yanked me out and pulled me in for a tight hug. "Oh, Chloe."

She let go maybe four more *Oh Chloe's* before releasing me. Then she snatched me up all over again. Spence stood to the side, swinging his keys on his finger. Vee pushed me away, still clinging to my hands.

"Why wouldn't you tell me? Or write or something? I mean, damn," she said, wiping her face. "Sorry, Mr. Vanderbrooke."

Robbie shrugged and took to the yard. Vee wiped her eyes, set her hands on my shoulders. "I haven't known what to do. It's all so awful."

"Look, Vee, sorry I didn't—"

"No. Don't apologize, Chloe. Don't you dare."

We sat there for a minute. Long enough for me to guess what they were thinking. *So she really killed that guy, huh?*

Even if I'd wanted to talk about it, I couldn't then. Not legally, emotionally, or even physically force the words from my mouth. They refused to form on my lips, even to my best friend. And in that moment I knew why I'd avoided them. It was right there. Now they all knew. They knew me. They knew about my rage and my secrets. About what had happened. They knew I wasn't normal.

I looked to the street. "I didn't know how to deal with it. I still don't, really."

"Oh, you dealt with it all right," Spence said and Vee smacked him. He jumped back. "What? Too soon?"

But Spence's jokes broke through the tears and seriousness. Besides, Lawrence had mentioned how the Nottaways had made some calls, which couldn't have hurt. I smiled, and Spence hustled over all dramatic-like, coming in for a group hug. "Come here, you."

There we were. Friends from another life. It was almost like nothing had changed, like I'd just returned from camp. That I hadn't gone to jail for murder, and we were merely planning another lake party or getaway to the coast.

Vee kissed my cheek, sweetly, but suspiciously. My horrible little actress was up to something. "So..."

She peeked to the car as we broke from our little huddle. My arms tingled at the sight of another head in the backseat. A breath escaped my mouth.

Vee squealed. "He wanted to see you. But he thinks you never want to see him again."

My eyes widened. "Dylan?"

"He has so much to say to you, but," Vee bit her lip, rubbing my arms. I stared into the safety of those eyes. She brought me in again. "Oh, Chloe. I love you so much."

It took a moment to get myself together. Because I wanted to have a good cry with her, but not now. I had to see what Dylan needed to say. I hugged her once more and nodded. I took a few slow steps towards the car. The wind blew against my face. I felt Robbie watching me, wondering if this was okay, within the realm of a girl out on bail. At the car, I looked back. Spence had Vee in his arms. I gripped the door handle when the other side opened and Dylan emerged.

We stood on either side, looking over the roof of the car. He looked like he had on the day he'd finally asked me to the dance. Cute as I remembered, hoping to please, but frightened, like he thought I might smack him.

So much to say. I mean, I knew it was him. And he'd absolutely crushed me that night on his roof. How he was all I thought about. And those thoughts of happier days—his warmth—got me through so many cold concrete nights. He shook his head.

"Chloe, I'm so...sorry. I just..." he glanced away. I looked down, walking to the other side of the car, tracing my fingers along the windows as he watched me, waiting for my reaction. Maybe my wrath. So I pulled him in and pressed my lips to his and tasted him. I tasted what I thought I'd never hold or touch again. I ran my fingers in his hair, felt the curve of his back and the strength returning to his arms.

Vee squealed and Spence laughed. I'm sure Robbie was squirming.

When we broke apart, he tried to talk. "Look, Chloe, it was me. I—"

I smiled at him, my eyes welling up. "How am I ever going to corrupt you?"

He pulled me in, tighter. "How am I ever going to save you?"

My breath caught and life blinked, slowly, so I could catch up. I couldn't say what my future entailed. A trial. Therapists. Doctors.

Appointments and judges—a lifetime of nightmares. But there, with his warmth in the sun, the smell of the fresh cut grass at our feet and a gentle breeze in my hair, I felt like the callouses might someday begin to heal, my scars fade, and after a while, I would feel again.

Maybe I would see Mom in the clouds. And slowly I could escape that big monster lurking inside of me. Because standing in front of that house I'd shared with Mom, I had a boy in my arms and a few people who cared.

And for a moment, all was right in the world.

LOOKING FOR MORE?

Read on for an exclusive look at Fanning's novel, *Please Don't* (November 2021, Immortal Works).

I find the letter in the mailbox, tucked between a colorful assortment of bills and threats. Its formality stands out; the envelope is thick and textured, stamped with the official town decal. A slightly askew address label in some no-nonsense font bears my home address.

I'm sweaty, my VIRGIL'S LAWN CARE t-shirt sticks to my back as a familiar dread sinks to my stomach. My hands tremble as I fiddle with the edges of the envelope, my heart *thump-thumping* in my ears as I tear it open and face my fate. Four neat little paragraphs from the Woodberry Board of Education, including a time and date for the hearing on my status to determine whether I will be allowed to attend Garner High next year.

Dear Mrs. Reams,

 While no legal action will be taken against Nathanial Reams, the Woodberry School District will recommend that he be expelled from Garner High School.

Right to the point, those guys. I gloss over it impatiently, skipping down the reasons listed. *Truancy...violation of school rules...assault.* Basically, it states I'm an all-around menace.

...For the safety of students and faculty due to actions and behavior listed...

Here it cites page numbers and sections of the student handbook.

This is where I stop reading. The school board is assuming I will be able to rouse my mother from bed, get her dressed and presentable, keep her sober and coherent—or upright enough to convince them she is. The board is assuming a lot.

Inside I find the regular messes. Dirty dishes, a half-eaten pop tart. A spread of saltines and cheese squares on the counter. My feet crunch over the scatter of crumbs on the floor where a trail of cotton balls, the kind from a pill bottle, lead to the trash. Balled up receipts, lipstick, pens, a key ring, jewelry—it looks like someone took a purse and shook it out all over the kitchen.

I clean the mess and start on dinner. While waiting for this letter, I've done a lot of thinking about my options—about breaking a promise and coming forward about what really happened at school. But whenever I'm tempted to do that, I hear two words in my head.

"Please don't..."

The first words Molly Martinez ever said to me.

Her voice cracked into a whisper when she said it. Her glassy red eyes, hiding behind strands of black hair that had fallen over her face, darted towards the door. It wasn't until then, as she eyed her escape, that I realized I'd never paid much attention to Molly.

Please don't *what?* I wanted to say. But I knew what she didn't want me to do or say. It wasn't hard to figure out. Not when she flung her book bag over her shoulder and scrambled off without looking back. When she left me alone with nothing to do but face what I had done.

Our chemistry teacher sat slumped over, groaning and holding his face, droplets of blood dripping to the floor. Later I'd find out his nose was broken in two places. But hey, I'd promised.

Please don't.

So I don't. I never said a thing to anyone. Except Molly. I begged and pleaded with Molly Martinez. I even got her a job cutting grass with me to help her family with the bills. But she never budged, never came forward.

Now I'm expelled.

I call Mom down for dinner. She slips into her seat across from me and curls her lip at the plate of chicken tenders and mac and cheese I've set in front of her. Not exactly black-tie scallops, but I'm working on a budget here.

I roll my eyes, because I'm not in the mood for this, for any of it. "Just eat, Mom."

She wiggles her nose, takes up her fork and starts picking around. The mac and cheese is runny, pooling into the chicken. I had to use water because I forgot to pick up milk. Just looking at it makes me want to throw the plate against the wall.

Mom must be thinking the same thing. She closes her eyes and whispers, "Yuck."

With her plate pushed to the center of the table, she covers her mouth with her napkin. I grip my fork tighter. Usually I can deal with it, but today, after the letter...

Her makeup looks as though it's been swiped on by a three-year-old. It's smeared across her cheeks, her lips, a glop on her eyelashes. Her shoulders sag. She sighs. "You haven't said a word about my hair."

I grab the back of my neck. This woman changed my diapers, wiped my butt, spoon fed me meals so I wouldn't starve. We have home videos, somewhere, if she hasn't destroyed them, of her feeding me when I was a baby. *Open up the hatch, Nat, here comes the carrots.*

I tell myself that person is still in there, knocking around somewhere. But I don't see her at the table. Haven't seen her in a while. I try to move things along.

"Sorry, I'm just tired, from work, cleaning up...whatever happened in the kitchen. Then cooking dinner."

"Nat, you sound like your father."

She has to know it's the worst thing she can say. I look away, tell myself to hold it together. Not to blame her for how my life sucks. Not to ask her how she can sit there and be so selfish.

Instead, I start in on my tenders while she puffs out her cheeks and looks around the room. It's all I can do not to slam my fork down on the table. Like Dad used to do.

Mom is all about Mom these days. She fashions herself a playwright, and when she's not drinking, she's busy clicking away on my laptop—the one Dad bought me a few years ago. At least it keeps her busy. Besides, if you try to argue with her she assumes the role of misunderstood writer, as played by mischievous toddler.

She's getting huffy, and I'm half expecting her to stick her tongue out at me. I set my fork down, gently, and make a point of considering her hair. Peroxide blonde, the hue of toxic sludge, sheared with a nail file or dull scissors. If she's going for the look of woman on the run, she's nailed it. I take a breath and try again. "Mom, your hair really does look nice."

Her eyes light up, animated. She cocks her head to the side, stroking her hack job hair. "Really. It's not too short?"

"No, it goes well with your, um, outfit."

She looks down. "You think?"

Today's theme is festive. Palm trees. She has a dozen or more of these scrubs, and it messes with my head because it reminds me of better times when she really was a nurse and went to work. When everything was, what? Normal?

When Dad took off Mom kept up with her appearance for a while. At least she wasn't gnawing off her hair and swiping on makeup. Months, a year passed, and I guess she thought Dad might be coming back—we both did—so she still wore normal clothes. Then, at some point after that, she said screw it. This is the result.

"Has um, Gary seen it?"

She grins. "Stop it."

Gary-the-Editorial-Guy is an older, early to mid-fifties dude from Mom's writer group. He wears brown polyester suits, the kind found at your local Goodwill. He's a nice enough guy, I guess. And he's hopelessly incapable of hiding his crush on my mom.

Seeing her smile makes me chuckle. I get back to my food. Mom crosses her arms and remains on hunger strike. This week I've only seen her eat yogurt and Fig Newtons. It's what I mean about having a toddler in the house, one who drinks all night and never blows out the candles.

I clean my plate and I tear into Mom's portion. I eat both of our dinners and wonder what we'll do tomorrow night. I get paid this Friday so at least I can pick up toilet paper and stop using fast food napkins. I can't tell you what Mom is using. Maybe she has her own personal stash.

Done sulking, Mom stands and drifts over to the fridge, humming a show tune. She fills a plastic cup with wine and shuffles to the den. I sit at the table, alone, wondering what I could have said differently.

I wanted to talk about my hearing, or what we're going to do about our tax delinquency, which is up to something like twelve-grand, last I checked. I even left the school board letter face up on the counter, its official letterhead screaming out its importance. But again, Mom is all about Mom these days.

I go back and forth between wanting to help her and hating her for not snapping out of it. Between wanting to leave and wanting to stay. I ride the waves of guilt and blame. When I'm at work, I do nothing but worry about her, when I'm home, I just want to leave.

Like Dad did.

Pick up the plates. Rinse off the runny cheese. Go make sure she's okay. Just like last night and the night before that. But tonight, the sink is too full, the counters are too sticky with wine and fig crumbs. It's too much.

Let the flies have their fun, I'm done.

Upstairs, I sprawl out on my bed, ready to indulge in my secret pastime. I pull out my phone and open the browser. There it waits for me. I don't even have to search for it. One swipe and it's there at my fingertips.

One More Makes Four!

It's not a math tutorial, but a parenting blog. One so choked full of product placement it sometimes crashes my phone. The usual onslaught of advertisements bombards me, and I have to close out windows and hunt for any real content, which is bogged down by sponsorships and branding. The side bars feature soaps, shampoos, diapers, clothing, apps, social media links, books, giveaways, contests, and on and on and on and on as far as I can scroll. Eventually, I find what I'm looking for: a picture of the family—Dad's family.

They pose with other bloggers and consultants. Everyone is all smiles, and it's hard to tell what the actual point of any of this is in the first place.

It's a cruel form of self-torture, reading about Kristen—my dad's wife, blogger extraordinaire—and how she feels about "mommyhood", as she calls it. In yesterday's post, she ranted about how hard it is to find decent free educational apps. And wherever there is a heartwarming story about her daughter, rest assured that lurking beneath her dribble is some sort of product placement. She reviews anything and has no problem using her kid, my dad, or the yet-to-be-born child to boost clicks. She's kind of a pimp like that.

I devour her latest post, complete with a picture of the happy family at the dinner table playing a board game. My dad is all teeth, giving a big thumbs-up. It's almost weird now to think about him as my dad, even stranger how the blonde chunkster is sort of my sister. While my mom has transformed into...whatever she's become, it seems Kristen has created a new version of Dan Reams—the ultimate family-dude. Tall, a bit of silver sliding in at the temples, but otherwise his hair is thick and stylish. He's kind of soft in the middle, but you can tell Kristen runs him to death. *Sponsored by Nike!*

I pore over some pictures of the family cooking out, zooming in and studying the details. Dan Reams wearing a new grilling apron by

Grill Masters™. I stare at his face. Our bone structure is similar. No one could look at his picture then look at me and not tell. We have the same jawline, nose, blue eyes, and broad shoulders. The more I study the pixels, the harder it is to figure out. The harder it is to let it go.

It would be so much easier to swallow if the guy was a drunk or in prison. That, I could accept if not understand. If he was just some loser who didn't want his family, maybe I'd be okay with it. Maybe I wouldn't be. But he's not a loser, he's like Dad of the Year. And it sort of kills me a little bit.

I can't even remember how I found this blog. I think I was Google searching his name and stumbled upon it. It's got thousands of followers. It's been viewed nearly half a million times. And I've been stopping by two or three times a day for the past six months. Again, probably not the healthiest habit, but hey, neither is pimping your kids for sponsors, right?

What the blog fails to mention is how Dan Reams took off for Indiana nearly four years ago, leaving behind a three hundred-thousand-dollar house and an eight-year-old Honda. Maybe he figured a house and car was enough, because he doesn't pay a dime of child support or call or write or even remember us for all I know. And Mom is either too proud or too delusional to try to get anything out of him, which means she's delinquent—in more ways than one—on property taxes, utilities, homeowner association fees, credit cards, and I'm sure a slew of other bills I don't even know about. Which leaves me here, waiting for something to happen.

For a while it was easy to ignore. My parents' fighting. Mom's drinking. Dad leaving. Bills piling up in the mailbox as I went about life like nothing was wrong. School. Basketball. Girlfriend. Parties. Anything to not think about what was happening at home. But it did happen. They decided not to be the parents I knew. People change, I get it, but when Dad quit the marriage and Mom quit life, it felt like they both quit me.

I close the app and sift through my contacts. Nearly one hundred of them, all ghosts after everything went down at school. I think about work and life and Molly Martinez. How these days I have no distractions, nothing to keep me from worrying. I think about whether I should even tell Molly about the hearing. I wonder if she knows what I gave up or what my future has become.

Suddenly I feel so alone it makes me shiver.

Acknowledgments

The working title for this book was *Why Go Home,* after the Pearl Jam song that sort of inspired the idea for this story. Many times I had to set this aside for a day or a month or longer because some things just aren't easy to write. And while I wasn't sure how things would end, I never gave up on Chloe. She is, if nothing else, a fighter. And as dark as things got for her, I'd like to think the ultimate message here is about family and hope.

Thanks to Dean Wilson for the early reads and encouragement. To Diane Fanning who never shies away from a little blood. To the many random lawyers I cold called with outrageous questions. To my Aunt Claire, who passed away many years ago but whose kindness lives on in her memory. Claire was who I thought of when writing Leigh, Chloe's mother. To my older sister, Ivy. Chloe learned a lot from you.

To Staci Olsen, as always, for believing in my work. To Holli Anderson, for having my back. To my wife, Anne, who thinks I capture the teenage girl eye roll just a bit too naturally. To Simon, who will have to wait a few years to read this one. To Bella, who, well, yeah moving on...

Lastly, to anyone out there who doesn't believe good things can happen to them, trust me, I've been out in the cold, in the dark, with nowhere to go and ready to give up. And yet somehow, I didn't give up. I didn't give in to it. So that's my advice. Don't give in.

I promise you it can happen.

About the Author

Pete Fanning is the author of *Justice in a Bottle* and *Runaway Blues*. He lives in Virginia with his wife, son, baby girl, and two very spoiled dogs. He can be found at www.petefanning.com, where he's posted over 200 flash fiction stories.

This has been an
Immortal Production

www.ingramcontent.com/pod-product-compliance
Lightning Source LLC
Chambersburg PA
CBHW050837190726
48286CB00007B/2124